CLEAN SLATE

Visit us at www.boldstrokesbooks.com

By the Author

Ladyfish

Clean Slate

CLEAN SLATE

by
Andrea Bramhall

2013

CLEAN SLATE

ISBN 10: 1-60282-943-8
ISBN 13: 978-1-60282-943-5

This Trade Paperback Original Is Published By
Bold Strokes Books, Inc.
P.O. Box 249
Valley Falls, NY 12185

First Edition: September 2013

CREDITS
EDITORS: Victoria Oldham and Cindy Cresap
PRODUCTION DESIGN: Susan Ramundo
COVER DESIGN BY SHERI (graphicartist2020@hotmail.com)

Acknowledgments

Thank you to everyone over at Bold Strokes Books, Rad, Vic, Cindy, Sheri, and everyone behind the scenes—you all rock!

Susan, Victoria, Cristin, Master Z, Kathy, Kim, and Dawn, for your beta reading and critique skills on the early drafts of this novel. Your help was invaluable to me and I can't thank you enough.

And everyone who takes the time to read this book—you are the ones I thank the most. Your continued support, encouragement, and enjoyment of my work are the things that keep me hunched over my laptop even on those increasingly rare British sunny days. Thank you all.

Dedication

Gran and Grandad,
Because you guys showed me the real importance
of all those beautiful memories that make up
this little thing we call life.

All my love,
A

CHAPTER ONE

A trio of naked women posed in a circular tableau. Morgan had lost count of the number of models she'd seen, first as a student, then as a teacher. She'd always been able to detach herself, to see soft breasts and thighs as a beautiful work of art. The long expanse of a bare back and rounded buttocks were worthy of study, not just lust.

The bright lights in the studio cast bold shadows across their skin, the scent of linseed oil, turpentine, and old paper filled the air. The scratch of lead on paper told her something about the artist as she wandered the room; long, confident, sweeping strokes filling page after page, or tiny, precise, slow marks that steadily built an image. She pointed to a sketch every now and then, offering advice about the tone, the shadows, curves, and angles, her eyes glancing between the pages of her students and the models before them.

Morgan wiped her palms on her jeans and ignored the trickle of sweat running down her back. It didn't matter where in the room she was, or which of her students she was talking to, she could feel a pair of blue eyes following her every move. Anna sat at the center of the tableau, her back against a pile of heaped cushions, her head resting along the length of her outstretched arm. The other arm lay across her stomach. Her small pink nipples puckered in the slight chill of the room, and her knee was raised, hiding her naked sex from direct view. One woman rested against Anna's leg, and the other rested her head on Anna's shoulder. Their limbs entwined and caressed Anna's, creating a beautiful vignette of femininity.

She stuffed her hand into her pocket and felt the worn edge of the envelope. She rubbed her finger over the tiny raised edge of the postage stamp. She knew the date stamp was faded, but it was already burned into her brain. June thirteenth. Six weeks ago. How could one piece of paper and some ink change everything? Yet it did. Her very own harbinger of doom carried on the wings of a postage stamp. The letter had thrown open the door to every painful memory she had, and promised nothing but heartache and danger. For her, and everyone around her.

She did the only thing she could think of to save the people she loved. Three weeks ago, Morgan had told her wife that she was leaving, that she wanted a divorce. The words still burned in her throat and made her stomach churn, as did the pain she'd seen in Erin's eyes as she'd packed her bags and slowly, quietly, closed the door behind her.

She knew leaving her family was best for them in the long run. Staying would only make them all miserable and put them in terrible danger. She knew they would hurt, but she was equally sure their pain would be temporary without her around. They were better off without her. Morgan quickly pushed away the thoughts that continued to plague her. *They deserve better than me.* She checked her watch and signaled for the class to begin clearing away.

"Morgan?"

She turned around as the model, Anna, swung her robe around her shoulders. She was only tangentially aware of Anna's breasts before the robe swept over them.

"I was wondering if you'd like to come for a drink with me?"

Morgan shook her head. "I'm not very good company at the moment."

"Oh, I'm sure you'll be fine."

"No, really—"

"It's just a drink. It might do you some good."

"Anna, really I don't think it's a good idea."

"It's my birthday. Surely you aren't going to make me go out alone?"

"Your birthday?"

Anna nodded.

"Why aren't you going out with your friends?"

"I will be tomorrow. But with work and stuff." She shrugged. "Tonight's not the best choice. I'd really like it though if you would come out with me. It's just a drink, Morgan."

Morgan thought about the empty flat that awaited her, and the loneliness that was clamoring at her heels. She shrugged. "Okay."

"Excellent. I'll just get changed." Anna walked to the storeroom they used as a dressing room and Morgan continued to clean up.

The last of the students packed up their gear, said good night, and left as she busied herself tidying away easels and supplies, rearranging tables and chairs, and getting the room ready for the next class to use it.

"Ready?" Anna tugged her long blond hair from the collar of her jacket and smiled as she walked out of her makeshift changing room wearing pale denim jeans, a tight pink T-shirt, and a black jacket. Morgan pulled open the classroom door and followed her out into the cool night air. They were only a few hundred yards from the Roundhouse pub and walked in silence.

Morgan led them into the crowded, noisy traditional English pub with a log fire, red velvet covered stools dotted around wooden tables, and quickly found them a space away from the dart match that seemed to be in full swing. She left Anna and went to the bar, returning a few minutes later with two glasses of red wine.

"Thanks." Anna took a hearty swallow before putting her glass down on the bare wood and picking up the unused coaster, slowly peeling the edges apart.

"I'm afraid they don't have a great selection of wines here. But this Shiraz should be palatable at least." Morgan sniffed the glass, closing her eyes to enjoy the aroma of berries, the slight peppery depth, and a hint of chocolate underneath it all, before taking her first sip. It had taken her years to fully appreciate the complexity of wine, but it was something she enjoyed. "Are you okay?"

Anna tossed the coaster back onto the table and smiled. "Just a bit nervous. That's all."

"Why?" Morgan cocked her head to one side.

Anna hesitated, her gaze flicking around the bar, never settling on anyone or anything. "I've wanted to ask you out for a long time."

Morgan looked at her, unsure how to respond. She pushed her fingers through her short black hair.

"I know you're married. It doesn't matter to me."

It matters to me. Morgan took a long drink and tried to ignore the uncomfortable ache in her belly. She wasn't sure how to react. She didn't want to tell Anna that she'd ended her marriage. That she'd walked away from fifteen years with Erin. She was too confused. She needed to think. No, she needed to stop thinking. She wanted to stop feeling. She stroked her fingers down the edge of the envelope again. Her wife and children deserved better than a woman living in fear, someone who had lied to them and kept part of herself hidden for more than a decade. She shook her head and pushed the feelings of self-pity and loathing away. *Enough with the pity party. You made your decision, now live with it.*

They talked about everything and nothing as they drank and whiled away the rest of the evening. Eventually, the pub signaled they were closing and they made their way out. As they stepped outside, a wave of dizziness hit Morgan and she gripped Anna's arm to steady herself.

"Whoa. Sorry. I only had a couple of glasses. I didn't think it was enough to get me drunk." Her head swam; the street lights blurred. "That wine must have been stronger than I thought."

"Don't worry. Hang on to me." Anna slipped her arm around Morgan's waist and held the other hand as Morgan wound it around her shoulders. "I've got you." They walked back to the college car park and Anna's car.

Morgan untangled her arms, feeling a little uncoordinated. "Good night, Anna." She turned to leave and started to fish in her pocket for her phone, intent on calling a taxi, knowing she was in no fit state to drive.

"Is that it?" Anna sounded disappointed.

"What do you mean?" Morgan frowned, finding it difficult to focus on Anna's face.

"I mean this." Anna twisted her fingers in Morgan's short hair, pulled her head down, and kissed her. Her tongue darted between Morgan's lips, seeking entrance.

Morgan pulled back. "Anna, no. I don't think this is a good idea."

"Don't think." Anna's lips closed over hers again and she pressed against her chest. Morgan wrapped her fingers round Anna's wrists and tried to pull her hands from her hair. "Why are you fighting me?"

"Anna. No." Morgan's hands were clumsy, her arms heavy as lead as she tried to push away from Anna, her dizziness and disorientation escalating by the second. *What the fuck is wrong with me?*

"Yes." Anna's voice was whisper quiet and breathless as she tugged Morgan closer to her.

Morgan felt herself falling, but could do nothing to stop the movement. She felt Anna's fingers in her hair, her cheek pressing against Anna's breasts, but she couldn't pull away. She closed her eyes, trying to regain her sense of self control, her strength.

"Get the fuck off her, you fucking dyke!" A fist slammed into her jaw, causing her to bite her tongue. Blood filled her mouth as the pain registered and she dropped to her knees.

"Jimmy, stop!" Anna screamed.

Another punch connected with the side of her head, and her vision blurred. She tried to look at the man, his fist poised to strike again.

"You fucking bitch."

She couldn't hold her head up anymore and the pavement felt cold beneath her cheek. A boot landed solidly against her ribs. Then across her shoulder and back. Saliva filled her mouth and she thought she was going to vomit.

"Jimmy, stop! That's enough. You're not supposed to hurt her!" Anna's pleading barely penetrated the fog clouding her brain. "He told you to get the pictures and that's it."

"The fucking bitch touched you."

"Don't be stupid, Jimmy. Whatever it was you gave me for her drink had her so weak she couldn't do anything. Another couple of minutes and she'd be passed out. This was all me. And I was doing it for you, you fucking moron."

He screamed his rage and kicked at Morgan's head and connected with her temple, making her head bounce off the pavement. Blood ran down her face and stung her eyes when she tried to open them. The dull thud of a car door slamming cut off Anna's voice before the car screeched away into the night. The streetlight faded slowly, narrowing to a pinpoint before the world went black.

CHAPTER TWO

Erin's heels clicked on the tiled floor of the hospital corridor as she made her way to the front desk. The smell of bleach, blood, and fear permeated the walls and tainted the air. The receptionist waited with her saccharine smile and eyes that held the last remaining vestiges of genuine care and concern. Manchester Royal Infirmary's accident and emergency department was humming with activity, and people waited in various stages of need all around her.

"Hi, can I help you?" The nasal voice of the receptionist carried easily over any noise in the waiting area.

"I'm looking for Morgan Masters. Someone called and said she'd been brought in."

"Are you a family member?"

"I'm her wife." She felt no need to tell her that they were divorcing. It was none of her business. Right now the doctors required consent from next of kin, and that was her until the divorce was finalized.

The woman rattled away at her keyboard and picked up the phone, speaking quietly before smiling at Erin and pointing to a bank of uncomfortable looking plastic chairs. "The doctor will be right out."

"Thank you." Erin sat down, determined not to let her growing panic consume her, and watched the people around her. An elderly man cradling his arm. A teenager wearing a hoodie, twitching in the corner. A mother cuddling a toddler, a wad of tissues held under his bloody nose.

"Ms. Masters?"

"Yes."

"I'm Dr. Reynolds. I've been treating Ms. Masters since she was brought in. Come with me, please?"

The young doctor wore dark blue wrinkled scrubs. Unkempt blond hair curled around his head, and a scruffy beard covered his lower face. He looked more like a surfer than anything else. *Christ, now I know I'm getting old. The doctor looks about twelve!*

He led her into a small room filled with chairs and a small coffee table covered with coffee rings.

"Is she all right?" Erin's heart pounded. No matter how angry she was with Morgan, she didn't want to see her hurt.

"Ms. Masters has been badly injured in some kind of attack. She has a substantial number of lacerations and contusions and some muscular strains. Nothing that won't heal, and nothing that will cause her any problems. But she has a very serious head injury. She has a skull fracture and an intracranial bleed. We need to operate to relieve some of the pressure. The amounts of alcohol and drugs in her system aren't going to help matters either. Do you know what she was taking?"

"Drugs? Morgan didn't take drugs."

"Well, there are drugs in her system. We'll send them off for testing if you don't know. We really do need to operate though."

"When?" Erin hugged herself, trying to quell the rising nausea.

"We're readying the operating room. We just need your consent." He held out a clipboard and pen for her.

Erin took them and scribbled her name as he pointed. "How serious is this? Will she die?" The panic she'd been fighting was pulling at her, and she pushed down the wave of nausea threatening to overtake her.

"There's a good chance she'll pull through, but we need to do this now."

"Oh God. Can I see her?"

"She hasn't woken up—"

"I don't care about that. Please, I need to see her."

"Just for a moment. Then I believe the police officers wish to speak to you."

Erin nodded, tears brimming in her eyes as she followed him out of the room. She ignored the two uniformed officers walking behind her and gasped when she saw Morgan lying on the bed. A breathing tube pumped air in and out of her lungs—wires monitored every bodily function and response. Thin plastic tubes fed her drugs and fluids. Her head was a mass of bruises and bloody tissue, the dark shock of hair Erin had so loved running her fingers through was matted with blood and sticking out at odd angles.

"You need to get better, Morgan." Tears burned her eyes but she refused to let them fall. "Tristan and Maddie need you." She brushed a lock of hair down on Morgan's head before giving in to the urge to take hold of her hand and let the tears fall.

Dr. Reynolds placed his hand on her shoulder, startling her before the orderly began to wheel the gurney out of the room. The reality that Morgan might not survive hit her and she felt her knees go out from under her. The strong hand of the doctor was all that kept her on her feet as he guided her to a seat.

"Are you all right?"

"No. I'm not all right. I'm not."

"Silly question. I'm sorry. If you want to wait in that room, I'll come and get you when we know anything." He pointed down the corridor before he followed Morgan's gurney out of the room.

She stared at the empty space, her eyes unfocused and glazed.

"Mrs. Masters?"

Erin turned her head slightly at the question, still unable to tear her eyes from the place she had last seen Morgan.

"I'm PC Lock and this is PC Ward. Can we talk to you?"

"Sure." She waited until they were seated. "I take it you're investigating what happened to Morgan?"

"We are. This was a very serious attack. Do you know what she was doing in the car park at the college tonight?"

"She teaches night classes there."

"Do you know what time she finishes?"

"The class usually finishes at nine, then she packs away, and usually leaves around nine thirty to go home."

Lock tilted his head to one side. "And what time does she normally arrive home?"

"About ten, but—"

"Were you not concerned that she wasn't home at her normal time?"

"Well, no. Sometimes she'll go for a drink with some of the other teachers and come home later, but—" Erin pushed her fingers through her dark hair, her frustration mounting.

"So tonight wasn't unusual?"

"No, but—"

"Do you know the people she goes drinking with?" PC Ward had his pen poised over his notebook.

"Will you please let me finish! Morgan wouldn't have been coming home to me tonight, so I wouldn't have been worried no matter what time it was."

"And why is that, Ms. Masters?" PC Lock leaned forward, bracing his elbows on his knees.

"Because she walked out three weeks ago."

"She left you?"

"Yes. Three weeks ago, she packed her bags and walked out on me and our two children. So I don't know what was going on for this evening. I'm not privy to her plans, or where she calls home at the moment."

They looked at each other. "Ah, and where were you this evening, Ms. Masters?" Lock asked.

Erin laughed and shook her head at the absurdity of it. "What? Just in case I had the urge to go out and bash her head in?" She tried to remind herself that they were just doing their job, and that the questions were just standard procedure. "I was at work until seven. I got home around seven forty-five, and then I spent the evening with my children. We did their homework, watched a film, and then I put them to bed. I went to bed myself at about eleven thirty after I completed a few house chores. I was in bed when the hospital rang me and asked me to come here."

"Was there someone else involved, Ms. Masters?" PC ward shifted in his seat as he flipped the page of his notepad over.

The question had plagued Erin since Morgan had left. Was that the secret she was hiding? Is that where she'd been staying since she walked out? So many questions that only Morgan had the answers for.

"I don't know. If there was, she never said."

"And for you?"

Erin laughed. "No, I'm not seeing anyone else."

"I'm sorry. We have to ask."

"I know. What else do you have to ask? Why did she leave?" She watched their reaction. "I have no idea. Morgan has a tendency to keep her thoughts to herself, and she was definitely keeping those quiet. What else?"

"The doctor told us that there were drugs in her system as well as alcohol. Do you know anything about that?"

"To the best of my knowledge, she didn't take drugs. If that's changed in the past three weeks…I have no idea."

"Where do you work?"

"Manchester airport. I'm an air traffic control officer." She opened her bag and pulled out a card. "My boss is Roger Siverton. You can get him on that number to confirm what time I left."

"Do you know of anyone who would want to hurt Ms. Masters?"

"You mean besides me?" She laughed at their raised eyebrows, the shock and her own growing unease making her verbally punchy. "Sorry, I'm tired and probably in shock. My mouth has a tendency to run away from me at times like this. But no, I can't think of anyone who would want to hurt her. She's an art teacher, for God's sake. You don't get bashed about the head for giving someone a bad grade. Wasn't it a mugging or something?"

"There was no theft. Her money, credit cards, phone, everything was untouched."

"So that means a personal reason for attacking her."

Lock shrugged slightly. "We don't know yet, but that seems more likely. What about friends or family? Would they be able to give us any more information?"

"Probably. Her friends anyway. Nikki and Amy have been friends with Morgan since they started school together." She scrolled through her phone to give them the telephone numbers. "She doesn't have much in the way of family. Her mother died almost twenty years ago, and her father is in prison. She hasn't seen him since his trial."

"And when was that?"

"Almost twenty years ago." Erin shifted uncomfortably in her chair. She hated thinking about Morgan's parents. Morgan had rarely spoken of them, never going into details, but it was obvious what she had gone through because of them. She couldn't stop the shiver that raced up her spine as she focused on PC Ward's next question.

"And they've not had any contact?"

"None to my knowledge. You'll have to ask Morgan or her father to confirm that."

"Thanks for your time. We'll be in touch if we need anything else."

"Sure." Erin waited for the door to close behind them before dialing her home number.

"Hello?"

Erin breathed a sigh of relief at the sound of her older brother's voice. "Chris, it's me."

"Oh, thank God. Maddie woke up a little while ago. She heard you going out."

"Is she okay?"

"Yeah, wanted to know all the ins and outs. I didn't know what to tell her, so I told her you had to go into work. Last minute. I swear that kid's not ten. She gave me the third degree about who—never mind all that. What's going on?"

"Morgan's being operated on at the moment. I won't know anything for a while yet. I've just finished speaking to the police—"

"Police? Why?"

"She was attacked. Beaten up by someone, I guess." Erin turned her head, trying to loosen some of the tension that was building.

"And?"

"The police needed information. I was the logical first person to speak to. I am her wife." She ran her fingers through her hair and let her head fall back against the wall.

"So what are you doing now? Are you coming home?"

"No. I'm going to stay and make sure she's all right before I leave."

"Why?" His voice was rough.

"What do you mean, why?"

"You know exactly what I mean. Why stay there, with her, after she walked out on you?"

Why indeed? "Because it's the right thing to do. We have children together. How could I come home and tell the kids 'sorry, your mother was in surgery last night having her brain operated on, but I don't know how she is now, or even if she made it out of the operating room alive.'"

The silence on the line told Erin exactly how much her comments had irritated her brother.

Erin pinched the bridge of her nose and willed herself to calm down. She knew he was right. It wasn't his fault, and she was taking it out on him. "I'm sorry, Chris. I'm tired and worried about her. I don't mean to take it out on you. They might need me to authorize some other operation or something too."

"You're a hell of a woman, Erin Masters. If you weren't my sister I'd have to marry you."

Erin wanted to laugh, but she didn't have the energy. "I'll call when I know something more."

"Erin, wait."

"What?"

"Are you okay?"

Erin didn't know how to answer. Everything was changing so fast she felt she couldn't keep up. "I don't know, Chris. I don't know what I'll do if—"

"Listen to me. You are the strongest woman I know. You can deal with anything this shitty life can throw at you. You always have done, and you always will."

"I know—"

"If you need me, I'm here for you."

"Thanks, Chris. I've got to go now."

Erin put the phone back in her bag and slid out of her jacket, determined to get comfortable while she waited. The harsh lights of the hospital hid the fact that it was three in the morning and there would still be a long wait for news. She curled up in the chair, tucking her legs under her, and let the hours roll by, playing over in her head the memories of their life together.

"What's wrong with you? You've been wandering around looking like I stole your puppy or something." Erin kissed the top of Morgan's head before she sat at the kitchen table. She smiled to soften her words, but she was getting tired of battling Morgan's ever increasing moods.

"Nothing's wrong." Morgan turned away.

"Then smile, and try to pretend like you're enjoying spending time with me and our children, and that we aren't making you miserable all the time."

Morgan's face drained of all color and her gaze dropped to the floor. "I can't help it."

"What can't you help?"

"I can't do this anymore. I won't make you all suffer because of me." Morgan stalked out of the room. Erin listened to her moving around upstairs for a few minutes, then followed her, grateful that the children were in the garden playing. She climbed the stairs and stood staring in shock as Morgan started throwing clothes into a suitcase.

"What are you doing?"

"You're an intelligent woman, Erin, what does it look like?"

She chose to ignore the sarcasm and try to get to the heart of the problem. "Why are you packing?"

"I'm leaving."

"What? Why? What are you talking about?" Erin crossed the room and grabbed the lid of the suitcase, intent on pulling it away from Morgan.

Morgan stared at her, her eyes brimming with tears. "I can't do this anymore."

"You can't do what? Morgan, sit down and talk to me. Tell me what the hell's going on." Erin ached to reach out and pull her into her arms, unable to maintain her own anger in the face of Morgan's despair.

"I'm making you all miserable, you said so. So I'm going to leave. Then you and the children can all be happy without me!"

Morgan threw more clothes into the case and reached under her pillow for her pajamas. Erin's mind scrambled to grasp what she was seeing. She'd seen Morgan withdraw from them more and more over the past three weeks and was at a loss how to reach her. Everything she'd done had only seemed to push Morgan further away.

Romantic dinners ended with Morgan sulking and disappearing into her art studio. Days out with the family resulted in her picking fights or wearing herself out playing basketball with the kids then falling asleep on the couch.

"Do you truly believe that any of us would be happier without you?"

"Yes!"

Erin reached out to touch her, swallowing her disappointment when Morgan shrank from her touch. "Morgan, we love you. I love you." She stepped slowly around the bed. Her approach cautious. Measured. Wary. Just like approaching a wounded animal, trapped in a corner. "Fifteen years ago when we fell in love, I knew that you were the woman I wanted to spend the rest of my life with. I know I'm not always very good at showing you that. I don't have the artistic soul you do, but I do love you with everything in me." She took hold of Morgan's hand. Her heart leapt with hope when Morgan didn't pull away. "Whatever the problem is, we can work through it together. No relationship is perfect all the time. This is a rough patch that we can get through. We can see a counselor or something, family therapy. Whatever you need, baby. Just talk to me and we'll figure it out."

"It won't work. I can't..." She wrenched her hand away from Erin and closed the case. "You don't understand. You'll never understand."

The path was set and Morgan's feet were already on it. Erin felt her heart beating its thunderous tattoo inside her chest, and the blood roared in her ears as she watched Morgan scramble down the stairs and reach for the door.

"Morgan, if you walk out that door, I'll never be able to forgive you. Stay, please, and we can work this out. Whatever it is that's hurting you, we can fix it. You have to stay. I don't understand...at least tell me why. We can fix it." The tears poured down her cheeks.

"You can't fix everything, Erin. I was broken a long time ago."

"You don't know that. You haven't even let me try. Please, Morgan. I love you. Don't give up on us like this."

Erin could hardly believe the words coming out of her mouth. She had never begged for anything in her life. Even when her world had been shattered as a child, she had stood proud beside her mother and brother, and worked hard to build a life that wouldn't break apart around her. One where she was secure in her job, the love of her children, and the partner she adored. She couldn't believe that she was watching it all blow apart and her heart was walking out the door.

"If you leave it's over, Morgan."

"That's the point."

"You planned this, didn't you? You picked a fight so you could walk out without having to explain what's really going on, didn't you?"

"I'll call to sort something out with the kids when I find a place to stay."

"I'm right, aren't I?"

"Good-bye, Erin."

She didn't slam the door behind her. The tinny click of the catch was all the more wrenching for its quiet mockery. "Damn you, Morgan Masters."

A knock on the door startled her from her reverie as Dr. Reynolds entered the room, a slight smile on his face. "She's out of surgery and it went well." He dropped into the seat opposite her. "We had to remove a small blood clot that formed and we relieved a lot of the pressure on Ms. Masters' brain. She's not woken up yet but I expect her to any time now."

"And she's okay?"

"Well, it's always difficult to say with brain injuries. We'll know more once she wakes up, and then we can see what she has to say for herself."

Erin couldn't stop the tears that slipped down her cheeks. "Can I see her?"

"Sure. I'll get one of the nurses to bring in a chair and you can sit with her if you like. Waking up to a friendly face would probably be nice for her."

Erin saw no need to correct his assumption as she followed him into Morgan's room.

CHAPTER THREE

Steady beeps and rhythmic humming were the first things Morgan was aware of when she woke. The throbbing in her head pulsed in time with the bleating machine. She opened her eyes but even the low lighting didn't stop the sharp pain lancing through her skull. She moved her head slowly to take in the dim details of the room. The wires and tubes attached to her skin were uncomfortably restrictive as she became aware of them. She tried to lift her hand to her face but a sharp pain in her shoulder caused her to gasp and moan, and she settled back against the pillows to let the pain subside.

She lost track of time cataloguing the aches and pains in her body as she tried to move; everywhere seemed to hurt, but her head was by far the worst of it. When she opened her eyes again, she looked around, moving her head gingerly, the ache growing with each movement until she saw a woman sitting in the chair by the window. Her head rested on a blanket that she had wedged into a pillow, her hair thick and dark as treacle, hanging in big soft waves over her shoulders and curling across one eye.

Her lips twitched as she slept, parting slightly as the tip of her tongue swept over the sensuous sweep of her lower lip. The top had a deep cupid's bow and a slight upturn at the corners. It was a mouth made for smiling, laughing; lips that were meant for kissing.

She'd wrapped a pale gray jacket over her shoulders and her feet were tucked under her legs, her skirt stretched tight across her slender thighs.

"Hi."

Startled by the soft voice, Morgan looked up from the woman's shapely legs. Pain tore through her head and she had to close her eyes until the waves of nausea passed.

"Take it slowly. Try not to move too much."

Morgan wanted to answer, but her tongue felt thick in her mouth. The woman seemed to expect this and spoke gently again, her voice soothing the burning in Morgan's head. It felt like forever before Morgan opened her eyes again without everything swimming out of focus. Her breath caught in her throat when she finally did. She hadn't been aware of the woman moving from her chair and was shocked when she looked up into the most startling blue eyes she had ever seen. Pale blue, like fresh melted water raging over glaciers, but there was nothing cold about the eyes watching her. Passion and heat and barely concealed anger were all carefully controlled but bubbling below the surface, and there was something in Morgan that wanted to open her up, in every way.

"I'm going to find the doctor. Stay awake, okay?"

She left the room and Morgan groaned softly from the pain vibrating in every part of her body. She tried to focus, to push away every needle sharp sting that sliced through her skull, and stay awake.

"Well, well. It's nice to see your eyes without having to pry them open myself." A scruffy looking man walked into the room, the woman from earlier following closely behind him. "I'm going to get you a little sip of water and see if we can get you to answer a couple of questions." He held a straw to Morgan's lips and instructed her to sip slowly before he pulled it away and placed it on the cabinet beside the bed. "I'm Dr. Reynolds. I've been looking after you since you came in. Do you know where you are?"

Morgan let the pieces fall into place and let out a relieved breath, the machines, the doctor. "Hospital." Her voice was scratchy, hoarse. It sounded odd to her own ears, and her ribs ached with each breath.

"Perfect. Can you tell me your name?"

"Morgan."

"Excellent. Just a few more okay?" He didn't wait for Morgan to answer. "Who is the prime minister?"

"John Major." She closed her eyes briefly and let out a long breath. "Boring bastard." The pretty woman gasped. "Sorry, I, like, didn't mean to offend. He's not that boring."

"It's okay, Morgan. I'm sure she wasn't really offended. What year is it?"

"Nineteen ninety-two. What's with all the questions doctor? Is my mum here?"

"Sorry, Morgan, I have to ask these because you had quite a bash on the head. Can you bear with me a bit longer?"

"Okay."

"Do you remember what happened to you?"

Morgan frowned as she tried to pull the memory from the fog. Her eyes widened and the heart monitor beeped faster. "No. I can't. What happened to me?"

"Morgan, I need you to stay calm. It's completely understandable with a head trauma that you can't remember what happened to cause it. I was expecting that. Please take a nice deep breath and calm down. You're doing fine. Okay?" He smiled gently as she followed his instructions and took a deep breath before exhaling loudly, groaning at the pain.

"Sorry."

"Don't be. Like I said, you're doing fine. Your ribs are pretty badly bruised. They're going to hurt for a while. What I need you to do now is remember three words for me. Pen, water, light. Can you remember them?

"Pen, water, light."

"Good. You up for some more questions?"

"Isn't my mum going to be worried about me? Is she, like, outside?"

"No, it's late Morgan. Your mum isn't out there."

"Oh, are you gonna call her then? To get her to come see me?"

"I'll talk to your relatives as soon as we finish up here."

"Okay. What else then?"

"How old are you Morgan?"

"Nineteen."

"And what do you do?"

"I'm at uni. I'm doing art."

"That's great."

"Yeah, when I finish university I'll be, like, a real artist. Maybe go to Europe and draw while I travel around."

"That sounds wonderful."

"Yeah. How long have I been here?"

"You were brought in three days ago. You've been unconscious ever since."

"No wonder my mum's had to go home then. I bet my dad was going mental." She grimaced. "Can I get another drink please? I feel like I've been on a weeklong pub crawl and got carpet instead of a tongue. What happened to me?"

He laughed gently as he put the straw between her lips. "Not too much though. I don't want you to get sick. With your head injury, that would not be fun at all."

"Suppose not. I'm knackered, doc. Any chance I can, like, have a nap and we do twenty questions later?"

"Sure. I could do with talking to some of my colleagues. When I come back, there'll probably be a few other people with me. That okay?"

"Sure. Just don't forget to tell my mum I woke up, and that I'm not a lazy git. All right?"

"Sure."

Morgan was already sleeping when the door closed behind them. She forgot to ask who the woman was who had been there when she woke up.

❖

"What the hell was that?"

"Ms. Masters—"

"Erin."

"Erin, I need to run more tests, but it would appear that Morgan has some memory issues—"

"No! Really? What gave you that impression? The fact that she thinks John Major is still the prime minister or that she wants to see her mother?"

"Does she not have an existing relationship with her mother?"

"Her mother's dead. So unless you've got an Ouija board handy, no one has an existing relationship with her."

"I see."

Erin pushed her hands through her hair. "Look, I'm sorry. I shouldn't snap. I'm just…" She couldn't find the words to describe what she was feeling at the point. Scared? Frustrated? Worried? Upset? Confused? None of them fit, yet all of them did. "She sounded more like our thirteen-year-old son than the woman I've been married to for the last fifteen years!"

"Right now, she believes that she is a teenager."

"How can that be? I don't understand."

"I need to speak to several people and run more tests. I also need to speak to Morgan more before we can find out exactly what's going on. What I do know is that the brain is tricky. Morgan has a grade three head trauma. In cases like this, memory loss of the event that caused the trauma is extremely common. Depending on the extent of the injury, the memory loss can be permanent or temporary."

"Perm—"

"If the trauma is extensive, it can affect longer term memories. Again, this can be permanent or temporary. At this stage, we don't know. She could wake up in a few hours and be back to normal."

"How likely is that?"

"The seizures she had may also complicate matters. I really need to speak with some of my colleagues."

"Sure. Yeah, okay."

"We'll need to speak to you too. We'll need to get her background from you so that we can check the things she does remember."

"I didn't know her twenty years ago, and there are a lot of things from that time she won't talk about."

"Is there anyone she still has contact with who knew her then?"

"Yes. She has a couple of friends that she went to school with. Should I call them?"

"Let me do some tests first and then we'll see. Maybe you should go home and come back tomorrow. We'll know more then, and there's nothing more you can do here tonight."

"I think I'd rather wait here. You may need me to answer questions or something."

❖

"Morgan, how are you feeling this morning? Can you remember the three things I asked you—"

"Pen, water, light. You've had someone asking me that stupid question all night. What's wrong with me? What's with all the bandages round my head? And who the hell cut my hair? I know it's not a hangover, doc, but it sure as hell feels like a bad one. Have you spoken to my mum yet? When's she coming in?"

"Morgan, this is my colleague Dr. Rebecca Bann. She's a psychologist here at the hospital, and she's going to help me out with your case. We need to ask some more questions. Are you ready for it?"

"Did you speak to my mum?"

"I have been in contact with your family, and you'll get to see them soon."

"Fire away then, doc."

Thirty minutes later, the two doctors were exchanging quick glances and Dr. Bann sat on the edge of the bed. "Morgan, thank you for answering all my questions, but I have something very difficult to tell you, and I want to ask someone else to come in while I do that, okay?"

"Erm, yeah. Okay."

Dr. Reynolds opened the door of the room and spoke quietly to whoever was outside. Morgan wiped her hands against the blanket, nerves making them clammy. When Dr. Reynolds came back into the room, she couldn't stop herself from smiling at the woman who came in behind him. She didn't notice that everyone was watching her for a reaction.

"Morgan, do you remember this woman?" Dr. Bann was studying her face intently.

"Well, yeah. She was here last night when I woke up." She dropped her voice and whispered slightly. "She seemed a bit shocked when I said John Major was a boring bastard. Is she a nurse or something?"

"No. Erin doesn't work in the hospital. But we'll get to that shortly. Can you remember the three things I asked you—"

"Water, light, pen. Doc, do you think we can, like, wait for my mum before you tell me the bad news?"

"What makes you think I have bad news?"

"The reinforcements."

"Right. Of course. I'm sorry, but I'm afraid that won't be possible. Morgan, this isn't nineteen ninety-two. It's two thousand and twelve."

Morgan smiled and started to laugh. "Oh, Doc, that's fantastic." Relief at the little joke coursed through her. "Two thousand and twelve. Bugger me, that's funny. Who put you up to that? I bet it was Nikki. She's a scream! So, like, what's really going on, doc?" She took a deep breath trying to calm the laughter that bordered on hysterical. *Two thousand and twelve, that's hilarious.*

They weren't laughing. *Why aren't they laughing, too?* They were just watching her. Watching as she giggled to herself, concern and pity written in every line on their faces as they waited. She didn't know what they were waiting for. Her reaction? Hadn't she just given them that, when she caught on to their game? When she guessed that Nikki would be the mastermind behind their little ruse? *Why the fuck aren't they laughing?*

Dr. Bann took a deep breath and started again. "Morgan, it's two thousand and twelve. You're thirty-nine years old, and John Maj—"

"Shut the fuck up. I'm not stupid. I went to uni this morning… well, whatever morning it was. I'm nineteen. Ask my mum!" She tried to shuffle up the bed, to get away from them, but the pain in her ribs and shoulder stopped her.

"Morgan, please calm down. You were hurt and it's affected your memory—"

"My memory's just fine, fuck you very much. Where's my mum?"

"Morgan, your mum isn't here." Dr. Bann pushed her glasses up her nose.

"Well, call her then. Tell her I'm awake and she can come and get me." Morgan tried to sit up using the non-aching arm.

"It isn't quite as simple as—"

"Simple? It's very fucking simple. You, like, pick up the phone, you press the numbers, and you wait until she answers. When she does, you tell her I'm awake and she can come get me. Simple."

"I don't think that will work."

"Why not? Don't tell me my dad hasn't paid the bill again and got us cut off. Rotten bastard. That's it isn't it? He spent it on booze again, I'll bet." She picked at the blanket over her legs. "Okay, I'll give you Nikki's number. If you call her, she'll go round to my mum's and give her the message. She owes me after that twenty year joke."

"Morgan, it isn't about the telephone being cut off." Dr. Bann took off her glasses, folded the stems, and tucked them into her breast pocket. Bann, Reynolds, and the woman were all casting glances between themselves.

"Then get her here. I want to speak to my mum. Is that difficult to understand?"

The woman, Erin, stepped forward and took hold of her hand. Morgan tried to pull it away, but she wasn't letting go. "Morgan, we can't get your mum here."

"Why not? She's my mum. She'll come."

"Morgan, she can't. She died."

Fear settled in the pit of her stomach, and it was all she could do not to throw up as she shook her head and whispered, "I don't believe you."

Erin's voice was quiet, soft as she soothed the panic growing in Morgan. "I'm so sorry, but it's true."

Everything felt wrong. The air rushed out of the room, leaving in its place a stale, bitter tasting substitute that burned the back of her throat and lay heavy in her lungs, suffocating her, even as she pulled in one breath after another. The smell of antibacterial soap faded, and the odors it covered clambered to the front. Blood. Urine. Sweat. Death. Each one vied to the front, desperate for her attention. The color drained from her vision, and Erin's ice blue eyes turned gray as she continued to stare at her. Blinking required more control than she could manage.

There was no doubting the look in Erin's eyes, and Morgan couldn't fight the truth she saw there. As wrong as everything else felt, Erin felt right. "What happened? Was she in this accident with me?"

Erin shook her head. "No, sweetie, she died nearly twenty years ago. You weren't in an accident; you were attacked." Erin stroked her fingers down Morgan's cheek.

"Twenty years?" Morgan lifted her hand to her cheek, smoothing her fingertips from the corner of her eye down to her lips, feeling for physical signs of aging. "No. That can't be right." Morgan shook her head and tried to sit herself up again.

It didn't make sense. None of it made sense, and she clung to the possibility that there was a mistake. "My mum's not dead. She can't be. There has to have been a mistake." Erin tugged gently on Morgan's hand, forcing her attention back to the present, away from the escalating panic rising inside her. She couldn't help staring into Erin's eyes. There was something so familiar in them. It felt so natural to seek comfort from this woman, to be touched by her. To believe her. "Who are you?"

Erin swallowed hard, and Morgan could tell she was debating how to answer her. Her eyes flickered down and her brow creased. Morgan didn't know how she knew, but she knew that these were signs of indecision in Erin. "It doesn't matter. What matters right now, is that you trust that what we're telling you is the truth, and that you let us help you get better."

"Trust you? How can I do that when you won't tell me who you are?"

Erin looked at the doctors, obviously searching for some sort of guidance. Shrugs and empty stares were all she got. *They don't know what to say. They don't know what's going to freak me out more. They're, like, telling the truth. No. That can't be right. Twenty years? Twenty years, just gone. I can't believe it.*

"If you aren't going to tell me, then you better prove what you're saying about it being two thousand and twelve."

Erin sighed. "That I can do."

CHAPTER FOUR

Erin walked slowly down the corridor. Her mind shifted between the two versions of Morgan. The one who'd ignored her tears and walked out of their home, and the one who had leaned into her touch in her hospital bed. Scared, alone, confused. Erin's desire to walk away and protect what was left of her dignity was at war with years of taking care of the woman she loved. Holding her was second nature, and loving her as natural as breathing. But she couldn't escape the fact that Morgan had walked away from her. She'd taken Erin's love and turned her back on it; no reason, no excuse. She was just gone. The anger welled in her chest. *Anger, that's good. I can live with that.*

Erin held a bag full of magazines and newspapers in her hand. *She wants me to prove it? Fine. I'll do this and then I can leave her to it. I only have to deal with her in regards to the kids—oh fuck!*

She won't remember the kids.

Gut-wrenching sorrow replaced her anger. The thought of having to tell their children that their mother didn't remember them swamped her. Her knees buckled and she put her hand on the wall to steady herself. Acid churned in her stomach, and she looked around for a bathroom. She barely made it before she lost her battle and threw up in the sink.

She cried as she pictured ten-year-old Maddie's dark eyes, so much like Morgan's, filled with tears. She could see Tristan fighting desperately not to cry, but the questions would burn so bright in his blue eyes. Thirteen and embarrassed by his mums, but still he would need to know whether Morgan would still love him. How do you reconcile loving the mother who doesn't even know you exist? How the hell could she answer that?

Later. I'll have to deal with that later. I can only do one thing at once.

She washed her face and slowly gathered herself physically and emotionally, readying herself for the next step—whatever the hell that was—before she made her way to Morgan's room.

She took a deep breath and pushed the door open again, then stepped inside. Morgan was staring out the window but smiled when their eyes met.

"Hi." Morgan's voice still sounded scratchy, and her lips were dry and cracked.

"Hey. Do you need anything?" She dropped the bag onto the table and pushed her hair behind her ear.

"Exit from the time warp?"

Erin smiled. "I meant a drink or something." She pointed to the water jug on the table.

"I know what you meant." She pointed at the bag. "What's in the bag?"

"Proof." Erin started to reach into the bag as the telltale emotions flittered across Morgan's face. Confusion. Fear. Panic. All so clear. Her vulnerability clutched at Erin's heart, and it was all she could do not to reach for her, to hold her.

Morgan shifted uncomfortably. "I, erm, I don't think—I'm not sure I want—"

"You don't want to see this?"

Morgan shrugged.

"Why not?" Erin waited, tapping her nails against each other. "Morgan, why not?"

"Because then it's, like, real."

Erin's heart ached at how terrified Morgan looked. "Not seeing this doesn't change that."

"It does for me."

Ah, denial. "Mm, but only for a little while."

"I know." Morgan closed her eyes and dropped her head back to the pillows. "But then it's not so scary for a little while." Morgan turned her head and stared out the window again.

"Hiding from it won't help."

"What will?"

"I don't know."

"So how am I supposed to know?"

Erin scrabbled for something to stop the spiral of doubt. "Tell me something that you remember."

"About what?"

"Anything. Whatever you were thinking about when I came in."

"Is this, like, a test?"

Like, like, bloody like. She sounds like Tristan! And he's only thirteen. No, I won't think about that now. I can't. She picked at a bit of lint on the blanket covering the bed. "No. You just looked peaceful when I came in. I thought you must have been thinking about something nice, that's all"

"I was remembering my mum."

Erin perched at the foot of the bed and waited for her to carry on.

"She's always—she was always on me, or at me to make notes of everything, at school, so that I didn't forget anything. She says—she said that you never know when something might be important." Morgan's voice caught and she coughed. "I don't remember anything now. Important or not."

Erin scrabbled for something reassuring to say. "The doctors think your memory may come back."

"Not really. They have no idea if or when that's likely to happen." Morgan smiled weakly at her. "They're not exactly encouraging. They don't seem to know too much about all this brain stuff." She shrugged. "The one who looks like an extra from *Point Break* just keeps saying 'the brain's tricky.'"

Erin couldn't help but laugh a little. "I know. How can I help?" Erin knew she'd made a mistake the moment the words left her mouth. It was an opportunity for Morgan to ask the questions that were burning so clearly in her eyes.

"Tell me why you want to help me?"

How do I answer that one without overloading her with information? Hasn't she had enough to deal with already today?

"We've known each other a long time, Morgan. There's a lot of…we'll cover it another time. When you've gotten over the shock of all this." *We'll cover it another time? What the hell happened to only being involved because of the kids?*

"Gotten over the shock? Somehow I don't think a cup of hot, sweet tea and a blanket's going to cut it, do you?"

"Look, the doctors have said not to dump too much information on you all at once. That you need time to adjust, bit by bit."

"But you aren't giving me any info—"

"For now, can you please just accept that we've known each other for a long time and that we care about each other? Isn't that enough of a reason for someone to be here with you when you're like this?" She watched as Morgan frowned, obviously thinking it over.

"So we're friends?"

Friends, lovers, partners, spouses, exes. Where do I start? "Yeah, we're friends."

"All right then."

"Good. Now should we have a look in the bag and see what's here?"

"Can I ask you another question?"

Jesus, what next? "Sure."

"What happened to my mum? And where's my dad?"

And that would be next. "Your mum died—"

"You already told me that. How?"

"I don't think this is the right time for this, sweetie."

"But you do know?"

"Yes."

"Were you there?"

Erin shook her head. "No, it happened before we met."

"So I, like, told you?"

"Yes."

"Then you should tell me. It was my story."

"I will. Just not today, okay?"

"No, I—"

"Morgan, I promise I will tell you when you're out of the hospital and we can have some privacy. But not here. Not now." Erin grabbed the magazine out of the bag and tossed it over to her. "Please?"

Morgan picked up the magazine and gasped at the front cover. "He's married? Prince William was in primary school last time I saw pictures of him. Was the wedding beautiful? I bet Diana looked stunning...what?"

"Sweetie, there's a whole lot of history you're missing. Let's start with the general knowledge stuff and see if anything rings any bells."

CHAPTER FIVE

Morgan ached all over. She tried to get comfortable, but pain radiated from her right shoulder or her ribs, pulling her up short. She pushed her fingers through her hair, grateful the bandage around her head was gone, wishing she could wash away the remnants of blood that stuck to her scalp and flaked onto her pillow.

She picked up the remote control and turned off the TV. She had the news playing constantly for the past three days. Images of wars, death, and destruction filled the screen. British athletes held up medals from the Olympics...in London. Flash floods up and down the UK washed away people's belongings and destroyed homes. America has a black president, and Prince Harry is flashing his bits after playing strip billiards. *Billiards? Get with it, Harry. It's supposed to be poker—or strip Twister! I'm pretty sure I remember playing that at some point.*

She replayed every moment of her life. Every childhood memory. Every school friend and teacher. Conversations, books she'd read, films she'd seen. Nothing sparked a memory from beyond nineteen ninety-two. Nothing seemed familiar now. *Well, nothing except Erin. Who the hell is Erin? Why was she here? Why does she feel like the only thing that's real anymore?*

The door swung open.

"Holy shit! What happened to you!" Morgan couldn't help staring. In the doorway stood her oldest friends. But they looked... different.

"The same thing that happened to you, shit for brains. We got old."

Morgan couldn't help but smile. *Now that's familiar!*

"Haven't you looked in a mirror?" Nikki crossed the room and wrapped her arms around Morgan's shoulders before she could say anything else.

"No, they said not to yet."

"Oh, we'll have to sort that out then. Now, don't go getting excited." She kissed Morgan's cheek. "This doesn't mean that I like you. But the missus told me to be nice to you 'cos you feel like shit." She pointed a thumb over her shoulder, then let go and straightened up. "Gotta tell ya, you look like shit too. They did a proper job on you, didn't they?"

"Yeah, feels like it. You all right, Amy?"

"So you remember us then?" Amy leaned forward and kissed Morgan's cheek.

"Yeah. Everything's, like, in place up until we started uni. Then it's just, like, nothing. Did I finish uni? What job did I do? What about you guys? I mean you're here so we're, like, all still friends, right?"

"Oh my God. Did we really sound like that?" Nikki dropped heavily into one of the chairs. "No wonder my mother was always telling us to stop saying 'like.' It's bloody annoying."

"You two did. I spoke proper English, like a good girl." Amy grinned.

"Yeah, look at you now."

"Hey!" Amy glared at Nikki.

"Okay, crap English aside, I really need to know stuff, you guys."

"Yeah, we heard. So how old are you in the last things you remember?"

"Well, I remember us all moving into the halls of residence. And us all being in the same room. And I think I remember the first term. Did we have a lecturer that always wore purple? Either purple pants, or a skirt, or something. And I mean, like, all the time?"

Nikki grinned again. "Yep, Ms. Sharpe. Very lovely lady. You had a huge crush on h—"

"What? No, I didn't." Morgan felt her heart beginning to race, and her palms were sweaty. No one knew she was gay. It was a secret. She wanted to tell her mum first. Before anyone else found out about her.

"Course you did. We all did." Nikki waggled her eyebrows comically.

"You don't know what you're talking about."

"Sure I do. I mean all three of us had a crush on her, M. We talked about it."

"You're talking out of your arse." Morgan glared at Nikki who frowned in confusion.

"Morgan, wait. Listen." Amy put her hand over Morgan's arm. "Stop a minute. It doesn't matter that you had a crush on your teacher. It was a long time ago, and so much has changed."

"Oh Christ. She doesn't remember the open door party." Nikki slapped her hand across her eyes.

"The what?" Morgan stared at her.

"We had an open door party after we all got back from Christmas break at uni." Amy said and rubbed gentle circles over Morgan's arm.

"What the hell is an open door party?"

"We all opened the door to the closet." Nikki sat back in her chair and waited.

What the hell is she waiting for? Opened the door to what clos—Oh, fuck. It's not just me!

Morgan stared, eyes wide, jaw slack, and her mind whirling. "Both of you, too?"

"Yes." Amy smiled and took hold of Nikki's hand. "We've been together pretty much ever since."

Nikki lifted Amy's hand and kissed the back of it. "My missus."

"Shit." Morgan watched them grinning at each other. The love between them was so obvious she couldn't help but smile too. But she couldn't get her head around what they were telling her. "Everyone knows about me? It's not a secret anymore?"

"No. Hasn't been a secret for a long time."

She was playing catch up about even the most intimate details of her life. The secrets she held close to her heart were common knowledge to everyone around her, and she hadn't had time to adjust. One thought played over and over in her head.

"Did my mum know? Before she died?" Morgan twisted the blanket around her fingers, needing to know the answer, but dreading it just the same.

Nikki and Amy exchanged glances before Nikki stared at the floor and Amy's eyes welled with tears. "Yes, she did. And she was okay with it. She was glad that you were happy." She wiped at the tears with one hand. "All she wanted was for you to be happy."

"I remember that. She used to say it all the time. That I had to do whatever made me happy, because life was hell if you're miserable. For everyone."

"Little ray of sunshine, wasn't she!" Nikki scrunched her face up.

"Nikki!"

"What?" Nikki held up her hands in a helpless gesture.

"It's okay, she was bloody depressing." Morgan's lips twitched in the faintest hint of a smile.

"See. Nothing wrong with your memory." Nikki winked.

"Tell me some of the happy stuff I've missed."

"Well since we've known you the longest, we figured we'd start at uni. You did pass, by the way." Nikki tugged on her collar slightly, then buffed her nails on her shirt as she said, "You copied all my notes and finished second in the class."

"If she copied your notes, how come you only ended up top ten percent of the class? Idiot." Amy shook her head at Nikki's crestfallen face before turning back to Morgan. "You ended up teaching art at college."

A teacher? How the hell did I end up as a teacher? I never wanted that. "So I never made it as an artist?"

"Well…" Amy started.

"Stuff happened and you kind of lost your…passion to be an artist." Nikki's cheeks paled as she spoke.

"It feels like you're walking on eggshells and you have no idea what to say or tell me because you don't know where it's going to lead next. What question it's going to spark, that you have, like, no idea how to answer. By stuff, do you mean after my mum died?" Nikki nodded. "Okay, I get that. And I'm guessing you're under orders not to tell me what happened to her yet, just like Erin."

"The doctors and Erin think it's best to take this a little bit at a time. I mean they probably have a point, don't you think?" Amy perched on the bed and reached for Morgan's hand again.

"Yeah, probably. But they aren't the ones who are scared, frustrated as hell, and have no clue who they are. They just keep saying a little bit at a time, and then show me newspapers and magazines. I can see how much everything's fucking changed. I don't need to keep watching the news or reading headlines for that. I mean, like, how the fuck did terrorists manage to bring down the Twin Towers? We were going to go there after we finished our first year. We were going to go to New York and see a show, and go up the towers, and the Empire State Building—"

"We did go." Nikki reached for a backpack and pulled out a photograph album. She turned pages until she was pointing to a picture of the two of them, arms slung around each other's shoulders, grinning into the camera. The backdrop had the Statue of Liberty behind them, and the Twin Towers in the background. "It was a great trip."

Morgan stared at the image and the self that she recognized stared back at her. She ran her finger over the plastic covered page and tried to bring up a memory to tie it to her. To make it concrete, real, something solid that she could grasp on to, but there was nothing. No feeling flickered at the thought of having been there, with her best friends, on the trip she and Nikki had dreamed of taking since they were children. Only frustration bubbled as she reached deeper into the void that had once been filled with a life. Her life. "Our dream trip that you remember and I don't. I don't know who I am."

Amy squeezed her hand gently. "You do know who you are—"

"No, I don't."

"Yes, you do."

"No, I don't. You just said I was a teacher. I don't even remember finishing fucking uni. I'm not a teacher!" The frustration she'd been fighting erupted into an explosion of anger and resentment. "I don't remember any of it. I don't remember me—her—whatever. I'm not her. I'm not your Morgan! I can't be!"

Amy tugged her hand. "The Morgan we know and love came from the same place as you."

"But I'm not her."

"Maybe not. But you're the same Morgan that we knew twenty years ago." Nikki leaned forward in her chair. "The same one who became a teacher—and a whole lot of other stuff too."

"I'm not—"

"You're not what? The same?" Nikki shook her head. "Everyone changes, M."

"Changes? This isn't even in the same league as a fucking change. My whole life is gone—"

"Really? You remember who you are up to a certain point, Morgan. You remember your whole childhood, don't you?"

"Yes, but—"

"But nothing. Sure, you've got a lot of catching up to do, but you aren't starting from scratch."

"You've got no idea, Nikki. None. I can't remember my mother dying. I can't remember her funeral. I'm assuming that I went. But I don't remember it. How can I be the Morgan you know—that you knew—when I remember nothing that made her who she was?" Morgan was shouting, but she didn't care. "I'm not her. I can't be her. I don't even know where to start."

"M, you aren't alone. Me, Amy, Erin, the ki—and loads of other people, all want to help you get your memory back."

"And if it doesn't come back?"

"Then we'll all do everything we can to help you adjust and make more memories. Maybe even better ones. We've got the perfect excuse to go back to New York then, don't ya think?"

"Why can you never let me feel fucking sorry for myself?"

Nikki laughed. "'Cos some things never change, M."

Amy pushed her hair behind her ears and fiddled with the blanket. "So when are they letting you out of here?"

"I don't know yet. They need to make sure I'll be okay on my own, and since I don't remember what my house is like, I can't tell them if I'm capable of managing. Erin didn't know what my place was like, either. I thought that was a bit odd, since she said we were friends, and we've known each other a long time, but—why are you looking like that?" Morgan's frustration grew as they exchanged looks again. "I'm getting really sick of everybody knowing what's going on except me."

"The place you were staying at was a really temporary place. It was very small and a bit…erm…well, a bit crappy to be honest. You were only staying there while you were sorting some stuff out." Amy held up her hands to stave off the questions. "Which I will tell you all about once you're out of here. Okay?"

Morgan frowned, and turned the page of the album. A picture of the three of them smiled back at her. She and Nikki both had hair full of gel to create that bedhead look they both craved. Nikki's eyebrow piercing twinkled in the sunlight, and Amy's long blond hair blew in the breeze. They all looked so young. So alive and carefree. She noted the tightness around the eyes of her younger self; the sadness in them that even her smile couldn't erase.

"I need to see what I look like." She pulled her eyes from the page and looked at Amy. "Please, I need to see."

Amy lifted her bag from the floor and rummaged until she pulled out her compact. "It's a little small, but it'll have to do for now." She handed it over.

"Remember, M, you've been beaten up. Your eyes are black, and you look like shit." Nikki leaned forward in her chair, elbows resting on her knees. "That makes everything else look worse, okay?"

"You telling me I'm ugly?" Morgan fiddled with the catch.

"Why change the habit of a lifetime?" Nikki grinned, but her eyes were serious.

She clicked the clasp open, then closed again. "Have I had any disfiguring injuries?"

"No. Just twenty years of living."

"Then it can't be all that bad." Morgan grinned at Nikki. "I didn't keel over when I saw you after all."

"Fair point." She pointed to the compact. "You gonna open it or do I have to do it for you?"

"I got it." She released the catch and raised the lid. The small circular mirror was far from ideal as she tried to find the right angle to see her whole face and found herself stretching. *Oh my God! My arms aren't long enough!*

Nikki sniggered as Amy handed her a pair of glasses.

"Oh you've got to be shitting me!"

"It's only for seeing things close up. Like reading and drawing and stuff like that," Amy said.

Morgan frowned as she unfolded the glasses and slipped them onto her face. *Jesus, no wonder I was struggling to read all those magazines and newspapers. I thought it was the damn brain fucked-up-ness. Instead, I'm just fucking old!*

She lifted the mirror again and gasped. It was her face, but it wasn't. The same sharp cheekbones and straight nose, full lips and strong jawline. But there were faint lines beside her mouth and softness to her jaw that hadn't been there before. Her hair was missing in patches and the stitches formed a neat uniform row across the red slice in her scalp. She shifted the mirror to look at her eyes. The lines were fine but very definitely there, magnified by the glasses. That wasn't what caught her attention though; it was what was missing from her eyes that struck her. She glanced at the photograph again, then back to the mirror. The sadness wasn't there. The lingering anguish that was so apparent in the eyes of her younger self was missing from her now. She couldn't help but wonder at the cause of it.

Amy cleared her throat. "So, Nikki and I talked about it, and we think you should come and stay with us for a while. We'll be there when you have questions—"

"Yeah, but will you answer any of them?" Morgan ignored Nikki as she chuckled from her chair, focusing solely on Amy.

"And we can help until you can cope with your injuries on your own. And yes, we'll answer anything we ca—"

"So who's Erin?"

"Anything we can, just as soon as the doctors say it's okay." Amy finished.

"They won't let you tell me about Erin?" Morgan frowned.

"I think Erin should tell you about Erin."

Morgan scowled at the smug grin on Amy's face. "You always were a killjoy, Amy."

"Something else that hasn't changed then, hey?"

Morgan turned and looked at Nikki. "I thought you said I was the teacher? She sounds way more like one than I do."

"Amy's a teacher too, smart arse. She was your boss. Head of the Arts Department." Pride shone in Nikki's eyes as she watched her wife.

"Oh, shit." Morgan groaned.

Amy giggled. "Exactly."

"I can get a sick note, I think."

CHAPTER SIX

Erin stirred her tea, dropped the spoon into the sink, and sat at the kitchen table.

"Mum, where's my basketball kit?" Tristan threw his coat over the banister as he walked down the short hallway. His long, lanky frame filled the doorway before he pulled a cupboard open and grabbed a handful of cookies. "Colin's mum said she'd pick me up in an hour."

Erin reached for his hand, stopping him as he headed for the door again. He turned inquisitive blue eyes to her and quirked an eyebrow in question. "Can you please text Colin and tell him you can't make training tonight?"

"We've got a tournament next week for this summer league." He ran his hand over his cropped dark hair. "If I don't train, Coach won't let me start—"

"Tristan, not tonight. I'll explain to your coach so you won't be penalized. Just let Colin know you can't make it."

"That's not fair. Maddie's at her swimming class."

"That was straight from summer club. Once she gets home, I need to speak to you both." Tristan stared at her. "It's important." He threw his arms up in dramatic defeat before stomping off to his room. The slamming door echoed through the house. She dropped her head into her hands and sighed. The battle of wills was something she really didn't need right now. A quick glance at the clock told her she had half an hour before Maddie was due home from her swimming lesson. She picked up the phone and dialed.

"Hi, Chris. It's me."

"Hello, baby sister. To what do I owe the pleasure?"

"Are you busy tonight?"

"Never too busy for you. What do you need? Are you okay?"

"Yeah. No." She laughed humorlessly. "I have no idea. I have to tell the kids."

"It's been a week, Erin. Why haven't you told them sooner?"

"Honestly? I was hoping I'd have something good to tell them."

"Hmm. Sounds more like you were avoiding it to me."

"Well, how would you like to have to do this? They hadn't seen her for three weeks before it happened. I figured another few days to give her a chance to recover wouldn't hurt any of them."

"I see your point. Logical as always. I still think you were chicken shit."

"Why, thank you for your esteemed opinion, Dr. Bain."

Chris laughed. "Finally you see why I became a psychologist."

"Yeah, all those years to be able to call me chicken. So worth it."

"You want me to come round?"

"You mind?"

"Hell, no. I'm on my way. Stick the kettle on."

She put the phone back in place and rubbed her hands over her face. She opened the fridge, trying to decide what to make the children for dinner, then pushed it closed; it could wait.

Twenty minutes later, Chris walked in. He was six foot three, with broad shoulders, dark hair, blue eyes, and an unmistakable resemblance to her. He wrapped his arms around her shoulders, holding her tight against his chest. Erin allowed herself to draw strength from him, secure that he had always been there for her.

He was two years older than her and had been the rock she depended on when their father had walked out on them. Twelve-year-old Erin had stood and watched, horrified, as bailiffs had removed their possessions, then locked the door to their house to cover debts their father had failed to pay, their mother on one side of her, and Chris on the other. The loss of their security—their home— highlighted her vulnerability, her dependence, and her helplessness as the truth of the betrayal sank in. She had idolized her father, and his abandonment cut her to the core.

"Are they home yet?" Chris rubbed her back before he pulled away.

"Tristan's upstairs. Maddie's due home any minute."

"Where's that brew then?"

Erin busied herself making tea before she joined him at the table as the front door burst open.

"Mum, I got a star for my drawing."

Erin and Chris grinned at each other as the little tornado that was Maddie Masters came barreling into the room, her Scooby-Doo backpack dragging behind her, her dark hair hanging in a long, wet, ponytail that soaked the T-shirt partially tucked into her dirt-smudged shorts. She held the paper out to her proudly, the gold star bright at the top of the page. Erin pulled her in for a hug and a kiss. The colorful landscape prominently displayed some of the artistic flair Morgan had so obviously passed down to her daughter.

"Well done, sweetie. Put it on the fridge. How was summer club?"

"Okay. We're doing kayaking tomorrow; you've got to sign a form to say I can go too. If you don't, I have to stay at the Brownie hut and make stupid masks with the little kids. I mean help the little kids with their projects." Maddie slapped the form on the table in front of Erin, then went to the fridge. She used one of the magnets to stick her drawing up before pulling the door open. "I'm hungry."

"When aren't you? What do you want?" Erin smiled and Chris chuckled as she took the milk out.

"Cereal," she said as put it on the counter and reached for a bowl.

"Okay, then I want you to go and get your brother. I need to talk to you both."

Maddie shrugged as she sat and quickly demolished her bowl of chocolate covered flakes.

Erin sipped her tea until Maddie dropped her bowl in the sink and raced upstairs to fetch her brother.

"She looks more like Morgan every day." Chris smiled.

"I know." She brushed the tears from her eyes and willed herself to stay calm. "I don't know how to do this, Chris."

"Just tell them the truth." He gripped her hand.

"And then what? I don't have answers to the questions they're going to ask. I don't have answers to the questions I've as—"

Maddie and Tristan stood in the doorway. Tristan had his hands on Maddie's shoulders and stood behind her protectively. His eyes were wary, while Maddie was curious. *The difference a few years makes.*

"Sit down, please."

Tristan took a chair opposite Chris, and Maddie sat across from Erin. "You wanted to talk to us?" Tristan's voice had the bored quality he was trying so hard to affect, when he was really burning with curiosity.

"It's about your mum." Erin's throat closed on the words, cutting off the air she needed to speak. She grabbed her mug and took a sip. "She was hurt a few nights ago—"

"And you're only telling us now?" Tristan stared at her, eyes narrowed to slits.

"Tristan, let me finish, then you can shout at me for not telling you sooner. Okay?" She waited, but he stayed silent, his arms crossed. She sighed. "She was hurt. Her shoulder was hurt, but that's going to be fine. It just needs some time to heal properly. She's got a couple of bruised ribs, and a few cuts. So all that is going to be just fine. She'll heal, and be out of the hospital in no time."

"Can we go and see her then?" Maddie's big brown eyes were brimming with tears.

Erin shook her head and pulled Maddie onto her lap. "It's not quite that simple, sweetie." *How do I explain? How do you make a ten-year-old understand this?* "You see she…it was…she hurt her head. And that's caused some other…" She swiped at the tears on Maddie's cheeks then glanced at Chris. He nodded, offering silent encouragement. "That caused a really bad concussion."

"But you said she'll be coming out of hospital." Tristan's anger was gone, clearly replaced by fear and panic.

"And she will be. She will. I promise."

"Then why can't we go and see her? She's our mum, too." Maddie's voice was so soft Erin could barely hear her. She glanced at Chris again. His face was set, and his eyes fixed on Tristan. They were both waiting for the reaction from him. Erin didn't know if it would be tears or rage he opted for.

Tristan stood, knocking his chair to the floor. "She doesn't want us anymore? Is that it? She left you, and she doesn't want us either."

Erin caught hold of his arm. "That's not it. She has amnesia." Tristan's eyes widened, his shock evident. Maddie just looked confused.

"What's that?"

Erin didn't take her eyes off Tristan, his face pale, beads of sweat forming on his brow. "It's when a person loses their memory."

"This is a sick joke. Right?" Tristan tore his arm from Erin's grasp and ran out of the room. Chris caught Erin's eye and went after Tristan.

Erin cupped Maddie's chin, tilting her face until she could see her eyes. She wiped the tears away.

"Do you understand, sweetie?"

"No."

Erin held her face against her shoulder, stroking her hair as she spoke. "When Morgan woke up, she thought she was nineteen. She doesn't remember anything after she was nineteen."

"But mum's older than you are."

Erin smiled gently at her reasoning. "I know, but she doesn't remember that."

"She just forgot it all?"

"Yes."

"Does she remember you?"

Erin swallowed the lump in her throat. "No, she doesn't remember me, sweetie."

"Does she remember us?" Hiccups interrupted Maddie's words.

Erin stroked her hands down the length of Maddie's back, then hugged her tight. "I'm sorry, sweetie, but no. She doesn't. She doesn't remember anything." Erin heard a whimper from the doorway and looked over as Chris wrapped his arms about Tristan's shoulders on their way back into the room.

His voice was tiny as he asked, "Will she get it back? Will she remember us again?"

"We don't know, Trist. The doctor's think it's possible, but they don't kn—"

"Does she still love us?" Maddie lifted her head from Erin's shoulder, her cheeks ruddy, and her eyes red rimmed and swollen.

Erin couldn't bring herself to look her in the eyes and tell her no. She couldn't find the words to break Maddie's heart even more than it already was.

All the anger and pain that Morgan had caused her—them—came flooding back to her. The nights she'd held Maddie, crying because Morgan had left them. Tristan's mood swings as he tried desperately to understand where it had all gone wrong, and why the mother he adored hadn't even phoned to speak to him. She felt discarded, and vulnerable, and unwanted. Morgan's abandonment stirred up every painful emotion of her own childhood.

She had trusted Morgan, built a home and a life with her, and believed that she would never subject their children to the pain Erin had suffered. Her own feelings of betrayal paled next to her children's pain. She knew she wouldn't be able to subject them to that risk again. It didn't matter how she felt seeing Morgan vulnerable and scared in the hospital. Some things were just more important.

Tristan's voice broke as he whispered the words Erin wished she could refute. "She doesn't remember us to love us anymore, Maddie. As far as she's concerned, we don't exist. You can't love someone you don't even know."

CHAPTER SEVEN

Morgan's scalp itched and her palms sweated as she waited. She shifted uncomfortably in the hospital issue wheelchair with its hard padded seat and wheels that made pulling it much easier than pushing. Dr. Rebecca Bann studied the file on her desk, papers scattered all around her. Her blond hair was pulled into a sloppy bun, a pen stuck out of it, and another pen danced between her fingers as she tapped it against the thick wedge of paper. The office had books along one wall and the blinds were drawn to stop the summer sun blinding her.

"So how are you feeling?" Dr. Bann looked up. She had an open face that made Morgan feel at ease; she was confident in her professional abilities and comfortable enough to talk to her.

"Mostly fine. Getting a shower this morning, like, really helped. I feel nearly human again. I'm still getting pretty bad headaches though."

"It's been a week since you woke up. In all honesty, I'd be worried if you weren't getting headaches. You head injury was very serious, Morgan. Your brain swelled inside your skull and we had to operate to relieve the pressure. Your concussion was very severe. Combine that with the seizures you had—"

"I didn't have seizures." She frowned and shifted forward in her chair.

Dr. Bann cast her eyes down then back to Morgan, as she pointed at a note in the file, obviously checking her facts. "Yes, you did. You won't remember them. You were in and out of consciousness, but you had several seizures. So the two things together have created areas of bruising and scarring in your brain." She got up and rounded the table, holding a thin metal and glass slate in front of her.

It looks like something out of Star Trek. "What's that?"

"An iPad."

Morgan frowned. "A what?"

"An iPad. It's a computer. Just smaller." She turned the screen toward Morgan. "This is the most recent scan of your brain." She pointed to some darker spots in different locations. "These spots are bruises; they'll get better over time. These are the parts that are affecting your balance and coordination. They're also affecting your concentration, lethargy, even the nausea you feel from time to time. The vertigo that you've been suffering from, is it getting better?"

"Yeah, a bit."

"Good. That correlates with the earlier scans and how the bruising is already decreasing."

"How come you didn't show me this before?"

"I did. The day after you woke up. Some of those memories may still be foggy; others will be crystal clear. Obviously, that one wasn't retained."

Morgan's leg twitched as she stared at the detailed diagram of her own brain, trying to make sense of what she was seeing. "You said bruising *and* scarring. I thought scars took ages to form."

"Yes, they do. But the scar starts to form the moment the injury occurs. Say you cut your leg, the moment your body starts to heal and form the clot bridging the skin back together, the scar is starting to form. It would take between six and nine months for it to fully heal, and it will be harder, sometimes raised too, but it's forming a scar from the moment the injury occurs." She pointed to a series of small white spots. "This is scar tissue forming on your brain. This area is known as the hippocampus, and this," she said, as she moved her finger to encompass the outside of the gray matter, "is the cortex. These are the areas of the brain that are involved with the formation and storing of long-term memories."

"Which is why I can't remember anything?"

"As far as we can tell, yes. It may be that as the swelling settles completely, your memories will return. It's very unusual to suffer amnesia in the way you're doing at the moment. Some of that may be due to the drugs that were also in your system. "

"I was doing drugs?" Morgan knew she was staring. "Doc, I did a little bit of weed, you know, like at parties and shit, but I didn't do anything else."

Dr. Bann looked back at her notes. "The tests showed that it was a derivative of Flunitrazepam, or Rohypnol. It's a kind of tranquilizer."

"Why the hell would I be taking a tranquillizer on a night out?"

"Rohypnol is called a date rape drug—"

"Rape! I was raped?" Morgan leaned forward in her chair and wrapped her hands around her knees. Her chest tightened and her pulse thundered in her ears.

"No. There was absolutely no evidence that you were sexually assaulted, Morgan. Not at all. We don't know why the drugs were in your system; this type of drug is legitimately used as a sleeping tablet. It's possible that you were taking them for this reason. But as you weren't prescribed any drugs by your GP, the police are working on the assumption that you were slipped the drugs by a third party."

"On purpose?"

"Yes. Morgan, it's okay. Please try to stay calm." Dr. Bann rounded her desk and put her hand to Morgan's forehead.

"But why would someone do that to me?"

"I don't know. And until the police find whoever did this to you, I don't think they do either."

"They didn't rape me?"

"No. Please try to calm down, Morgan. I'm sorry I scared you like that."

Morgan shivered. "It's okay."

Dr. Bann moved back behind her desk. "Changing the subject, have you recovered any memories beyond the age of nineteen?"

"No. You're the expert here, Doc. What chance do I actually have of remembering everything?" Morgan tried to calm the irrational desire to scratch at her skin and clung to the tiny flame of hope that burned inside her, waiting, yearning, for something to ignite.

"The brain is—"

"Tricky. Yeah, I know. You all keep saying that, but it doesn't help me." The glimmer of hope flickered and died, anger taking its place.

"I'm sorry, Morgan, but the scar tissue tells me that it is very unlikely that you'll recover all your memories. Some things may get left behind completely, but you could regain the majority of them over time. Or they may never come back at all. Talk to your friends and family. See if they can help trigger—"

"You've told everyone not to say anything about my life that might shock me, so they've told me, like, diddley fucking squat! I want to know who I am! Who everyone out there expects me to be!" Morgan leaned forward in her chair. "I've been told I was practically living in a hovel. Why? I was working, right? Teacher, at a college. Got to have been earning a decent amount, but I was living in some crummy flat that's so awful my friends won't let me go back there. How the hell did I end up there?"

"Morgan, I don't know." She put the iPad back on the desk and leaned her hip against it.

"Then who the fuck does?" Morgan collapsed back into her chair, her anger dissipating as quickly as it flared. She rubbed her hand over the jumping, twitching muscle in her thigh.

"Your friends are the people who will help you fill in the blanks. Quite obviously, it's causing more harm than not now, to keep anything from you."

"About bloody time." She smiled. "So tell me what I was doing when I got hurt?"

"I don't have all the detai—"

"I thought you said keeping stuff from me was causing more harm than good."

"But I understand that you had been teaching a night class and were attacked in the car park."

Morgan frowned. *Okay, teaching, late July, night class. I can buy that.* "Right, so what happened?"

"I don't know." She sat back in her chair. "Haven't the police talked to you yet?"

"No."

"Are you worried about talking to them?"

"No." The twitching in Morgan's leg increased until it was bouncing in a fast rhythm against the footplate of her wheelchair.

"Really?" Dr. Bann paused in her reading and cocked her head to one side as she studied Morgan.

I feel like a microscope specimen. "I don't have anything to tell them, so what's to worry about?"

"Hmm. The police should give you more information when you talk to them."

"Right." Morgan continued to fidget under the doctor's intense stare. "What?"

"Do you want to go home?"

The leg jumping stopped. "I can?"

"Well, there's nothing more that we can do with regards to your injuries. They'll heal as well at home as they will here. The symptoms of your concussion are getting better. You're not vomiting. Your memory…" She shrugged. "I think surrounding yourself with familiar things will be far more beneficial to you than staying in a sterile hospital room."

"Will it help me get my memories back?"

She laughed. "It can't hurt, Morgan. Have your friends take you places you used to frequent. Do things you used to enjoy. Many amnesia patients say these things can trigger memories."

"Really?"

"Sometimes. It's not a guarantee, Morgan. You may regain some of your memories, or none. It may do nothing but give you a nice afternoo—"

"Like you said, it can't hurt. It's not like I'm going to end up any worse for giving it a try, am I?"

"As long as you don't go banging your head again, you should be absolutely fine."

❖

Nikki was sitting with her feet propped up against the bed, her hands clasped behind her head, as the orderly wheeled Morgan back into the room and helped her back into her bed.

"I've been thinking about this," Nikki said after the door closed behind the orderly. "You know all the shit that makes us who we are? Is it how we were born or everything we live through? Nature or nurture. Innate or environmental."

"And, Einstein? Did you reach a conclusion?" Morgan's lips twitched.

"Not a bloody clue, but it's fascinating really. I mean, are we the sum of our memories, and experiences? Or is there something else? And then what really is a memory? Everybody's memories are always different, aren't they? If you ask two people to tell you about the same event, there's always a difference."

"Did you switch to Philosophy at uni?"

"Ha ha. No, I was just thinking, that maybe this is a good thing. You can let the stuff go that you want to. I mean, we've all got shit that we wish we could forget, right? And you really have."

"Speaking of all that shit, the doc says you've got to tell me now."

"Did she?"

"Yep. So start talking."

"What else did she have to say?"

"I can go home, and that you should help me do stuff that I used to like, and did all the time."

"So I gotta take you to strip clubs?" Nikki rubbed her hands together gleefully. "Result!"

"Nice try, studley." Amy shook her head at them both as she walked in. "I brought some clothes for you. I figured they wouldn't be keeping you too much longer."

Morgan pulled the clothes out of the bag Amy handed her.

Nikki was laughing. "You need a hand?"

Morgan flushed. "No, thanks."

"Nikki, go and tell the nurse we'll be ready to go in a few minutes. I don't know what paperwork they need to do, so you can get the ball rolling."

"Why do I have to go?"

"Jesus, just because Morgan thinks she's nineteen, does not mean you can act like the spoiled bloody teenager you were back then, Nicole Rogers. Now scoot."

Morgan stared as Nikki hurried out the door. "Boy, have you got her well train—"

"And don't you start either. Come on, sit up. Let's get you dressed before she gets back, and you start behaving like teenage boys again."

"She started it." Morgan decided silence was the better part of valor and followed Amy's instructions. They'd changed together so often throughout their friendship she didn't feel the least self-conscious, though seeing her body all bruised and bandaged and... old, made her wonder what Amy saw when she looked at her.

An hour later, Nikki helped her walk up the driveway to a semi-detached house with ivy climbing up the sides of the front door, buddleia blooms under the window, and roses growing in a small flower bed cut in the middle of the lawn.

"It's really pretty."

"Amy loves the garden. She's growing tomatoes and peppers in a greenhouse out the back." They took the small steps into the house slowly. "You used to come and draw here sometimes."

"I did?"

"Yeah. It wasn't your favorite place though. You loved the park. You'd sit for hours drawing people around the duck ponds, and kids on the playing field."

Morgan frowned.

"Any of that sound familiar?"

"No."

"Maybe if we go there it would."

"Nikki, I need to know what happened to my mum."

"Now?" Nikki helped her into a cozy sitting room with cream walls, wooden flooring, and an overstuffed peach colored sofa that swallowed Morgan when she sat down. "I think I need a drink first."

Morgan looked around while she waited for Nikki to return. A painting of two children hung over the fireplace. Cherubic faces grinned off the canvass, the little girl's dark hair and eyes shining, her dimples cutting deeply into both cheeks as her shoulders scrunched, laughter and love radiating off her. The little boy was sitting side on, looking over his shoulder as he faced the girl, his eyes as blue as the Aegean Sea and his dark hair sporting an awkward cowlick that obviously wouldn't stay down. He rested his hand on the girl's shoulder, his smile just as wide as hers.

Nikki pulled a small table near to where Morgan was sitting and put a mug down for her before sitting on the other side of the sofa.

"That's a nice painting."

Nikki paused, her drink halfway to her lips. "You did that."

"I did?" Morgan stared at it again. "Who're the kids?"

She swallowed heavily as Amy came into the room. "That's Tristan and Maddison."

Morgan ignored the pained whimper from Amy. "Who are they? They must be special to you to have the picture there." Out of the corner of her eye, she caught the near-panicked look that passed between them, but chose to ignore it. She was determined to find out what had happened to her mum now. She needed to start there before she could move forward.

"They're our godchildren. In that picture Tristan was seven and Maddie four."

"They're cute."

Amy got up and walked out of the room.

"Is she all right?"

Nikki shrugged, her eyes downcast as she took another drink. "She has a bit of a headache, that's all. So you're stuck with me for this one. That okay?"

"I just need to know." Morgan picked up her mug, content to cradle the warmth in her hands, hoping it would thaw the chill that had settled inside her.

"I understand that, but part of me thinks you're better off not knowing."

"I don't under—"

"I know." Nikki smiled sadly. "You remember what it was like for you at home? Before you went to uni?"

Morgan nodded. She remembered the violence between her parents, her mother's misery, and her father's anger. She remembered every excuse he gave: "she pushed me to it," "it wasn't my fault," "it was an accident." Time and again. "I remember."

"When you went home at Christmas break, they had another fight. Your mum was fighting back, and it made your dad even worse. You remember that tankard glass he always had his Guinness in?"

"Yes." Her voice barely a whisper.

"He smashed it."

"Oh, God." Her vision narrowed until all she could see was Nikki's lips forming the words. Time seemed to slow down, and the sound became elongated as it reached her. Stretched thin, taut, poised, like a rubber band ready to snap.

"There was a huge fight and he slashed her neck open." Nikki motioned with her hands how the broken jagged edge of the glass had sliced open the side of her throat. "The ambulance people couldn't stop the bleeding. When they got there it was already too late, but they tried."

"He killed her." The words didn't even reach her own ears. They didn't need to. She knew the truth of them down to her very soul. "Why?"

"You know how they fought—"

"I mean, why was she fighting back? She never fought back. She said it only made things worse." Her hands shook, sloshing hot liquid over her. She quickly put the mug onto the coaster and wiped her hand on her jeans.

"I wasn't there, M."

"But you know. Don't you?"

"It doesn't matter anymore. They fought, he killed her, now he's in jail. End of story."

Morgan stared at her. "It isn't though, is it? Don't fob me off, Nikki. I need to know."

"Why?"

Why is she being so fucking stupid? Of course I need to know. "So that I can be me again?"

"And you think knowing all the gory details of this will help that?" Nikki put down her own mug.

"Well, yeah." Morgan's frown deepened.

"For the past twenty years, you've told me time after time, that you wished you didn't know. You wanted it wiped out of your head. You wanted to be free of it all." She reached for Morgan's hand. "You can be now. Do you really need to know more than that?"

Morgan let the warmth of Nikki's palm slowly heat her own. Did she? What difference would it make now? Nothing would bring her mother back. Her father was already in jail. What more could she gain from knowing the details? Peace of mind?

"I really said that I wished I couldn't remember it?"

"Yes. Many times."

"Why?"

Nikki stared at her, the internal battle over how much to say raging clearly in her eyes. She blinked, shaking her head. "Because you were there, Morgan. You saw it happen."

Her heart pounded in her chest as she tried to drag air into her lungs. "I let her die?"

"No. God, no. No one could've helped her. There was nothing anyone could've done differently to save her except your dad. Nothing."

Blood rushed through her ears, deafening her. "But if I was there—"

"No. The ambulance people, the police, the doctors, coroner. Everyone." Nikki tugged her hand gently until Morgan was looking at her again. "Everyone always said there was absolutely nothing you could have done that you didn't do. You called nine nine nine; you held her neck to try and stop the bleeding. You did everything in your power to save her."

"But it didn't work."

"No. Not everyone can be saved, M."

"But—"

"No, no buts. You've spent twenty years feeling guilty because you survived that night and your mum didn't. Tell me one thing."

Morgan didn't say anything as she looked at her. Was that what she'd seen in the eyes of her younger self? Guilt for surviving when her mother hadn't? Was that the shadow she had seen in her own eyes? The one she didn't see in the mirror now?

"Would your mum have wanted it the other way around?"

"What? For me to die?"

Nikki nodded.

"God, no."

"Then don't feel guilty for surviving; for doing what she wanted."

Morgan closed her eyes, not wanting to shed the tears that filled them. "I don't think I want to know any more right now."

CHAPTER EIGHT

Morgan paced in front of the window, stopping every few minutes to stare out at the garden. She picked up the leaflet Amy had given her, thumbed open the page, and then tossed it back onto the windowsill. The stages of grief. Shock and denial. *I passed through that in the hospital. Well...maybe.*

Pain and guilt. *Apparently, I've lived with that for twenty years. Do I want to go there again? Fuck, no. Nikki said I did nothing wrong, I have to trust her, right? Or I have nothing. She said I shouldn't feel guilty, that my mother wouldn't want that. Amy said the same thing this morning.*

She knew she either needed to trust them or make them explain everything that happened, which would probably pull her into the same hole she'd been living in. The same self-destructive cycle that left her lonely and depressed, according to Nikki. *Another stage I've already been through, and let's face it, I'm angry. So there's another one off the list.*

She grabbed the paper, screwed it into a ball, and launched it across the room. *So why the fuck don't I feel any better?* The walls of the guest room were a pleasant off-white, but they seemed to be getting closer and closer to her with every minute she was there. The need to get out, to stretch her legs, and breathe fresh air, gnawed at her. She found Amy in the kitchen.

"Can we go out somewhere?"

"Where?" Amy finished loading the dishwasher.

"I don't know. Anywhere." Morgan ran her hand through her hair. "Can you take me somewhere that I used to like going?"

Amy smiled. Her green eyes sparkled and she pulled her hair out of its ponytail. "You feel up to a walk?"

"Yeah. My ribs aren't too bad."

Amy looked at her skeptically. "After a week? Hmm."

"I'll be fine. Honestly. I need to get out for a while."

"Well, it's a lovely day, I know just the place."

They walked slowly, Morgan following the quiet directions Amy gave her, until they were walking down a dirt path, with horse chestnut, sycamore, and beech trees on one side of them, and a small duck pond on the other. There was a field on the far side of the water, and what looked like a family playing football.

"You used to come here nearly every weekend."

"So, I lived around here?"

"Yeah. Before you moved to the flat you lived only a few streets away from us."

"Why did I move?"

"To be honest, Morgan, I still don't know."

"What do you mean?"

Amy shrugged. "You never explained. You just went all hermit on us and hid out in that flat." She pointed to a bench at the head of the pond. "You used to sit there and sketch." They sat side by side, watching a pair of swans floating majestically across the water, their heads bent close together making the shape of a love heart between them. Her fingers itched to capture the scene; the proud birds, the ripples spreading across the water, and the playing field in the background. The view was good across the water and the playing field, and she could easily understand why she would have chosen this spot.

"I wish I had my pad with me now."

"That's wonderful to hear."

Morgan frowned at her.

"The last few weeks, before the incident, you stopped drawing."

"Why?"

"Something else you didn't explain."

"What did I explain?"

Amy laughed. "Bugger all, really."

The sound of excited children drifted over as a boy celebrated a goal on the field. He ran in wide circles with his arms held aloft, fingers pointing to the sky, until he stopped suddenly. His arms dropped to his sides and the girl chasing him ran into his back, the force of her momentum almost taking them both to the ground.

"Shit. Morgan, we should go." Amy reached for Morgan's hand.

Morgan stayed seated, feeling stubborn. "Why? It's lovely here. I feel like I can think for the—"

"Maddie, no!" A woman's voice yelled from the other side of the field as the little girl sprinted around the edge of the water, a huge smile on her face.

"Morgan, please. We need to go. Now."

"Isn't that the girl in the picture? The one over your fireplace?"

"Maddison. Stop! Come back here, now!"

Morgan looked beyond the girl and recognized the woman running across the field after her. Her pulse quickened as Erin neared, despite the look of fear on her face.

"Morgan, plea—"

The girl closed the final distance.

Morgan expected her to approach Amy.

She was wrong.

"Mum!" The girl wrapped her arms around Morgan's neck and dropped a sloppy, sweaty kiss on her cheek. "Are you better now?"

Mum? Me? Morgan felt her arms rising automatically to hold the child. She pulled her back a little to look at her properly. The girl's face was the mirror image of her own face when she was kid. *Mum?*

Then the girl was gone, her little arms ripped from her neck as Erin lifted her into her arms and cradled her against her body.

"What the hell are you doing?" Erin's eyes flashed angrily and her face was flushed. Her dark hair curled against her forehead and neck. Morgan thought she was beautiful, even though she looked ready to rip Amy's head off.

Amy grimaced. "Erin, I'm sorry. I had no way of knowing you were going to—"

Erin didn't look at her, her eyes were firmly fixed on Morgan's face. The girl was sobbing against Erin's neck as she patted her back and kissed her hair. "It's okay, sweetie. It's okay."

"She called me 'mum.'" Morgan looked from Erin to Amy, her mind unable to comprehend the magnitude of it all. "Why did she call me mum?"

A giant of a man walked up to Erin's side and took the girl from Erin's arms. He wrapped his other arm around the boy's shoulders. "I'll take these two home. We'll be okay till you get there. Won't we, guys?" Neither child responded. They just stared at Morgan, desperation clear in both their little faces.

Morgan stared at them, the lovely family unit. Beautiful Erin and her handsome husband. Their gorgeous kids. The boy was a miniature version of them both. *Why did the girl call me mum?*

"Thanks, Chris." Erin stroked her hand down the boy's cheek. "Will you look after your sister for me? We'll talk when I get back. I promise, Tristan."

He turned watery blue eyes up to her. "She doesn't remember anything, does she?"

Erin wrapped her arms about his shoulders and held him. "I promise we'll talk when I come home."

"Don't bother." He pushed away from her and set off running across the field.

"Tristan!" Erin started after him. He stopped at the gate to the park, hung onto the railings, and buried his head in the crook of his arm.

"I've got it. You need to be here." Chris stopped Erin from chasing Tristan and gestured at Morgan. "I can handle this." Chris carried Maddie away and headed for Tristan. The sobs racking his body were visible across the field.

Erin pressed her fingers into her eyes before taking a deep breath and turning back to Morgan as the man, Chris, ushered the children out of view.

Amy touched her arm. "I'll wait over there." She pointed to another bench, halfway along the pond.

Erin shook her head. "Chicken."

"I know. Sorry." Amy walked away slowly.

Morgan stared across the field as Erin sat down beside her. "Is he your husband?"

"No, Chris is my brother."

Morgan felt a surge of relief but didn't have time to dissect it. There were too many other things that needed to be addresses. *She called me mum.* "She has my eyes."

"Yes, she does."

"I don't understand. They're my children?"

"*Our* children."

Morgan snapped her head round so fast it sent a pain shooting through the base of her skull. She winced as she lifted her hand to rub the back of her neck. "We're together?" Despite the twinge in her neck, and the shock, Morgan felt like her world finally made sense. Of course Erin couldn't take her home to the children straight away. It would be far too traumatic for them. They needed time, to adjust, to get to know each other again. She smiled, knowing instinctively that this was where she belonged. Beside Erin. She felt a sense of peace that she hadn't known since waking up. The black hole of her past suddenly didn't matter quite so much, because she was sitting beside the most important part of it. She couldn't stop herself from reaching for Erin's hand.

Erin flinched and pulled away before dropping her gaze to the ground. "No. Not anymore."

The peaceful feeling evaporated, leaving her with the anger that was becoming all too familiar. "Because of this?" Morgan pointed to her head.

"What?" Erin frowned.

"The whole memory thing?" She turned away from Erin and stared out across the water; the swans were swimming along, ripples spreading across the surface of the water behind them. "Is that why you don't want me?"

"*You* left *me* before this happened."

She turned around to face her again. Erin's crystal blue eyes were red rimmed, and the thought that she'd been crying hurt Morgan deeply. She wanted to soothe her pain, as she was sure she must have done in the past. The attraction she felt for Erin was undeniable, but there was something deeper that called to her. It had been there the moment she woke in the hospital, and it was still there now. Instinct, intuition, whatever name she gave it, it all meant the same. She knew that Erin made her whole. The thought of leaving her stole the breath from her lungs, and chilled her to the core. "I'm sorry. That was a really stupid thing to say. Why did I leave?"

"You said you were making us miserable and walked out. That was the last time I saw you before you ended up in hospital."

"That doesn't make sense."

Erin laughed. "Funny, that's just what I said."

"The kids aren't little babies—"

"We were together for fifteen years. Tristan's thirteen, and Maddie's ten. Is that what you wanted to know?" Erin pulled the band out of her hair, swept up the loose tendrils, and then re-secured it at the back of her head. She crossed one leg over the other.

"Among other things."

"Like?"

Morgan shrugged. "Everything, I guess. What do you do? Where do we—did we live? We had a whole life together."

"Our life together doesn't really matter anymore. You walked out on that. Before your accident, we hadn't seen hide nor hair of you for three weeks. *Our* life together doesn't exist anymore. Our children are a different story." Her voice was sharp, and Morgan flinched.

"They know? About the memory thing?"

"Yes, I told them. I don't think it had really sunk in what it meant before now. For Maddie especially."

"Will she be okay?"

Erin was silent so long that Morgan didn't think she was going to answer.

"I have no idea. They're used to having you around. Having us both with them every day." She twisted the ring on her finger around. "I have no idea how to help them with this. It was hard enough telling them you left us and not being able to give them a reason why. But now you don't even remember them. I don't know what to do."

Erin looked lost. Morgan reached out her hand and slowly covered Erin's, stopping her from playing with her ring. Third finger, left hand. "Did I give you this?"

Erin's cheeks colored. "I should have taken it off before now." She started to pull her hand away.

"No, don't." Erin's skin was soft beneath hers, and warm. She tried to pretend she didn't hear the sharp breath as she traced her fingers over her knuckles and twisted the ring until the small diamond faced out. "When?" She heard Erin swallow, but she couldn't tear her eyes away from the white gold band, glinting in the sun.

"Two thousand and four." She cleared her throat. "Civil partnerships were introduced, effectively allowing gay and lesbian couples to get married. Tristan was your best man, and Maddie was our bridesmaid." Erin's voice broke. "He was so proud when he stood at the altar next to you."

She wanted to entwine their fingers, press their palms together, and never let go. Instead, she traced her finger lightly over the veins in the back of Erin's hand. "Now he hates me."

"No, he still loves you. They both do. That's why they're hurting." She pulled her hand away.

"How can I help?" The words were out before she thought about it, but she didn't regret airing them. She realized that she'd do anything to be close to Erin, to spend more time with her.

Erin laughed again. "You want to help?"

Morgan frowned. "Why is that so hard to believe?"

Erin stared at her. Morgan had never felt so exposed as she sat in front of the woman who knew her better than she knew herself. The woman who had held her, kissed her, touched her. The woman who was a beautiful stranger. She wanted to connect with her, to feel some of the warmth that must have been between them, but there was a wariness in Erin's eyes that told her it wouldn't be so easy.

"You said in the hospital that we were friends."

"We were." She uncrossed her legs and put her hands on her knees. "We were everything to each other."

The bitter sorrow in her words stung, and Morgan wished she knew a way to take that pain away. "But not anymore?"

"I can't forget how much you hurt me, Morgan."

"I'm sorry."

"Oh, God. If only it was that easy. You don't even know what you're apologizing for. Hell, you don't even know me!"

The pain and vulnerability that had been clear only moments before were replaced by anger. Morgan knew she was getting ready to leave, and she was desperate for Erin to stay. Even just a little longer. "I didn't know you fifteen years ago either, but we changed that."

"Fifteen years ago we were in the same place. Now you think you're nineteen, and I'm a thirty-six year old single mum, with two kids, a failed marriage, a mortgage, a full-time job, bills to pay. Do I need to carry on?" Erin stood and looked over at Amy. "I need to go and see to my children."

"You said they're our children."

"Don't make this harder than it needs to be." She didn't look back as she walked away.

CHAPTER NINE

The mechanical whirring of the washing machine hummed in the background. The muted TV flickered from one scene to the next, dragging Morgan's attention from her maudlin thoughts before they sucked her back down into the vortex of questions and emotions that seemed disconnected from reason. Every time she closed her eyes she saw Erin's face, eyes red rimmed and filled with pain one moment, smiling gently at her the next.

She could still feel warm little arms wrapped around her neck. Maddie. *My daughter. Our daughter.* Morgan wished she could remember what it felt like to wrap her own arms around the girl; she'd been too shocked to do so yesterday at the park. She wished she'd been able to erase the pain from Tristan's face. Her son. *My children.*

"Morgan?" Nikki's voice was quiet, but strong enough to get her attention. "There are two police officers here. They want to talk to you. Do you feel up to it?"

Morgan shrugged. "Now's as good a time as any. It's not like waiting's likely to help." A wave of vertigo gripped her as she stood up. Nikki reached for her hand to steady her, and simply waited until Morgan was ready.

"Is that any worse?"

"No. I've just, like, got a bit of a headache right now. That doesn't help with the spinning world feeling."

"You sure you're up to this?"

"I'll be fine."

Nikki kept hold of her elbow as they walked through the house. Two police officers were sitting, talking to Amy, and they stood when Morgan and Nikki entered the room.

"Ms. Masters, I'm PC Lock, and this is PC Ward." He held his hand out to shake, and then indicated his colleague. "We need to ask you some questions about the night of your attack."

"Sure." It wasn't a question, but she felt she needed to respond. "Have you spoken to the doctors who were treating me?"

"Not since you were released. Can you tell me what happened on the night of Wednesday, July twenty-fifth, two thousand and twelve?"

"No." Morgan shook her head. "I'm sorry, but I don't remember anything."

"We need your help if we're going to catch the person who did this to you."

"I get that. But I really don't know. If you spoke to my doctors you should know that I have amnesia. I'm not being stubborn, or secretive, or protecting someone, or any of that crap. I really don't remember a thing."

The two police officers glanced at each other. One of them, Lock, reached into his pocket and pulled out a picture. "We got this off the CCTV footage from the college. Their system takes still pictures every few seconds in rotation. So we have images of what happened to you that night. The quality isn't good enough for facial recognition, but would you take a look and see if it jogs your memory?"

"It can't hurt, right?" She took the picture from him and it landed like a blow to the gut. The air hissed out of her lungs, and her hand shook.

Nikki was looking over her shoulder. "Fuck."

It was grainy, and distorted, but it was clearly Morgan, her head pressed against a woman's breasts. The woman had her head thrown back, a look of pleasure on her face, and Morgan's arms were wrapped around her.

"That's you, isn't it, Ms. Masters?"

Morgan looked up from the picture, her mouth hung open, but no sound came out.

"Do you know who the woman is with you?"

Morgan shook her head.

"Do either of you recognize her?"

"No." Nikki pulled the picture from Morgan's hand and passed it to Amy.

"No." Her face paled as she handed it back to PC Lock and he pulled another picture from his pocket.

"We never got a full view of this man, but this is the man who attacked you. Do you know him?"

"PC Lock, I don't even know my own children. Do you really think I'm going to recognize this man?" She took the picture he held out to her, and the rage on the man's face made his features difficult to make out. "If I do know him, I have no idea who he is."

Nikki and Amy studied the picture for themselves, also at a loss.

"He shoved the woman into the car and drove off with her. It looked like she was struggling and she seems to know the man, but we can't confirm that until we identify her. I've circulated the pictures of her face and his with the college security people in the hope that someone might recognize either of them, but so far no luck. I've also had them run the pictures through the database of staff and students. No one seems to know either of them."

"The picture you showed me?" Morgan's pulse raced at the thought of anyone else seeing her like that.

"We cropped you out of the picture. Data protection." He plucked a business card out of his stab vest. "If you do remember anything, please call me right away."

"It's been more than a week. Why haven't you already found out who they are?" Nikki's accusation hung in the air.

"We are doing all we can, but we don't have very much to go on. We have no idea where Ms. Masters met her. We can't find anybody at the college who recognizes either of them, and Ms. Masters can't give us anything else at the moment," he said, as though this explained everything. "Like I said, it appears on the footage as though she knows the man. We're checking other CCTV footage to see if we can track down where they were that night." They both stood. "We'll keep you informed, Ms. Masters."

"What about the drugs?" Morgan asked.

Lock shrugged. "There's no way to tell how they got in your system until we can identify these people as you can't tell us anything. There was nothing distinctive to the drug makeup that would help us to identify the source or the person using it. At this point, it doesn't help. I'm sorry."

Morgan was silent as they left. Nikki was barely back in the room before she turned to face them both. "Did you know?" Her shock was lifting, and in the pit of her belly she felt disgusted with herself. The image of her body pleasuring some stranger in a car park was burned into her brain.

"Know what?" Nikki said.

"Did either of you know that I was screwing someone else?"

Amy shook her head.

"No." Nikki's face was red as she glared at Morgan. "If I had, I would've told you that you were a fucking idiot!"

"Was I having an affair? Is that woman why I left Erin?" Morgan stared at her hands. Hands that yesterday had held Erin's. The same hands that had stroked another woman's skin. *But I'm Erin's.*

"You didn't tell anyone anything. You could've been screwing the pope, for all we knew!"

"I really didn't tell you anything?" There was no anger left in her to direct at Nikki. She felt empty, numb, and cold. "I don't want to be the Morgan in that picture."

"What do you mean?" Amy said.

"The woman in that picture, she was the one Nikki said was depressed and lonely. And she didn't have any family with her, she ran away from Erin, and those kids, and no one has any idea why. And I don't want to be like her. I don't want to be her. She sounds, like, fucking miserable."

"I don't know; she had her good points." Amy got out of her chair and knelt in front of her, gripping her hand.

"Yeah? Like what? Because all I've heard so far is that she was a fucking waste of space who didn't know a good thing when she was fucking living it!"

Amy frowned. "She was a good mum—"

"Good mums don't walk out on their kids. How long before the attack did I leave?"

"Three weeks." She let go of Morgan's hand and stood up.

"And how many times did I call them? How many times did I go and see them? Because Erin said they hadn't seen me or heard from me since I walked out the door. That sound like a good mum to you?" Morgan didn't even look up. She wanted the anger back. She wanted to feel the heat of rage's fire. Anything but the numbness that was enveloping her.

"You were a good teacher."

"Really? Did I become a teacher because I failed at being an artist?"

"No, you didn't fail."

"Did I even try?"

"What?" Amy frowned, her confusion evident.

"Did I try to make a living as an artist? That was my dream." They waited staring at her. "Well? Did I even try?"

"No."

"So, I wasn't a good teacher. I didn't want to be a teacher. Being a good teacher takes passion. Pride. Not just falling into it. Right?"

Amy blew out a frustrated breath. "Morgan, right now, it doesn't matter what either of us say—"

"You're damn right it fucking doesn't! I was a piece of shit!" The coldness in Morgan's voice broke, like the ice cracking over a frozen lake. Underneath, the fire of fury gripped her and wrung all logic from her mind. "It's no wonder Erin doesn't want anything to do with me. I don't want anything to do with me! Those kids have a mother who loves the bones of 'em, they—"

"They used to have two." Amy flung her words out like stones, and Morgan felt the sting of each one as it hit its mark.

"What?"

"You're right, Erin does love the ground those kids walk on. But so did you. You did just as much for those kids as she did. Every damn day of their lives, until the day you walked out." Amy jabbed a finger at Morgan's chest. "You changed their nappies and got up in the middle of the night just as often as Erin did. Picked them up from school, took them to swimming lessons, parents' evening. Kissed skinned knees and held them when they cried. You did all that for them." Amy grabbed her shoulder and spun her to look at the painting. "Look at that picture. Look at those kids. Do they look like they're unhappy to you? Look at the painting. Every time I see it— every single, fucking time—I see the love you have for those kids in every brush stroke." She let go. "The little girl who wrapped her arms around your neck yesterday, did she look like she didn't want to be near you? Like she wasn't used to being held in your arms and being told—by you—that everything will be all right, because you love her. Did it?"

Nikki reached over and held Amy's hand as Morgan stared at the picture.

It's there, around their eyes, they're looking at me. Looking for me. And it's like looking in a mirror. Adored. Devoted. Loved. It's all there, right down to those dimples. Can you love without knowing someone? She stared at the faces of her children again, and knew, without a shadow of a doubt, that she could. She did. She always would.

"You made some huge mistakes, Morgan. Mistakes you may not be able to fix, especially with Erin. But those kids love you, and they need you, and no, it won't be fucking easy, but you know what?" Amy pointed her finger at Morgan's chest. "It doesn't matter whether or not you find it easy. They're your kids and you damn well better do the right thing by them. After everything you and Erin went through to have them…" She let her thoughts trail away.

"What do you mean?"

Amy shook her head and dropped onto the sofa.

"Nikki?"

"You went through months of those bloody painful injections so that you could harvest your eggs. Erin's brother, Chris, he donated the sperm. It took four tries for Erin to get pregnant with Tristan. Every time she was devastated when they didn't—when she wasn't pregnant. You even offered to try carrying the baby if it failed again. That's how much you loved her, 'cos let's face it, you pregnant? I nearly had a heart attack when you suggested it."

"But she did get pregnant?" *Way to state the obvious, Genius!*

"Yeah. She had a pretty rough time with Tristan. But not as bad as she did with Maddie."

"What happened?"

"Erin got preeclampsia. The placenta abrupted and she had to have an emergency Cesarean section."

"Jesus." Morgan sat back in her chair, wincing as she landed awkwardly and jarred her tender ribs. "I don't know what that means."

Nikki rolled her eyes. "A placental abruption means the placenta comes away from the wall of the uterus." Morgan still looked blank. "It can be fatal for both the baby and the mother if they don't do a C-section. Fast."

"I nearly lost them both?" Morgan felt the blood drain from her face.

"Yes."

"I feel sick."

"That's more like it." Nikki grinned. "If I remember right, that's exactly what you said then."

"I don't want to lose them."

"The kids?"

"Any of them."

Nikki whistled. "Seriously. Do you remember them now?"

Morgan shook her head. "I don't need to. I feel them." She pressed her hand to her chest. "I love them."

"Is that enough?"

"Did I have more than that when they were born? The first time I held them?"

"No. But they are used to more from you."

"Then I'll learn." Morgan looked from Nikki to the painting again. "I have to. I can't lose my family."

CHAPTER TEN

Nikki grabbed Morgan's arm as she turned away from the picture and headed for the door. "Where the hell are you off to?"

She paused and looked over her shoulder. "Actually, I have no idea. Where do they live?"

"Who? Erin? The kids?"

"Well, yes."

"You want to go round now?"

"Didn't I just say that?"

"But it's the middle of the afternoon. What are you going to do if there's no one in? Or better yet, what are you going to do if one of the kids answers the door?"

Morgan frowned. *I didn't think about that.* "So what do you suggest?"

"Maybe it would be a good idea to see when it's convenient for Erin to talk to you."

"I like that." Morgan stroked her chin unconsciously. "Thoughtful, shows I'm thinking about what's best for her and the kids. Good idea. So...how? Do you have her number, 'cos I don't—"

"Remember it? Yeah, I know. Do you want to call or text her?"

"Text?"

"Yeah, on her mobile—right. Sorry." Nikki held up her mobile phone and waved it. "Modern invention that's revolutionized communications. No one talks anymore, we text, e-mail, SMS, IM, Skype, tweet, or Facebook."

Morgan looked at the tiny box in her hand. "When did you learn to speak Russian?"

"Trust me, M. You want your family back, you gotta get down wiv d'kids!" Nikki crossed her arms over her chest and slouched back, a shit-eating grin on her face.

Morgan stared at her, her jaw hanging slightly, and she knew the look on her face said what-the-fuck.

"It's gangsta rap. Tristan loves it."

"My kid's a gangster?"

"No, it's a kind of—you know what, it doesn't matter right now. We'll educate you later. Do you want to call or text Erin?"

"What do you suggest?"

"Text. It doesn't put her under pressure to say something straight away. Gives her time to think. Also, if she's at work, she can get the message when she finishes, or when she's on a break, rather than it going to voice mail."

"Oh, yeah. That's good thinking. Give her the chance to prepare. Girls like that, right?" Morgan held up her hand to high five Nikki.

"Oh my God, it's like watching *American Pie* or something. Please tell me you two weren't this bad before?" Amy rolled her eyes and shook her head.

Nikki grinned. "Nah, I had you." She leaned over and kissed Amy. "She was worse though."

"Hey, I was not. What's American pie?"

Nikki shook her head and clapped Morgan on the back. "Okay, I've just asked her if she's free to talk to you."

"Now what?"

"We wait."

"And this is how you all communicate now?"

"Yep. Great, isn't it?" The phone beeped. "Wow, that was fast." Nikki stared at the screen and frowned.

"What? What is it?"

"Screwfix has a sale on. Twenty-five percent off cordless power tools and—"

Amy grabbed the phone. "Give me that. You'll give her a heart attack." She scanned the message quickly. "Morgan, she was teasing. It's from Erin. She wants to know why."

"Can you tell her that I want to talk to her about the kids, and I want to see them, and I love them. And that I want to see them—"

"You already said that." Nikki winked at her.

"Yeah, but I really mean it."

Amy's fingers danced all over the small phone. "I said you wanted to talk about the kids."

"What about the rest of—"

"No, just that."

"But how's she going to know that I want to see them?"

"M, Erin's a clever girl. She can figure that one out."

"Oh, right. Yeah, course she is." She pushed her fingers through her hair. "What does she do?"

"She's an air traffic control officer."

"Huh?"

"She directs all the planes that land at Manchester airport or fly over the airspace. Last time I talked to her about this she told me that the airport handled about eighteen million passengers a year, plus freight planes, and the planes flying through their airspace too. She's a busy lady. Lot of people's lives in her hands during every shift."

"Like in that Bruce Willis movie. *Die Hard*?"

"*Die Hard 2*. That was the one at the airport."

"Right." Morgan started pacing before a wave of dizziness hit her. She stumbled and just managed to catch hold of the mantle shelf before she fell. Nikki was beside her and leading her to the sofa in a heartbeat.

"Take it easy, M. Are you going to throw up?"

"Don't think so." The phone pinged. "What does she say?"

"I'll look in a minute. We need to make sure you're okay first."

"I'm fine. Just the damn balance thing. What does she say?"

Amy checked the message. "The kids aren't due home till around six. If you can come now, then fine. If not, it'll have to wait."

"Okay." Morgan tried to pull herself up, but Nikki held her in place.

"Tell Erin we'll be there in half an hour. It's only three, we've got time."

"But—"

"But nothing. You need a few minutes, or you're going to end up puking in my car. And that'll just piss me off." Nikki scowled. "Erin's five minutes away. I'll drop you off in half an hour."

❖

Erin grabbed magazines off the coffee table, and looked for somewhere to put them. With no suitable storage space immediately available, she lifted one of the sofa cushions, dropped the magazines, and let the cushion fall back into place. She jumped when the doorbell rang.

She walked quickly to the door then paused, one hand on the door handle and the other against her stomach, her unconscious attempt to soothe the butterflies raging inside her. Nerves or anger, she couldn't tell.

She took a deep breath and pulled the door open, and all she saw were the coal dark eyes that still haunted her dreams and she couldn't pull her gaze away. She could hear her heartbeat pounding in her ears and she felt the heat of her blush coloring her cheeks.

Anger had sustained her since Morgan had left, but it dissipated when she saw the vulnerable Morgan whose soul she had fallen in love with fifteen years ago, the woman who still turned her knees to jelly and made her skin burn with a look.

She wanted to thread her fingers through Morgan's hair, just to feel it on her skin. Morgan was just the same as before, tall and slim, chiseled cheekbones and full lips. The aged leather jacket mingled with the heady musky aroma that was entirely Morgan, and brought back memory after memory of their time together. Yet there was something so different about her too. The dark brooding energy that had crackled around her was gone, and in its place a restless nervousness that made her seem younger, gentler than before.

Erin backed away from the door and turned her back, leaving Morgan to enter behind her as she tried to gather her thoughts, determined to deal with the past later. Not now, when it was staring her in the face.

She glanced up at the clock. Three thirty. *Fuck it.* She pulled open the fridge and grabbed a bottle of wine, half demolished from the night before. She poured a large glass, and held it up to Morgan in silent question.

"No, thanks." Morgan's eyebrow quirked.

"Don't look at me like that. This is an unusual situation." She took a large drink before sitting at the table. She kept her hands wrapped around the glass, afraid if she let go, she wouldn't be able to stop herself from touching Morgan. "So you wanted to talk about the children."

"Yes. Can I sit down?"

She waved her hand in the direction of the chair opposite her own.

"Thank you for letting me come round."

"You're name's still on the mortgage." Erin couldn't help herself. She felt disconcerted, seeing Morgan in their home, looking around her and not recognizing anything. She looked down at the table. They had argued about its size at a furniture auction. Morgan was certain it would fit, Erin was equally sure it would be too big. When they got it home Morgan had ended up cutting a three-foot section out of the middle and fixing it together with support batons underneath, using a mixture of wood glue and sawdust to hide the crack that ran the length of the new center. It had taken her and Tristan all day, but they'd been happy with the result. Erin had taken Maddie shopping with her for a new tablecloth.

Morgan licked her lips. "I'm sorry."

Erin shrugged. "We can change the mortgage."

"No." Morgan frowned. "I mean I'm sorry about yesterday. Are the kids okay?"

"Not really." She took another drink.

"Where are they?"

"Out."

"Oh."

Erin watched her push shaking fingers through her hair, and felt the table shuddering, and knew it was because Morgan's leg was jumping. It always did when she was nervous. "What do you want?"

"I—I want to see the kids."

Erin almost spat out the drink she had taken. "Do you now?"

"Yes."

"Why?"

"Because they're our children. I want to see them. I want to know them."

"And if that's not what they want?"

"They don't want me?"

Erin didn't say anything. The strong lines of Morgan's face were set with determination, only to slacken, her brows pulled together and her jaw dropped. Fear morphed into loss, and the sorrow in her soul shone from her eyes.

"Then I wo…" She started to push away from the table. "Then I'll leave you all alone, I guess." She walked down the hall.

Erin heard the door open. *That's it, Morgan, walk away. Leave me to pick up the pieces again.*

She swallowed the rest of her drink and stood, determined to finish the bottle. *It's got to be five o'clock somewhere, right?* She poured the wine and turned around. She startled and dropped the glass, holding her hand against her chest. Morgan was standing in front of her. Tears dampened her cheeks.

"I thought you left."

Morgan shook her head. "I know I probably deserve your hatred. I'm sure I earned your contempt, and I've got no right to even think about asking you to forgive me for whatever I did to you. But what about our children? Don't they deserve everything we can give them?"

"And what can you give them? Lessons in how to sound like a stupid teenager?"

"I know I have a long way to go. I have a lot of growing up to do again, or maybe for the first time. I don't know. I'm, like—I'm really trying to do that. I've got a lot to relearn. About me. About them. You. I can't even text!" She shuffled forward a pace and then stopped. "I don't know who I was before, but from everything I've learned, I really think I can do better. I can *be* better." She took another step closer.

"And you think I'll risk our children on 'I think'?"

"No, but right now, you know me better than I know myself, Erin. Was I a bad parent to them? Are they better off without me in their lives? I don't just want to see them and walk away. I want to be there for them, with them, always. I want to know them, and for them to know me. The good and the bad. Isn't that what families do? Help each other through the hard stuff. If you can tell me, right now, that they're better off without me, that I was a bad parent to them, then I'll go. You have my word. But if I wasn't—if they loved me—if they still love me, don't they deserve to know that I love them too?"

The passion in Morgan's voice made Erin's heart beat faster. It burned in her eyes and flushed her cheeks, and it would be so easy to believe the words as they tumbled from her lips. But passion couldn't replace the one thing that Morgan had destroyed in Erin. Trust. Such a simple word for something so fragile and so complex. So difficult to build, but the easiest thing in the world to destroy. "You don't even remember them. You walked away from them and didn't look back. You never even gave us a reason. You left, and you don't even remember why."

"I love them. I loved them before they were born, and I will love them till the day I die. Whether they want to know me or not, doesn't matter. I might not remember them, Erin. But I know I loved them. I still love them. I can feel it, even if I don't know why. I want the chance to know them too."

She didn't know how to read Morgan's eyes. There was panic, and love, and hurt, all pleading with her, begging her for a chance. "I don't know—"

"Please."

This wasn't the Morgan she knew; her Morgan. This wasn't the woman who had turned her back on the life they'd built and walked away. She looked the same, sounded the same, but she wasn't.

"Please ask them. If they don't want to know me, I'll respect that."

"I'll talk to them." Erin didn't know if it was Morgan's request she was giving in to, or her children's wounds she was trying to heal, but she couldn't say no. "But if you hurt them again, I swear to God, Morgan, I'll make sure you don't see them. Do you understand me?"

"Perfectly." She bent down slowly, careful to avoid a wave of dizziness.

"What are you doing?"

"I was going to clean up the glass so the children won't hurt themselves later."

"I can do that."

"I know. But I want to help." She knelt and gathered the largest pieces into a pile. "Do you have something to wrap this in?"

Erin's heart ached at the easy domesticity as they cleaned the mess together. The awareness of each other's movements—instinctive. The simple touch of Morgan's hand brushing her own—electric.

CHAPTER ELEVEN

Erin parked the car outside the sports center and plucked her handbag off the passenger seat. She walked slowly to the main entrance, and dodged a steady stream of children as they bounced balls and exited the building. She smiled when the automatic doors opened and she saw Tristan counting out the change from his pocket before giving it to Maddie.

"Just a drink though, Mads. Mum'll be here soon, and she said we were going for pizza."

"But I'm hungry." She turned her big doe eyes on him. "Just a small bar of chocolate, Trist. Please."

"You know mum'll kill me."

"I promise not to tell."

Erin cleared her throat and placed a hand on her daughter's shoulder. "You promise not to tell what?" She was sure she could hear the "uh-oh" as Maddie turned her head.

"Nothing."

"Those big eyes don't work on me, young lady. Now stop pestering your brother for chocolate and get a drink for you both." She winked at Tristan as he pulled himself off the uncomfortable plastic bench and swung his kit bag over his shoulder. She wanted to hug him, but his friends were too close, and the potential for embarrassment far too high. "How was practice?"

He shrugged. "Okay."

Maddie struggled to lift the heavy trap door on the vending machine to retrieve their drinks. "Tristan, help."

He rolled his eyes, but dutifully dropped his bag and did as he was told.

"Come on, guys. Pizza's calling." She held out her hand for Maddie and smiled proudly as Tristan picked up both of their bags and walked beside her. It still shocked her that he was shoulder-to-shoulder with her already.

"Mum, Tristan's got a girlfriend!"

Oh my God, please let this be one of those hold hands in the cafeteria-type girlfriends. Or better yet, the ones they never actually even hang around with. I'm not ready to deal with real girlfriends yet!

Tristan's face paled even as his cheeks flushed. "I do n—"

"She's really pretty and got blond hair and they were kissing in the corridor outside the changing rooms."

Kissing! Oh, shit, this is real girlfriend territory. Breathe, Erin, breathe! "Maddie, we've talked about telling tales. It's not nice." She put her hand on his shoulder, as she tugged on Maddie's hand.

"But they were kissing—"

"And one day you'll have a boyfriend or girlfriend of your own, who you'll want to kiss, and you won't want your brother telling me about it then, will you?"

"Boys are yucky."

"And Tristan thought girls were yucky at your age. Now what do you say?"

She looked at Erin, then at Tristan. "Sorry, Trist."

He shrugged and dropped his chin to his chest, trying to lengthen his stride and walk away from them. Erin let her hand slide from his shoulder to the strap of the rucksack he was wearing to keep him with them.

"Please don't run off. It's nothing to be embarrassed about."

He didn't say anything, but she felt his resistance lessen.

"Your little sister's just got a very big mouth."

He grunted his agreement. "Should have let her fill it with chocolate." They reached the car, and he waited for her to unlock it before dropping the bags into the boot. "Then I'd get more pizza too."

Maddie climbed into the back as Tristan opened the passenger side door. Erin checked the backseat through the rearview mirror.

"Put your seat belt on, young lady. Or you can pay the fine when the police pull us over."

Maddie giggled. "I don't have any money," she said as she pulled the belt over her shoulder.

"Then you should definitely wear your seat belt." She smiled when she heard the reassuring click, and Maddie's feet swung a few inches from the floor.

"Listen, I was thinking about getting our pizza takeaway tonight. You both okay with that?"

Tristan shrugged again, but Maddie frowned.

"I like going to the restaurant."

"I know, sweetie, but tonight there are some things I need to talk to you both about, and I thought it would be better at home."

Tristan turned in his seat, his eyes wide. "It was just a little kiss, Mum. And we'd already said no tongues or anything. She's—"

Tongues! He's talking about kissing with tongues.

"It's not about that, darling." *Tongues!* "We can talk about your girlfriend if you want to, but I need to talk about some other stuff, too. So, takeaway?"

"What've we got to talk about?" Maddie leaned forward as far as her belt would let her.

"Not while I'm driving. I have to concentrate. I've got precious cargo in this car." Maddie's smile widened and Tristan's eyes lost the look of panic. "And how can I think when Tristan's stinky basketball kit could be sold to medical science for a small fortune? I'm pretty sure he's breeding a new species in there." He huffed good-naturedly in his seat and Maddie giggled. Erin smiled at him and pointed to her handbag. "Trist, grab the menu out of my bag and you two decide what you want before we get there."

"Can I have garlic bread, too?"

"To share."

"But I'm hungry."

"And your eyes are bigger than your belly."

Thirty minutes later, Erin carried plates and paper napkins into the sitting room. Maddie and Tristan had already opened the boxes on the coffee table, and Maddie had a slice of garlic bread with melted cheese in her hand, a huge bite missing from it, and her cheeks bulging as she chewed. Tristan was laughing and calling her a hamster. It felt so good to see them laughing and teasing; she didn't want to spoil the moment. She knelt next to the table and grabbed a slice of pizza.

"She's called Isabelle."

Erin choked on her pizza slice. "Your girlfriend?"

He nodded. "She's in the year above me, but her birthday's in August so she's only really a couple of months older."

An older woman! Oh, God. "Does Isabelle go to your school?"

"No. I met her at the basketball center. She's on one of the girl's teams."

"Where does she live?"

"Offerton."

"Not too far away then."

"No. I want to ask her to the pictures one night."

Erin couldn't help but smile, thinking how different her own school days had been. She had known by the time she was Tristan's age that she wasn't interested in "going out with the boys" like her friends were. She had a huge crush on her form tutor, Mrs. Cavendish. Taking her girlfriend out wasn't an option then. She was determined to make the transition from childhood to adulthood as painless as possible for all of them. She knew there would be bumps along the way, tantrums, fights, mood swings, and stressful, restless nights. However, they were good kids, and she knew that they would deal with it. "You do?"

"Yeah." His voice was quieter, and his eyes seemed glued to his plate.

"When do you have in mind?"

He shrugged again. "Dunno. Can you drive us?" The blush coloring his cheeks was so endearing she wanted to pull him into her arms.

"I think I can manage that. Text her later and see when. My shifts are on the calendar. Try to pick a day off or an early, please, son. I want to make a good impression on my future daughter-in-law."

"Mum!"

Maddie giggled. "Do you know what her favorite flowers are, 'cos you have to give her flowers."

"Good thinking, Maddie. Girls love flowers." Erin smiled and let Maddie high-five her.

"Really?" Tristan's voice squeaked a little, something they all ignored. Erin and Maddie both nodded. "I wish mum was here to ask about this. She'd know what girls like."

Erin knew it was the best opening she was going to get. She dropped her pizza onto her plate and wiped her hands on a napkin.

"That's sort of what I needed to talk to you about." She grabbed a can of pop, peeled it open, and took a sip. She didn't want to look at them as they waited for her to speak, but she knew she had to. Tristan's eyes were wary, and his shoulders had grown tense. Maddie looked scared, her big brown eyes already misting with tears, and a frown marring her little forehead.

"Your mum came round this afternoon. She wants to know if you'd like to see her."

"Has she remembered us?" Maddie crawled around the table and on to Erin's lap.

"I don't think so exactly."

Tristan snorted. "What does that mean?"

Damn good question, Trist. "Well, she hasn't gotten her memories back, but she's found out a lot of things in the last day or so. About who she was before she got hurt, and what her life was like. The things—the people—who were important to her. And she said that she loves you both, very much—"

"She doesn't know us. She can't love us!" Tristan glared at her.

"I said the same thing to her."

"Yeah, right." Tristan tossed his slice of pizza onto the box.

"I did. And she said something that made a lot of sense to me."

Maddie wiped her nose with her sleeve. "What?"

"Use a napkin, sweetie." She grabbed a tissue and handed it to her. "She said that neither of us knew you when you were born, but we still loved you then." She wiped the tears from Maddie's cheeks and smiled at Tristan. "We didn't know who you were going to be, what you were going to look like, or if you'd have stinky feet. But it didn't matter. You were our children, and we loved you. From the very second we knew I was pregnant, we both loved you."

She shifted until her back was resting against the sofa and shifted Maddie more comfortably into her arms. "She was the one who held you first. Both of you. She cut the cord, and she kissed you, and she loved you." She kissed the top of Maddie's head, not taking her eyes off Tristan.

"Covered in gunk, screaming blue murder, and looking like Winston Churchill, she loved you." She smiled at the hiccupping laugh that came from Maddie's chest. "That hasn't changed. From the moment she found out about you again, she loved you. Again. Still. I don't know which it is. But that's the truth of it." She stroked Maddie's hair while she watched Tristan try to understand.

He picked up his slice of pizza again, picking the toppings off and dropping them onto the box. "So what does she want from us?"

"The chance to get to know you again."

"And if I don't want to?"

"Tristan, she doesn't want to force you to do anything. She just wants the chance to know you both. To be a part of your lives."

"But she left us!" Tristan threw his slice of pizza into the half-empty box and grabbed a napkin to wipe his hands. "She didn't call or anything. Why? She couldn't have loved us that much. She left us."

"Yes, she did. And I know this is really hard, but I want you to think about something for me." She waited until she had his attention again.

"What?"

"If she hadn't been hurt, if she still remembered you, and she'd come back saying that she was sorry, and wanted to see you again. Would you want to?" *I know that's what I wanted more than anything. I wanted my dad to walk in and make the pain disappear. You have the chance to do that. Please take it.*

"Yes." Maddie wrapped her arms around Erin's neck and sobbed, her whole body shaking.

Tristan wasn't so easy. It was so much harder for him to let go of the hurt and anger. The napkin he'd wiped his hands with steadily became a pile of confetti as he pulled it apart and tore it into pieces.

"I'd still be pissed at her."

"Don't swear. You have every right to feel angry about that. And I wish she could talk to you about her reasons to help you deal with that, but she can't. You didn't answer the question, Tristan. Would you want to see her?" *Come on, kiddo. I know you want this.*

He shrugged. "S'pose so."

Hallelujah! "So, will you give her a chance now?" She could feel Maddie nodding against her neck. "Good girl." She smoothed her hair down and patted her back. "Tristan?"

"Do I have a choice?"

"If you see her and it doesn't work out, I'll talk to her, and make her back off. But right now, I think you should give her a chance."

"That's just mum speak for 'no, you don't have a choice.'"

Erin couldn't stop the corners of her mouth twitching into a small grin. "I think it's the right thing for you."

He tossed the wadded up confetti napkin on to the table. "What if you're wrong?"

"Then I'll apologize, and I won't make you see her again."

"What if she tries to make you? I mean genetically we're her kids, right? Her egg and then they put us in you."

"True. As for her forcing you to see her, my only concern is you two; how this affects you both. If seeing her is too much for you, too painful, then I'll fight her in court if I have to. We both adopted you, so that legally we both have equal rights and responsibilities as your parents. I will do everything in my power to protect you. If that means fighting her in court, I will." She held her arm out and beckoned him over, silently praying that he'd welcome the affection.

He didn't hesitate. He crawled to where she sat cradling Maddie. He leaned against the back of the sofa and wrapped his arm around Erin's back, and stroked Maddie's leg with his other hand. Erin couldn't help but smile at the protective gesture.

She rested her cheek on the top of Maddie's head looking at Tristan. "I love you both so much, I will do everything I can to make this better for you. You're my life."

"Love you too, Mum." Maddie's muffled voice reached them from Erin's chest.

"When do we have to see her?" Tristan patted Erin's back seemingly unaware of the comforting gesture he was doing.

Erin smiled. "We didn't discuss that. When would you like to see her?"

He shrugged again. "Don't know."

"Can we see her now?" Maddie lifted her head.

"I don't think that's the best idea, sweetie."

"Why not?"

"Well, I think I need some time to sort out a time and place, and maybe you both need some time to think about it too."

"Why?"

"Well, you have to remember, sweetie, she doesn't remember all the things that you do. And that's going to be hard for you all."

"But I forget things all the time. Like I forgot that I was supposed to take my library books back today, but Mr. Hughes said it would be okay, as long as I remember them tomorrow. So it wasn't too hard."

"Maddie, this isn't like forgetting your library books." *I hate this.* "She won't remember when your birthday is, or what sports you like to play. Or you being the princess in the pantomime at Christmas. She doesn't remember your middle name, even though she picked it."

"She won't?"

"No, sweetie. That's what amnesia is. She doesn't remember being a teacher either, or my birthday, or Tristan's. It's everything. And it makes me upset to think about, so I have to expect that it's going to make you upset in some ways too."

"Does she remember her birthday?" Maddie's lower lip quivered.

"I think so, yes."

"Will she ever remember it all?" Tristan picked at his jeans.

"I don't think anyone really knows."

"What did the doctors say?"

"I don't know, darling, I was only there at the beginning. I don't know the final prognosis. You could ask her when you see her. It'll give you something to talk about."

She held them long after her legs had gone numb under Maddie's weight. She didn't want to let them go. Ever.

CHAPTER TWELVE

Morgan stared at the picture of Tristan and Maddie as Amy tapped away on her computer and Nikki sat reading in the living room. She studied every inch of their faces, cataloguing every similarity and difference that connected her to them. Maddie's dark eyes shone in a way her own hadn't as a child, happiness and mischief prevalent. Tristan's blue eyes were almost identical to Erin's. She couldn't stop the questions bouncing around her head. "How did I meet her?"

Nikki looked up from her book. "Who?"

"Erin. How did we meet?"

"She was in a band we went to see. You said she was the most gorgeous woman you'd ever seen and that you knew you belonged together." Nikki rolled her eyes.

"She still is." Morgan looked at her hands, picturing Erin's beautiful face. "I can see her as a singer. Does she have a lovely voice?"

Amy turned away from her computer and shook her head as she laughed. "She wasn't a singer. She played the drums."

"What? No way!"

Amy nodded, and Nikki grinned.

"But she...it just..."

Amy crossed her legs and leaned back in her chair. "Don't jump to conclusions. Erin hates stereotyping, and you did exactly the same thing then. She totally blew you off the first time you went and spoke to her."

"Why?" Morgan frowned, thinking how little things had changed.

"You offered to carry her heavy gear to the van. She said she could do it herself, and you looked mighty skeptical." Nikki stretched the word mighty out to three syllables. "So she told you to piss off."

"Erin was lugging the stand box outside, and you decided to show her how strong you were. So she had this big oblong kind of box, and you went to take it off her." Amy grinned. "You got your arms around it, and she told you to let go, or you'd end up dropping it. This wounded your pride, of course. You jerked this damn box out of her arms, and tried to keep hold of it. You couldn't, the damn thing weighed about a ton, but when you dropped it, it landed on your foot and you ended up breaking your toe."

"She stood there looking at you, with that eyebrow arch thing, looking all I-told-you-so. She looks totally femme, skirts and dresses and shit, but I can't beat her in an arm wrestling match." Nikki flexed her biceps, and then pointed at Morgan. "Weedy-arty-farty you, with those spindly little arms didn't stand a chance!"

"I made a complete arse of myself." Morgan laughed, trying to cover how uncomfortable she felt. *I was a prize idiot.*

"Yep."

"So how did we end up together?"

"She picked that big box up, finished packing her transit van, and told you to get in," Amy said.

"What?"

"Yep, that's what we said. She said that she wasn't going to be responsible for you ending up crippled if you'd broken your foot, and that she was going to drop you off at the hospital to get it x-rayed. What you did after that was up to you." Amy tucked her hair behind her ear.

"Then what happened?" Morgan glanced between them, not sure she liked the knowing looks, or the shit-eating grin that Nikki was wearing.

"She helped you hobble to the van and told us we could jump in the back if we wanted to go with you. She still hadn't even told you her name. You were so used to women falling at your feet with that tortured, brooding artist thing you had going on, it floored you that she wasn't interested."

Morgan tried to picture herself confident with women and used to attention, but it felt wrong. *The other Morgan. The one I'll never know.* She shook her head. "So then what happened?"

"She dropped us all off at the hospital and made sure you booked in, then she left us to it." Nikki sipped her drink.

"I still didn't get her name?"

"Not for lack of trying." Nikki laughed. "You tried everything, offered to paint her picture, dinner, drinks, a picnic, walk in the countryside. You might have even offered to have her babies right there and then. I can't remember. We'd been drinking all night. But she just kept shaking her head and laughing at you. Every time you moved your leg you practically cried. Wuss."

"So how did we get together?" Morgan stared at the picture again. It was a strange feeling, listening to her own history, but feeling like it was someone else's.

"You stalked her." Amy smirked.

"Huh? How? I didn't even know her name"

Nikki threw her head back, laughing. "Notice it wasn't, no, I wouldn't stalk some poor unsuspecting woman, but how did I stalk some poor unsuspecting woman?"

Amy laughed. "You followed the band. Every gig they did for months."

"And you started lifting weights." Nikki grinned and pointed to Morgan's arms.

"Shush," Amy said. "Eventually, one of the band members told you her name, and you started showing up with placards, like you were going to some sort of major concert or something. Erin's the greatest; Erin, I heart you." She made a heart shape with her fingers. "Erin, will you marry me. God, it was sickening. Funny, but sickening."

"The poems were funnier." Nikki sniggered.

"You think?"

Morgan blanched. "Poems?"

"Yep, you wrote her little love poems and left them with a single rose on her drum kit during the interval." Amy smiled sweetly.

"*I* wrote poems?"

"Amy uses the word poem very, very loosely. More like…dirty limericks."

"Oh God." She grimaced. "I continued to make an arse of myself."

"For months. It was great."

"Thanks. What did I finally do to convince her to go out with me?"

"You apologized to her," Amy said.

"What? I don't understand."

"Well, it turned out that all the time you were pulling your little stunts she had a girlfriend."

"Oh, God." Morgan covered her eyes with one hand.

"Yep. Course you didn't know this. But all the band members were talking about your little…okay, big…signs of adoration, and apparently, her girlfriend wasn't impressed." Nikki sniggered. "Anyway, long story short, when you found out she had a girlfriend you went pale, and then went and apologized for being an arse."

"And then what?"

"She told you that she broke up with her girlfriend because she was being an arsehole, and asked you if you wanted a drink."

Morgan grinned. "Then we got together?"

"No." Nikki shook her head. "She still thought you were an arse."

"Behave." Amy rubbed Nikki's hands. "She did start to hang out with us a bit. She came to the quiz night at the pub and stuff." Amy wrapped her hands around Nikki's. "I don't really know how it happened in the end, but you'd been friends for a few months when you turned up one day and said you'd screwed everything up. That you kissed her."

Morgan waited. "And?"

"Well, obviously you didn't screw it all up, because that was fifteen years ago and you were together from then on."

"Till I screwed it up."

Neither of them spoke. They didn't have to.

She needed answers to questions she didn't even know. If knowledge is power, in a game of chess, she wasn't even a pawn.

"Amy, can I use the computer?"

"Sure. Anything I can help with?" Amy saved her work and closed the file before she slid out of her chair and waved Morgan over.

"Well, I don't know really. I want to know everything. But I guess I should focus on what's important."

"And that is?"

"Well, the kids of course." *And Erin.* Morgan tapped in her search request and sat back to wait for the results; the almost instant appearance on the screen startled her. "Damn, that's fast."

"Oh yeah. It's not dial-up anymore, M. Broadband and WiFi now." Nikki chuckled.

"Broadband everywhere? I thought it was, like, just big business and stuff that was getting that. What's WiFi?"

"Wireless Internet."

"So why isn't it WiI instead of WiFi?"

Nikki laughed. "I don't know. It just is. Look it up if you're so curious."

Fuck! Even the Internet's changed! "Maybe later."

Morgan typed in her name and was instantly rewarded with a barrage of results about her attack. Notices of police looking for witnesses and requests for information about persons of interest were dominant, and the grainy black-and-white image of the blonde's face stared back at her.

Amy swore under her breath and Morgan turned to face her.

"You really didn't know there was someone else?"

"No." Amy scowled at her then stared at the picture again. "She does look familiar to me though. I just can't place her."

Nikki joined them. "Common face. Probably seen someone who looks like her."

Amy shrugged. "Maybe. But I'm not...never mind. If I do know her it'll come to me."

Morgan scrolled down the page, clicking from one to the next until she found an old news report with her name in bold type and her father's next to it. She hovered the mouse over the link.

"M, are you sure you want to do that?" Nikki put her hand on Morgan's shoulder.

"No. But there's stuff I need to know."

"I thought you didn't want to know anymore. I can tell you what happened if you really want to know."

Morgan held her breath for a moment. Did she really want to know? Did she really want to see all the details…feel all the details while Nikki told her? Was that what she needed? She balked at the prospect of reliving those emotions. She didn't want to *feel* her mother die again. She didn't want to know how it felt to see her father murder her. She needed information, facts, pure and simple. She wanted the information in as unemotional a way as possible. *If it reads like a car manual, so much the better.*

"I want the facts. Not the emotions that went with it all. You guys were there, you lived it with me, and you're emotionally invested. I need to know it, but not relive it. Do you understand?"

"Yes. But I don't think that's really possible."

Morgan turned her head to look at her. "Why not?"

"Because they were your parents."

"Yes, but I still won't see it like I did before."

Amy closed her hand over Morgan's as she gripped the mouse. "Morgan, those newspaper articles weren't very factual. There were some pretty awful things printed. If you want the facts, and only the facts there is another way."

Morgan turned her head. "How?"

"The transcript from the Crown Court."

"You can get those?"

"Absolutely. We could probably find out online."

Morgan relinquished the mouse to Amy and watched her expertly maneuver to the required site. "Your solicitor can apply for the transcript."

"I have a solicitor?"

"Well, we all kinda do."

Amy turned to look at her. "Becky?"

"Her name's on that approved list. Look." Nikki pointed at the screen.

"You call her then. Last time I spoke to her was at your birthday party." Amy blushed crimson.

"You haven't spoken to her for three months? How come, babe?"

"Erm…she was totally plastered and kept making comments about her intentions toward various people at the party. You being one of them." Amy shrugged. "I may have told her that you wouldn't go near her with a ten-foot barge pole, and that you have a little thing called taste."

"Oh shit." Nikki tried to suppress her laughter.

"She probably doesn't remember it though. She was drunk."

"Maybe we should find another solicitor."

"Hey, this is for Morgan. Becky would want to help her." Amy turned to Morgan. "She's really your friend anyway."

"She is?" Morgan looked between the two of them as Amy nodded. "How do I know her?"

"You dated her in uni." Nikki clapped her on the back.

"I did?" Morgan knew she was blushing when Nikki pointed to her face and laughed.

"Oh boy. This is going to be fun." Nikki pulled her mobile from her pocket and crossed the room.

"Amy? What happened with this Becky and me then?"

"Oh, it was just a few dates. Nothing major. She's been a pretty good friend through the years. We've always gone to her for legal stuff. You and Erin even had her draw up the adoption papers for the kids."

"Why did we need adoption papers?"

"Well, biologically they are yours and her brother's. Erin carried them both, but legally that wouldn't give her any rights as a parent. At the time, the only way around that was for both of you to adopt them after they were born. That gave you both equal rights as parents."

"Oh."

"Yeah, Becky's good though. She made it very straightforward."

Nikki laughed before she said good-bye and crossed the room again. "Becky says you're forgiven, babe." She kissed the top of Amy's head and smiled at Morgan. "And that it'll take her a few days, but she'll have the transcript by the end of the week. She'll bring it over; she wants to see how you're doing."

"Okay."

Amy pointed at the computer. "You want to look at some other stuff?"

"Yeah. I've got twenty years to catch up on." Morgan took hold of the mouse and started surfing.

CHAPTER THIRTEEN

The air traffic control room was buzzing with activity. Controllers called flight data to the various planes they were in charge of as they traversed the skies over Manchester and landed at the airport. Banks of computer screens were filled with graphic images of planes, most with more than two hundred people aboard, being expertly guided safely around the sky. Erin passed behind one of her controllers and gently tapped him on the shoulder, waited for his nod of acknowledgment, and then moved on, signaling the end of his shift and that his replacement was ready to be briefed to take over. The switch was seamless and the people up in the air were passed safely from one pair of hands to another.

She looked from screen to screen, deciding where to shift people, who needed a break, and where she needed to be to contain any potential hazards. The huge screen in the middle of the center wall gave her the full overview of their control space.

"Erin."

She turned her head toward Roger without taking her eyes from the screen. "What's up?"

"I've just finished talking to the police."

She clenched her jaw and tried to push away her annoyance. She hated the thought of them intruding into any aspect of her life, but having them in her place of work and talking to her colleagues needled at her far more than she had expected. She shook her head and blew out a heavy breath. "Well, I did warn you that I gave them your name."

"No, no, that's fine. I know you told me. They've asked to speak to you."

"I'm in the middle of a shift; they can see me later."

"They were quite insistent, my dear."

She looked away from the screen and met his eyes.

"Go ahead." He smiled at her. "I'll take care of this while you're busy."

She inclined her head at the screen. "You might want to keep an eye on the BA903 flight. Tom doesn't seem to have it on the right path at the moment. If he doesn't shift it in the next ninety seconds, we're gonna have a close call."

"I've got it. They're in my office."

She pulled off her headset and passed it to him before leaving the control floor. She climbed the stairs to Roger's office. The door was open, and the two uniformed officers stood and offered their hands as she entered and attempted a smile.

"PC Lock, PC Ward. What can I do for you today?"

"Ms. Masters, we won't keep you long. We just have a couple of questions for you."

"Okay." Erin sat in Roger's chair and waited.

PC Lock pulled some papers from under his stab vest. "I have a couple of pictures to show you. If you could tell me if either of these people are known to you, it would be a great help." He placed the first picture on the desk in front of her.

She stared at the grainy image; a bald headed, angry man stared back. The angle was awkward, but the snarl marring his features was unmistakable. She tilted her head to one side, unconsciously trying to get a better look at him.

"No. I don't recall ever seeing him before." She pushed the picture back toward him. "Is he the man who attacked Morgan?"

"Yes."

"Can't you do facial recognition or something?"

"The image isn't good enough I'm afraid." He placed another page on the desk. "Do you recognize this woman?"

Erin lifted the picture off the desk. Black, white, and gray squares filled the page, making up the cropped image of a blonde with her eyes closed, a look of pleasure on her face. The image cut off below her neck. Which, presumably, was where Morgan was. Her heart pounded against her ribs and her mouth went dry.

"What does she have to do with Morgan's attack?" Her hands shook.

"Do you know her?"

Erin shook her head, unable to tear her eyes from the picture even though she could no longer focus on it. She placed it back on the desk and pushed it toward him. Every doubt Erin had harbored over the past weeks came flooding back. She no longer doubted; she was sure that Morgan was seeing someone else, and the bitter taste of duplicity turned her stomach.

"Who is she?"

"We don't know. We were hoping you might have some idea." He put the photographs away.

"How was she involved?"

"We have very little information at this point."

"Was she seeing Morgan?"

"We have no idea. Ms. Masters is unable to confirm or deny that."

"Of course not."

"Well, thank you for your time, Ms. Masters." They stood and held out their hands for Erin to shake.

"That's it?" Manners had her shaking hands with the two men before she even finished asking the question.

"Yes. If you do think you recognize either of them, please call me. Do you still have my card?" PC Lock patted his pocket as though trying to locate another one.

"Yes, I do." She stood as they opened the door.

"Thank you for your help."

Erin closed the door behind them before she sank back into her chair, covered her face with her hands, and let the tears fall. Her heart ached more as every tympanic beat resounded with the deep vibrations of sorrow and loss; the sour notes playing in the symphony of the perfidy against her. The betrayal sliced deeper than she ever thought possible; her soul bled.

CHAPTER FOURTEEN

The slamming of a car door startled Morgan awake. The TV had been turned down, and a blanket wrapped about her as she dozed in the chair beside the fireplace. *Thank you, Amy.* Voices in the hallway grew closer to the door. It was easy for her to pick out Amy and Nikki, but the other high-pitched, slightly nasal voice was new to her. The door opened and Nikki led in a tall blonde with striking blue eyes, wearing a sky blue power suit and three-inch heels.

"Ah, Sleeping Beauty's awake," Nikki said before turning back to the blonde. "Coffee?"

"Love some, thanks." The woman smiled and sat on the sofa as Nikki left the room. "So how's the head, M?"

Morgan frowned, still wondering who the woman was. "Oh, it's getting better. Fewer headaches, and the dizzy spells are more or less gone now."

"Excellent. Any developments with the investigation?" She placed a heavy looking briefcase on the seat next to her and flipped the catches open to remove a thick folio.

"If there have been, the police haven't told me."

"Right, well, I suppose they don't have very much to go on."

"They have pictures of the guy," Morgan said, feeling more than a little defensive. "It's not like I'm deliberately trying to block their investigation."

"Oh, I know, chick. It's gotta be hard for you too."

"Do you want sugar, Becky?" Nikki called from the kitchen, and the pieces shifted into place for Morgan. Becky. Transcript. Answers. She felt herself relaxing. Her frown disappeared, and she smiled at the woman.

"No, thanks, I'm sweet enough."

"Yeah, right," Nikki hollered back.

"You didn't have any idea who I was, did you?" Becky looked directly into Morgan's eyes.

"I'm sorry, but, no, I didn't." Morgan dropped her gaze.

"They told me you wouldn't, but I guess I was hoping they were wrong." She smiled sadly.

"Were we close?" Morgan looked up again, wishing she could find some connection.

"At one time. Now I like to think we're good friends." She lifted the folio and waved it slightly. "I hope this helps you find what you're looking for."

"Did you read it?"

"No, chick, I didn't."

Nikki entered the room and passed out mugs before sitting down.

"Why not?"

Becky shrugged. "I have a lot of these pass through my hands every day. Professionally, reading one of them is suicide for me unless I'm involved with the case. Yours is no different. Unless you want me to read it."

Morgan looked at the thick file. The thought of wading through page after page of legalese trying to find the pertinent facts made her head ache, but she knew it was something she needed to do alone.

"No, thanks. I need to do it."

Becky nodded. "Okay, but if anything doesn't make sense, just text me. If I'm in court, I'll get it afterward and get back to you."

"Thanks." Morgan brought her cup to her lips, then changed her mind. "I think I'm going to go and take a little look at this. See if anything…I don't know. Maybe it'll help me to remember something." She put her cup down and picked up the folio.

"You sure, M?" Nikki caught hold of her hand as she passed. "You okay?"

"Yeah. I'm fine." She pulled the door closed behind her.

❖

Morgan sat on her bed. The warm sunlight filtering into the room caught on the crystal wind chime hanging over the window; the light split and the colors spread across the walls, ceiling, and over the bedspread. The gentle breeze through the open window caused the faces of the prisms to move, and the refracted light danced around the room. Once whole and astonishing, the light was no less beautiful in its separate parts; just different, changed.

"Beautiful, isn't it?"

Morgan turned to see Becky standing in the doorway, smiling.

"Yes."

"What were you thinking?"

"That the light changes through the prism, but it is no more or less than it was before. All the parts that make up the white light are still there. Just separated. Kind of like people. The way we have different sides. They all make up this whole person, but I'm not like that anymore. I'm missing some of the colors that made me whole."

"Is that really what you think? That you aren't whole anymore?"

Morgan shrugged and stared at the shifting pattern across the ceiling.

"Did Amy or Nikki tell you we dated?"

Morgan felt her cheeks heat and knew she was blushing. "Yes."

Becky crossed the room and sat on the edge of the bed. "Okay, on one of our dates we went to the Whitworth Art Gallery, and we saw this installation piece. I can't remember who the artist was, but it was called *The Theory of Memories*. It was this steel meshed net suspended from the ceiling, and across different parts of it were these little…well, blobs really."

Morgan laughed. "Blobs?"

"Yeah. They were supposed to represent the events that get caught in the net of our memories. The net symbolized the way some things slip through the gaps and we never remember them, and other things get caught and never go anywhere. Parts of the net were close together, and others were set very far apart." She reached for Morgan's hand. "We talked about it afterward. You were very taken with the piece. I was taking it very literally and thought it was quite an insulting piece. But you didn't think that. You pointed out that the net and the event blobs were made of the same material, which meant absolutely bugger all to me. But you told me it represented the artist's ideal that we are all the same. We all come from the same place and are made of the same things, so how can anyone be better or worse than another. You said that everyone's memories work differently. Everyone remembers everything differently. Some remember in minute detail, some vaguely, and others retain nothing that would seem to be important."

"But I did have these memories and now I don't. I don't remember the piece you're talking about. I don't remember dating you, or anyone else. I don't remember my children. These are things I had. Memories that made me who I was."

"But they weren't all that made you who you are, Morgan. There is more to a person than what they remember."

"Like what?"

"Heart. To love and love well is far more important than remembering all the details that made you the person you were before." Becky let go of Morgan's hand and pushed her hair behind her ears. "The Morgan I knew was terribly wounded. There was this sadness about you that I always wanted to take away. In the twenty years I've known you, only your children and Erin came close to wiping that shadow from your eyes." She looked up and met Morgan's gaze. "It's gone now. Maybe widening that net was a good thing."

"Are you telling me I shouldn't read this?" She pointed to the file Becky had given her.

"No. I'm saying you have a choice about what you know now. You can choose what's important to learn, and what isn't. You get to decide what influences you from here on out. Not many of us at our age get that option, chick."

"It doesn't feel like an option. It feels like a prison sentence."

Becky laughed. "I'm an alcoholic. I know all about feeling like I'm trapped in something and that I don't have a choice. But I do. I go to AA meetings, and my sponsor taught me something. Want to hear it?"

"You're an alcoholic?"

"Yes. And you were the one who made me get help. After Nikki's birthday…well, it was a few months ago now, but I haven't had a drink since then. And that's because you cared enough to help me. Now I'm going to tell you something that I hope helps you."

"What?"

"God grant me the serenity to accept the things I cannot change," Becky said, her voice barely more than a whisper. "The courage to change the things I can." She looked Morgan in the eye. "And the wisdom to know the difference."

Morgan closed her eyes and let the memories she had of her parents play out. Her father with his fists raised, ready to strike; he towered over her mother as she cowered in a corner. Fear bubbled in the pit of her stomach as she watched scene after scene in her own head.

She felt fingers wipe away the tears she didn't know she'd shed and a soft kiss was pressed against her forehead.

"Know the difference, chick."

The door closed with a soft click, and Morgan wept, mourning the loss of her mother and those final precious yet debilitating memories of her. She mourned the loss of the woman she might never be again.

CHAPTER FIFTEEN

Erin rinsed the lunch dishes under the tap before loading them into the dishwasher.

"I've been thinking."

She spun round at the sound of Tristan's voice, clapping her hand to her chest. "Jesus, you scared me."

"Sorry." He pulled open the fridge and helped himself to a can of pop.

"What have you been thinking about?" She dried her hands and turned the kettle on to boil.

"It's the first footie game of the season on Saturday." He popped open the tab and took a drink, holding his soccer ball against his hip with one arm.

"I know."

"Do you think mum will come and watch me play?" He didn't look up from the top of his can.

Erin felt like the air had been sucked out of the room, and her lungs burned as she schooled her face into a smile for Tristan's benefit. "I'm sure if you asked her she'd be there."

"Erm…I don't…I'm not sure…" He looked toward the door, out the window, at the ceiling, anywhere but at Erin.

"Do you want me to ask her for you?"

He dropped his gaze to the floor and nodded his head once.

Erin felt her heartbeat speed up at the thought of hearing Morgan's voice. She didn't want to talk to her. She didn't want to try to be civil to her. She wanted to scream, and shout, and she wanted answers. She wanted to know who was so important to Morgan that she had left their family for her, but hadn't bothered to show up at the hospital.

"Will you ask her?"

Erin swallowed her anger and smiled at Tristan. "Of course."

"Now?"

"Okay." Erin pulled her phone from her pocket. She took a deep breath to steel her nerves as she dialed Amy's number.

"Hello?"

"Hi, Amy, it's Erin. Can I speak to Morgan, please?"

"Sure, she's in the garden. One second."

Erin closed her eyes and tried to push away the picture of the blonde as she focused on the sound of Amy opening doors, her footsteps striking the wooden floors, her muffled voice as she spoke to Morgan and finally Morgan's voice.

"Hello, Erin."

Erin's breath caught in her throat and tears burned her eyes. The happiness in Morgan's voice was unmistakable. She opened her mouth to speak, but she couldn't find the words to say what Tristan wanted her to ask. All she wanted to do was shout, to scream at her and demand answers. She wanted to know why Morgan had betrayed her. How she could have done it. She wanted to cry at the unfairness of knowing that Morgan wouldn't be able to answer her even if she wanted to.

"Hello? Erin, are you there?"

Fear colored Morgan's words, and a part of her rejoiced at it. She wanted to strike out and hurt Morgan just the way she was hurting now.

"Mum, talk to her," Tristan said.

She cleared her throat. "Sorry, yes, I'm here."

"Oh, good. I thought I lost you for a minute there."

Erin laughed at the unintended irony of the statement. "I'm calling to see what you're doing on Saturday."

"Well, nothing."

"It's Tristan's first soccer match of the season. He wondered if you'd like to come and see him play."

"I…" Morgan paused then cleared her throat. "I'd love to."

"Good. I'll let him know you'll be there." She smiled at the beaming grin on Tristan's face.

"Erm…where do I go?"

"I'll text Amy the details." Erin wanted nothing more than to end the conversation and try to forget. For a moment, she envied Morgan, but just for a moment. Tristan's wide smile was more than enough to erase that thought. The price was far too high for her, no matter what the pain.

"Okay. Thank you."

"Don't thank me. He asked."

"And I'll thank him when I see him."

"Right. See you Saturday."

"Good-bye, Erin."

Erin disconnected the call as Tristan kissed the top of her head and ran out into the garden kicking his ball. She stared at the blank screen in her hand, and wished she had never seen the woman's face. *How the hell am I going to be able to face her on Saturday?*

CHAPTER SIXTEEN

Morgan shuffled back and forth trying to spot Erin. The morning was surprisingly cool for late August; the wind whipped through the trees and across the field. It had been two weeks since she'd visited Erin and asked to see the children, and almost a week since Erin had called her. She'd wanted desperately to see them immediately, but had acquiesced to Erin's request for time. She wanted to help them adjust to everything. As much as it made sense, it ripped at her heart to wait.

The soccer game started ten minutes ago and she didn't want to distract Tristan. She finally spotted Erin sitting in a collapsible camping chair by the sideline, and the child's version next to her was empty.

"Hi. Sorry I'm late. I got a little lost."

"It's okay." Erin didn't take her eyes off the game.

"How are you?"

Erin shrugged, still staring at the field.

Okay, that's definitely a cold shoulder. I'm not that late.

"What about you? Remember anything else? Anything new on the investigation?"

"I'm good. The dizzy spells are getting fewer and further between, and most of the other stuff seems to be pretty much normal now. As for the investigation…" She shrugged. "They have a couple of pictures of people they think are involved, but I have no idea who they are, so it really hasn't helped anything."

Erin turned her head and looked into her eyes. Morgan felt as though she were under a microscope being studied, her gaze was so intense. She wished she knew why the anger and hurt sparked in those beautiful blue eyes. She wished she knew how and why she had caused so much pain.

Morgan crouched beside Erin's chair. "For everything I did to hurt you, I'm sorry. I know you think that doesn't mean anything because I don't know what I'm apologizing for, but it does. I'm apologizing for hurting you. I know I've done that. The how and the why are things I wish I knew, but I don't. All I know is that I did. And that's reason enough for me to say I'm sorry to you for the rest of my life."

Tears filled Erin's eyes. She reached for her bag and let her gaze fall as she retrieved a tissue. She wiped her eyes and pointed at the pitch. "They're one nil up. He saved a penalty."

"He did? Already?"

"Yes."

Morgan scanned the field and found Tristan shouting instructions to his defense and clapping his oversized gloves as the wall lined up to block a free kick. She watched him squat down to check all the angles and shout for the wall to move over. The referee blew his whistle and the other team tried to curl the ball around the wall. Morgan felt her heart pounding as it sailed over the heads of the boys and straight toward Tristan. He jumped, arms outstretched, and finger tipped the ball over the cross bar. He rolled with the landing and was back on his feet in seconds organizing his defense for the corner kick that would follow.

"He's good. How long has he played goalkeeper?"

"Three years for this team. He played for another team before that. Midfield."

"Why did he switch?"

"He prefers it, and he's good in goal—tall, jumps higher than the rest of his teammates, probably because of his basketball training too. You worked with him for months on his skills, and how to land without hurting himself." Erin kept her eyes fixed on the field.

"We were close?"

"Very. He's angry at you for leaving and not calling, not coming round. Don't expect this to be easy, Morgan."

"I don't. I'm amazed he wanted me to come here."

Erin laughed. "You've been to every game he's ever played. If you hadn't been here today, it would have been the first one you missed. It would have killed him."

"He's amazing."

"They both are. Even though he wanted you here, he might not speak to you. Or he might get moody and sulk."

"He can scream at me if he wants to. I'm so grateful he's giving me a chance. Where's Maddie?"

"Toilet."

"Should I go and see if she's okay?"

"No. She's on her way back now." Erin pointed across the field to the row of Portacabins and the girl skipping toward them. "There's another chair if you want to sit down." Erin pushed at the canvas bag at her feet.

"Thanks." Morgan picked it up, pulled the chair out, and unfolded it. She sat next to Erin, watching Maddie cross behind Tristan's net, and then carry on. But Tristan was looking across the field at Morgan. He raised his hand as if to wave, but dropped it before he got halfway. He turned back to the game and shouted more instructions to his teammates. Out of the corner of her eye, she could see Erin holding her hand out to Maddie, as she stopped skipping and slowly walked the remaining distance toward them. She cuddled in close to Erin and stared at Morgan.

"Hi." Morgan smiled warmly. Her heart pounded as she looked at her daughter. She had long, dark hair, big brown eyes, watching her cautiously, and dimples just waiting to pop when she smiled. Her leg twitched and jumped while she waited.

"Hi."

"I, erm…" She cleared her throat. "I brought something for you, Maddie."

She cocked her head to one side and waited.

"Right, I—I used to love these when I was your age, and I thought if you didn't already know loads of cool tricks, I could maybe, teach you some." She reached into her pocket and pulled out a yo-yo. It was bright pink with glitter all over it.

Maddie's eyes lit up, but she looked to Erin before she reached for it. Erin smiled and nodded, subtly shifting so that Maddie was closer to Morgan and could see much easier.

"Do you know how to work a yo-yo?"

Maddie shook her head.

"No?"

Maddie giggled as she shook her head this time. "Nope. You never taught me old toys before."

Erin pressed a hand to her lips, trying to stifle the laughter that bubbled out. She winked at Morgan when their eyes met.

"Old toys, eh?" Morgan tied the loop in the end of the string and slipped it onto her middle finger. "Well, young lady, I'll have you know that this 'old toy' can be a lot fun." She flexed her shoulder and let the yo-yo go. She went through a quick repertoire of a straight forward roll, walking the dog, sleeper, around the world, the three leaf clover, and then the pièce de résistance, the pinwheel. Maddie's eyes were huge, her hesitancy forgotten as she crept closer and closer to Morgan.

"Can you teach me all of those?"

Morgan slid the string from her finger and helped Maddie put it on. "Well, let's give it a try and see." Twenty minutes later, she looked up as Maddie executed her first walk the dog on her own and caught Erin watching her before she turned back to watching the game. She smiled and then went back to helping Maddie with her new toy. Every few minutes, she would look up to see how the soccer game was progressing. By half time Tristan had saved another five shots, and his team had scored again. They all ran to the sidelines, grabbed drinks, orange segments, and sat down to listen to their coach.

"Maddie, do you want something to eat?" Erin ran her fingers through her hair as she spoke.

"Yes, please." Maddie wound the string up and slipped the loop back on her finger.

"I put a banana and a packet of crisps in your bag this morning."

"Can I have a hotdog?" She looked up and grinned cheekily.

"What's wrong with the banana and crisps?"

"Nothing. But I like hotdogs."

"Okay, straight there and back."

Maddie made a cross over her chest. "Promise."

Erin fished her purse out of her coat pocket. "Do you want anything?" She glanced over at Morgan.

"I'll go with her."

"Yay!" Maddie wiggled as Morgan quickly got out of her chair.

Maddie reached out and grabbed hold of Morgan's hand and led her toward the concessions stand. The warmth of Maddie's fingers penetrated her own as she skipped along.

"I've got important stuff to tell you."

Morgan smiled down at her. "You do?"

"Yep. The third of October."

"What about it?"

Maddie frowned slightly. "That's my birthday. Mum said you don't remember it. So I made you a list. It's in my bag, on my chair."

Morgan stumbled slightly as she stared at her. "I'm sorry, Maddie."

"What for?"

"That I can't remember. It must be very upsetting for you."

"Well, yes. But you can learn my birthday, so it's okay. I'll teach you the important stuff."

"That's good. Can you teach me texting too?"

Maddie giggled. "I'm not allowed a mobile till I go to secondary school."

"Oh. Why not?"

"I can't remember. It was just what you said. Tristan's got one. He's always texting his girlfriend, so he can teach you."

"Tristan has a girlfriend?" *My son has a girlfriend? I don't know whether to be proud or terrified.*

"Yep. She's called Isabelle, and she's older than him, and she's got pretty blond hair and they were kissing at the basketball center, but no tongues."

Terrified. Definitely terrified. "Oh. Does your mum know about Isabelle?"

"Uh huh. She told me not to tell tales."

They reached the hotdog stand and she scanned the menu.

"Can I help you?" The woman wore a baseball hat and a white striped navy apron over her ample body.

"Three hotdogs, please."

"You want onions on them?"

Morgan looked at Maddie, who shook her head. "No, thank you. Do you want a drink, young lady?"

"Hot chocolate, please."

"And what will your mum want?"

"Coffee, with milk and two sugars."

Morgan turned back to the woman. "One hot chocolate and two coffees as well."

The woman was efficient as she filled their order and put the polystyrene cups on the counter. "Milk and sugar is over there." She pointed to the other end of the counter. "Do you want lids for these?"

"Yes, please." Morgan doctored the coffees and wrapped the hotdogs for Maddie to carry, and struggled to put the hot cups in a triangle to carry herself without spilling them. She turned and took a couple of steps.

"Mum, why don't you ask the lady for a cup tray?"

"A what?"

Maddie rolled her eyes and retrieved one from the woman. Morgan quickly put the drinks in and took one of the hotdogs from Maddie, so she had less to carry.

"Thank you."

"What for?" Maddie looked at her curiously.

"I didn't know about these." She waved the loaded cup holder.

"Did they not have them in the olden days?"

Morgan tried not to laugh. "No, I don't remember these."

"Oh, right. S'pose there's lots of stuff like that. Do you know about microwaves?"

"Yes, I know about them."

"What about DVDs?"

"What's that?"

"It's what we watch films and stuff on."

"Oh, videos."

"No, silly. Nobody has them anymore. Mum threw out the old ones of our baby movies when she got them put on DVDs last year."

"I'd like to see them."

"Well, DVDs are everywhere."

"No, I meant your baby films."

"Oh, I'll ask mum. I think she's got some of them on her iPad."

"Your mum has an iPad?"

"Yep. You got it for her for her birthday last year. You put pictures of us all on it for her and all her favorite songs and films and stuff. She cried and said you were wonderful, and then she kissed you and we all went out to a restaurant."

"I'm beginning to think food is very important to you, young lady."

"Mum says I'm a dustbin."

"Does she now?"

"Yep, and that Tristan has hollow legs, 'cos he eats so much."

She skipped the last twenty yards to Erin and handed over the hotdog. She wriggled onto her chair and grinned as Morgan handed over her hot chocolate. She put it in the drinks holder and unwrapped her hotdog.

"Coffee?"

Erin glanced up. "Thanks." She took the drink and peered around Morgan. "They just conceded another penalty and one of Tristan's teammates has been sent off."

"Why?"

"He fouled the other boy. Clearly. So when the referee gave him a yellow card he started mouthing off. That's his mother on the pitch arguing with the referee now."

The woman was waving her arms as she told the man what she thought of his refereeing skills and where he was in the evolutionary scale. Another man walked over to her and grabbed her arm, trying to pull her away.

"That her husband?"

"Nope. That's her new boyfriend. I believe he's the fifth new boyfriend that has accompanied her to matches since Christmas."

"Ouch. How's your hotdog, Maddie?"

"S'good, fanks," she said around a mouthful.

"Don't talk with your mouth full." Erin took a bite of her own.

Maddie made a show of swallowing. "Sorry, Mum."

The woman was escorted off the pitch and the referee placed the ball on the penalty spot before indicating that the striker could come forward to take the shot. Tristan was on his line, knees flexed, arms out at his sides, bouncing lightly on the balls of his feet as he watched the striker spin the ball then place it on the spot. He took several steps back, staring first at the ball, then at Tristan.

Tristan smiled, shimmied his hips, and waited. The referee blew his whistle and the striker took off running for the ball. He blasted it toward the goal with all the power he could muster. Tristan moved as soon as his foot connected with the ball, jumping high and to the left. He stopped the ball with his chest and curled his arms in to secure it as he hit the ground.

Morgan and Erin jumped to their feet, yelling proudly. Morgan spread her arms wide with glee; it felt so natural to pull Erin into her embrace as she celebrated. She didn't even think about it until Erin froze in her arms, her body stiff and unyielding.

"Let me go, Morgan." Erin's voice was little more than a whisper.

"I'm sorry. I got carried away." She let her arms drop and backed away.

"I'm not here for you. I'm here for our children." Erin's voice was only just loud enough for her to hear.

Morgan swallowed her disappointment. "I'm sorry." For a brief moment, she'd felt Erin's body against her own, smelled apples in her hair, and heard her quick intake of breath. She felt as if she were home. She didn't want to think about the loss of contact, or that even the briefest, most innocent, of touches was so unwelcome. They sat down again and Morgan felt the wall between them as solidly as though it were real.

Maddie finished her drink and rummaged through her backpack. She knelt next to Morgan and handed her a piece of paper. "Here's the list I made for you. It's got all the important stuff on it."

Morgan took it and glanced down the list. Birthdays, middle names, sports, favorite colors, games.

"What's a Wii?"

"It's a game."

"What kind of game?"

"Erm, all sorts. There's running ones, and kickboxing, and I like the dancing one, and Tristan likes the snowboarding one."

Morgan knew she was frowning, but she was getting more and more confused. "Maddie, I don't understand. Are these sports you both do?"

"It's a computer games console. Like the SEGA Megadrive, with that blue hedgehog you and Nikki used to play all the time." Erin smiled and ruffled Maddie's hair. "It's interactive and they love it. I'm sure they'll show you."

"Okay, thanks."

"Can I ask you something?" Maddie's hand was on her knee.

"Of course."

"What should I call you now?"

"Oh, erm." She ignored Erin's gasp, and tried to think what would be best for Maddie. Such a simple question, but every answer was a minefield. "What did you call me before?"

Maddie cocked her head to one side. "Mum."

"Is that what you want to call me now?"

Maddie nodded. "Yes, but I don't know if I'm supposed to."

"Why not?"

"'Cos you don't remember being my mum."

The air suddenly felt thicker, harder to breathe, and tears filled Maddie's eyes. Morgan's fingers shook as she stroked Maddie's cheek. "I feel like your mum, baby girl." She took hold of Maddie's hand. "If you want to call me Mum, you go right ahead. If that doesn't feel right yet, you can tell me, and we'll think of something else."

Maddie crawled onto Morgan's lap and wrapped her arms around her neck. Morgan didn't care how much her ribs ached from the move, or how much her shoulder throbbed, there was no way she was letting go. She wrapped her arms around the precious bundle and closed her eyes. She sucked in a deep lungful of Maddie's sweet scent, apple shampoo like Erin's, talcum powder, and soap. She ran her fingers through the silky tresses and let her tears fall freely, oblivious to everything and everyone around her.

❖

Tristan was the last player to leave the pitch, after congratulations from the rest of his teammates. He walked slowly toward them. Morgan smiled and hoped she didn't look as scared as she felt. He walked to Erin first and grudgingly accepted her congratulatory kiss. Maddie wrapped her arms about his waist and declared him the "bestest goal keeper in England." He smiled at her enthusiasm and turned slowly to face Morgan.

"Hi." Morgan stepped toward him, but froze as he took a step back and pulled Maddie in front of him, tickling her ribs as he did.

"Hello." His voice was cool, distant, and so unlike the passionate young man who had been shouting at his teammates for the better part of the last two hours. It cut Morgan to the core.

For the second time in an hour, she hid her disappointment, and smiled through the pain she felt. "Thank you for asking me to come. You played brilliantly. Those penalty saves were fantastic."

"You missed the first one."

She felt herself blushing after being called on her overly exuberant response. "Sorry, I got lost. But your mum told me, and I saw the second one. You played really well, Tristan."

"Thanks."

"Trist, look at this." Maddie pulled her yo-yo out of her pocket and held it up. "It's an olden day toy, and Mum showed me how to do tricks. Watch." She started to work through the simple tricks that Morgan had shown her, but Tristan kept looking at Morgan.

"Maddie, I need to go to the ladies. Come with me?" Erin held out her hand.

"But I'm showing Tristan my yo-yo."

Erin cocked her head and raised an eyebrow.

"Okay, I'm coming." She followed behind Erin, wrapping the string tight around the core as she went, her tongue poking between her teeth as she concentrated.

"Subtle." Tristan dropped heavily into Erin's chair and fished a bottle of sports drink from her bag.

"As a ton of bricks." She smiled and sat back down. "You really did play brilliantly."

He shrugged. "Just doing what I do."

She almost laughed at the cocky attitude, but she knew she had to tread carefully, and teasing him wasn't going to work right now.

"I heard you play basketball too."

"Yep." He took a long drink from the bottle and then fiddled with the lid.

"Are you good?"

He shrugged again. "I'm all right."

"You enjoy it?"

"Wouldn't play if I didn't." He pushed the cap on firmly and tossed it into the bag.

"Right."

"Mum said she doesn't know if you'll ever get your memories back."

"No. That's pretty much what the doctors say. When I was in the hospital, I had some seizures, because of the concussion. Well, they caused some brain damage, I suppose. There's scar tissue on my brain. They think that's part of the reason why I can't remember stuff."

"So you're never going to remember?"

"Some things might come back, but some of it won't. And there's no way to tell what will or won't." They sat in silence for a few minutes.

"Was it scary?" He picked at the dirt under his nails.

"Yeah. I thought it was a joke at first. Now it's not so much scary as sad."

"Why?"

"Because I've missed so much."

"Like what?" He slouched further down in his chair, looking out across the empty field.

"Like holding you when you were little. Seeing you take your first steps, your first words, first day at school. Everything."

"But you didn't miss all that. I remember you taking me to school and stuff."

"I don't," Morgan whispered.

He dropped his chin to his chest, seemingly lost in thought. "So what do you want from me?"

"I just want to spend time with you. To get to know you. Just to be in your life. As your mum if you want me to be. If not, however you want."

He looked at her. "So it's up to me?"

Morgan swallowed, dreading his rejection. "Yes. If you want me to leave you alone, I will. I know that I hurt you, although I can't remember why, and I know this must be really, really hard for you. I don't want to make it harder."

"You wouldn't try to make me?"

Morgan shook her head. She knew her voice wouldn't hold if she opened her mouth.

"I need to think about it."

She inclined her head. "Okay."

He stood up and started to pack away the folding chairs. Erin and Maddie walked across the football pitch, hand in hand.

"Everything okay?" She touched Tristan's shoulder.

"Yeah. I need to go and get a shower."

"Okay." Erin picked up her bag. "Maddie, say good-bye."

"But I don't want to go yet." She ran to Morgan and wrapped her arms about her waist. "Can you come home now?"

Morgan knelt and hugged her. "You'll see me again soon, baby girl. I promise. Your mum and I, we'll talk and sort something out." She looked up at Erin. "Right?"

Erin blinked. "Yes."

"You can speak to me whenever you like. I'm staying with Nikki and Amy. Do you know the number there?"

"No."

"It's in the book, sweetie." Erin stroked Maddie's hair.

"See. It's already there. And I'll call you too."

"Promise?"

"Promise." Morgan made a cross over her heart.

"Love you, Mum."

Morgan's heart filled with joy and broke with anguish as she held Maddie to her chest. "Love you too, baby girl."

CHAPTER SEVENTEEN

"You look like you've found a penny and lost a tenner."
Chris patted Erin on the back and perched on the bar stool
next to her. "Pint of lager, please," he said to the bartender when she
held up a glass toward him.

Erin shrugged and finished the last mouthful of wine. When
the woman put Chris's drink in front of him, she raised her glass,
indicating her desire for another, and then fished in her pocket for
her purse.

"I'll get these." Chris paid for their drinks, and Erin took a
long swallow. Chris raised his eyebrow, but refrained from saying
anything. "Who's looking after the kids?"

"Sitter." Erin sipped her wine and wondered how long Chris
would wait before he started in with his questions. She knew she
needed to talk, to vent, and figure out what was going on in her head.
Chris was always the best one to help her with that. Even off the
clock, he couldn't seem to stop being a shrink. But she didn't want
to talk. She wanted to get drunk and forget everything. She laughed
at the irony.

"What's the joke?"

"I was just thinking that I wanted to get drunk and forget
everything. But since forgetting everything is part of the problem, I
don't think that's going to help."

Chris smiled. "Probably not." He bumped her with his shoulder.
"Want to find a table? Bit more private."

She nodded and followed him away from the bar. He found them a small table in the corner and pointed for her to sit first.

"So how did the footie match go?"

"About the way I expected it to."

Chris sipped his drink, obviously waiting for her to continue.

"Maddie was shy at first, but Morgan brought a yo-yo and started teaching her different tricks. She called her Mum again." Her voice was husky and thick with emotion.

"And how did Morgan react to that?"

"She held her and cried." She ran her fingers through her hair. "It obviously meant the world to Morgan."

Chris leaned back in his chair, comfortable, relaxed. "And Tristan?"

"Played brilliantly. Saved—"

"Don't change the subject. How was he with Morgan? How was he afterward?"

"He didn't make a scene; he was…cordial, with her. He seemed much happier after she assured him that she wouldn't push. She let him know that if he didn't want to see her, she'd accept his decision."

"And what was his decision?"

"He told her that he wanted to think about it."

"Ah, make her sweat."

"Yep." Erin put her glass back on the table and picked up an unused coaster and slowly peeled the layers apart.

"Okay, now you can tell me how he played."

"He saved two penalties and really put on a show."

"That's my boy!" Chris grinned. "Was it appreciated?"

"Morgan was so excited she was jumping around like one of the kids when he saved the second penalty. She even hugged me." She watched Chris's eyebrow twitch. She waited for him to question what she was doing letting Morgan touch her. She expected him to get angry with her for not stopping it before it happened, at Morgan for daring to try. But he didn't say anything.

"So she said she won't push for access?" Chris grabbed his glass and took a long drink.

"She said that she knew it was hard for them both, and she didn't want to make anything any more difficult. She was there if they wanted her, but if they didn't, she wasn't going to force the issue."

"Do you believe her?"

"What do you mean?"

"Well, technically, biologically, they're her children—"

"Legally they're both of ours. We adopted them both when they were born, so in the eyes of the law, we both have joint rights and responsibilities."

"I know. And that's my point. Legally, she can push this and get access, even joint custody."

"And you think I don't know that?"

Chris held his hand up. "Hey, I'm just making sure you're looking at all sides here. I'm pretty invested in this situation too."

Erin closed her eyes and brought her temper back under control. Fear drove her to snap at the smallest excuse. "Sorry. I know you're only trying to help."

"Do you believe that she'd back off?"

"She sounded sincere."

"But?"

"Morgan's stubborn. If she's determined to see them…" She didn't want to think about fighting Morgan in court. Standing across from her and telling a judge that seeing her own children wasn't in their best interests. She could only imagine how much that would hurt all of them. The thought of losing her children was too much to contemplate.

"Tell me again how she was with Maddie."

"She brought her a yo-yo and spent ages teaching her how to do tricks with it. She took her for hot dogs, and Maddie had made her a list." She sipped her drink. "Birthdays and stuff. So Morgan could learn them."

"How did Morgan react to that?"

"She was grateful. She thanked Maddie for being so thoughtful, and later she asked Tristan about some stuff that was on it, so she must have thought it was beneficial."

"Hmm." He took another drink. "Now, forgive me if I'm wrong here, but that doesn't sound like a woman who wants to do anything to hurt those kids."

"No, it doesn't. I want to believe her."

"But you don't."

Erin sipped her drink. "No."

"Why not? She never hurt them before."

"Yes, she did. She was gone for three weeks and never called them once."

"But she's here now, and that's what we have to deal with, Erin." Chris lifted his glass again. "Look, Morgan left, you don't know why, she can't tell you now, and you're pissed off with her. I get it. Before the accident, she was dragging her heels in regards to the kids. That upset them, and you don't want to see them upset again. I get it. And trust me, I'm fucking furious with her. But Morgan loved those kids. Whatever her reasons, she would not have left never to be seen again. She loved them far too much for that. And you know it."

"Do I?" She swallowed the last of her drink. "Until six weeks ago I would have sworn she loved me too much to think about leaving me. I thought we were rock solid. I built my whole world around her. Then she walked out." She pulled her bag onto her lap and pulled out the picture of the blond woman that she had printed off the Internet.

Chris picked up the page. "Who's this?"

"The woman Morgan left me for."

Chris dropped the paper like it had burned him. "What?"

"You heard me."

"How do you—where—I don't—no."

"What do you mean, no?"

"Morgan wouldn't cheat on you."

"Well, explain that then." She pointed to the picture.

"Where did you get this?"

"Off the Internet."

"What?"

"Oh for God's sake. The police came and asked me if I recognized her or this guy. Said they needed to speak to them about Morgan's attack."

"And?"

"I didn't know her."

"So why is the picture on the Internet?"

"They've posted the pictures and are asking people to come forward if they know who they are."

"Okay. And how does that make her the woman Morgan left you for?"

"They're looking for her because she was with Morgan that night."

"Okay. And?"

"Look at her face."

Chris raised an eyebrow at her but did as she asked. "What am I meant to be seeing?"

She stared at him. "Her eyes are closed."

"So?"

"Her head's tipped back and her mouth is open."

"Maybe she's laughing."

"Does that look like laughter to you?"

Chris shrugged. "I don't think it matters what it looks like to me, does it?"

"She looks like she's being fucked."

"You said this was from a car park CCTV camera."

"So?"

"Well, I'm just going to clarify here for a second. You think Morgan left you for this woman because the police want to ask her questions about Morgan's attack based on this picture from a car park CCTV camera that you think is showing them—presumably her and Morgan—having sex in the car park before she was attacked. Have I missed anything?"

"No. That just about sums it up."

"Okay. Let me put another angle on this for you." He waited until she looked at him again. "What if this woman was having sex in the car park with the guy they want to question? What if Morgan disturbed them and that's why she was attacked?"

Erin felt her jaw drop and the air rush from her lungs. Could that be the truth? Could she really have it wrong?

"Ask yourself this, before she left was she acting like she was seeing someone else?"

"How the hell would I know how someone acts when they're fucking around?"

"They say the wife always knows."

"Oh, do they? Well, they are talking out of their collective arses then aren't they?"

"So you didn't think she was having an affair?"

"No." She kept her voice quiet, but the relief was making her hands shake around her glass. "So no, I don't know anything anymore. I'll be back in a minute." The bathroom was empty when she walked in. She bent over the sink and splashed water on her face. The paper towel was harsh against her skin as she wiped away the water and looked at herself in the mirror; the dark circles under her eyes telling the tale of sleepless nights and worry.

Chris had fresh drinks waiting when she got back. "You okay?"

Erin shook her head and sipped her wine letting the fruity flavor settle on her tongue and warm her throat as she swallowed. "No. I really don't think I am." She laughed bitterly.

"Why are you questioning yourself like this?"

"I think I have very poor judgment when it comes to people."

Chris frowned. "How do you figure that one?"

"I trusted Dad, and look what happened there. I trusted Morgan…I loved her." She placed her glass on the table and picked up another coaster and slowly peeled the edges apart. "Like I said, bad judgment."

He laughed. "That's it? That's your reasoning?"

Erin looked up at him. "Isn't that enough?"

"No, baby sister, it really isn't." He took a drink. "Dad wasn't your judgment to make. It was Mum's. And what he did is not the same as what Morgan has done."

"How do you figure that?"

"He left us homeless, penniless, and he didn't even say good-bye. He practically crawled out the window in the middle of the night, before the bailiffs could come and take his boxer shorts! I remember that day just as well as you do. Watching them lock our house so we couldn't go back inside. Seeing them load up everything but the essentials. I felt that too, Erin."

"He left, she left."

"It's not that simple, Erin. The basic facts aren't even close to being the same. Morgan walked out after a fight. Maybe she was coming back, maybe not, you don't know either way. Her wages were still being paid into your joint account, she had no debts that she left you with, and she left you in the house."

"Even if she wasn't seeing someone else, she still walked out!" She tossed the mangled coaster back onto the table.

"Yep. I seem to remember a time when you had another big row with her, and you walked out."

"I did not!"

"Yes, you did. You were pregnant with Tristan, and she refused to go and get you something or other at four in the morning. You turned up on Mum's doorstep and it took her three days to convince you to go home."

"Oh for God's sake, I was pregnant!"

"So?"

"So, I was hormonal. I had a reason."

"Not a very logical one." He folded his arms across his chest, a smug smile shaping his lips.

"It was still a reason."

"How do you know that Morgan didn't have a reason?"

"She said she did. But it was even worse than the pregnant one."

Chris grinned as he took another drink. "You never said she had a reason."

"Because it was stupid."

"Well?" He put his glass down again. "Let's hear it."

"She said she was making us all miserable, and she couldn't stand to do that to us."

He frowned. "Okay, that is a pretty crap reason, but I don't think it's worse than the pregnant one. Definitely on a level."

"Why are you sticking up for her?"

He shrugged. "I'm not. I'm just trying to understand. I'm pissed off with her, too. I put a lot of trust in you both when I agreed to donate for the kids. I feel betrayed, too. But I think I know Morgan well enough to know that this—her leaving like this—that's just not her. If it was, I would never have agreed to help you have your family. And I do trust my judgment, Erin. Didn't her mum suffer from depression?"

Erin sipped her drink. "She did."

"Okay, hear me out on this. What happened with Morgan's mum and dad, it was horrific, right?"

"Yes."

"And she was there? She saw it?"

"She always thought it was her fault."

Chris cocked his head. "Why?"

"I don't know. She wouldn't tell me. She hated talking about it. She refused point-blank to tell me anything but the facts: he killed her, Morgan testified against him, and now he's in prison."

"That's something you both did then."

"What?"

"You didn't exactly give her all the gory details about Dad, did you?"

"What more did she need to know? He left, we never saw him again. End of story."

"God, Erin, you can be such a pain in the arse sometimes. We both know that affected you—us—so much deeper than that."

Erin closed her eyes as the memories hit her. Her mother stood to one side of her, Chris on the other, his arm wrapped about her shoulders. She stood horrified as the bailiffs locked the door to their house. The loss of their security—their home—highlighted her vulnerability, her dependence, and her helplessness as the truth of the betrayal sank in. The father she had adored—worshipped—had cared so little, he had left them with nothing and hadn't even said good-bye.

Chris interrupted her thoughts. "Did he hit her?"

Erin shrugged and took a sip of her wine. "She wouldn't say, but I think so. She has a wicked scar down her shoulder blade. When I asked about it, she said she was cut with a broken glass. She would never say anymore than that."

"What was Morgan like before she left?"

"Moody. She didn't crack a smile for weeks. She looked worried. Maybe scared. But she wouldn't talk to me. I don't think she talked to anyone. Amy and Nikki didn't have a clue what was going on either. Well, they said they didn't."

"You don't believe them?"

"I do. It was frustrating. The not knowing."

"I know there were parts of her past she refused to talk about, but she wasn't usually so tightlipped. Did something trigger the change?"

Erin glared at him again and sipped her drink. "I don't know, maybe some blonde."

"Well, it's a fairly big change in behavior, and the actions that followed were out of character too. If this was one of my patients, I'd be thinking about treating for depression."

"You think she was depressed rather than having an affair?"

"Do you?" He sipped from his glass.

"I hate it when you do that."

"What?" Chris wiped beer froth from his upper lip.

"Answer a question with a question. It's such a shrinky thing to do."

"Sorry." He smiled. "So do you think she was depressed?"

"I have no idea."

"But it makes more sense now, doesn't it?"

"Than her fucking someone else? Not really."

"I'll say this once so listen to me very carefully." He waited until she met his eyes. "Morgan wasn't having an affair. I'll stake anything you want on that. Swear to anything you like. Morgan loved you and the kids with everything in her. Why she did what she did—well, I'm guessing we'll never really know now. But when the police find out who these people are, there will be some other explanation for that picture than the one you assumed. I know Morgan wouldn't have cheated on you. And so should you."

"I thought I did."

"But her behavior was so out of character that now you doubt everything?"

"Yes."

"I understand that. But if you doubt everything, do yourself a favor."

"What?"

"Doubt that your assumption is right too. Give yourself the possibility that the explanation for that picture will not be one that is incriminating for Morgan. Whatever it might be."

"You do know what you're asking of me here, don't you?"

"Yes. I'm asking my science loving logical baby sister to have faith."

"Hmpf."

"Trust in what you and Morgan had, Erin. Trust it. It was something I always dreamed I'd one day find."

"Something I—we—had. Not anymore."

Chris drank his beer and watched her. "Depression prevents people from thinking logically. What seems simple and understandable, becomes the most difficult thing in the world to grasp. Even small things turn into insurmountable obstacles. You said she looked scared sometimes."

"Scared of what though? That I couldn't deal with the situation if she was suffering from depression? That I'd be like her dad and hit her?" Erin could scarcely believe what he was saying.

"No, I know it seems ludicrous. But she grew up in that environment. I think she was scared for the kids."

Erin frowned.

"That they'd grow up like her if they saw their mum the way she saw herself."

"That's just backward. She left, thereby hurting them, to stop them from being hurt. We're back to stupid reasons again, Chris."

"Not really. It comes down to which is the greater hurt, doesn't it?"

"English. Plain and simple. Speak it now!"

"If you've got a plaster over a cut, you know that taking it off is going to hurt, how do you do it?"

"Why are we talking about plasters now?"

"Answer the question."

She rolled her eyes. "Rip it off fast. Get it over and done with."

"Exactly."

"Exactly." She mimicked. "And that's important because?"

"It hurts less in the long run."

"And?"

"Oh, Erin, use that big brain of yours and think for a minute. Stop feeling hurt and angry and think."

She felt her jaw drop and her eyes grew wide as the realization of what he meant hit her. Was it possible that Morgan ran because she was afraid she was going to lose them or hurt them? What possible reason could she have for believing that? Did she really believe that? Erin thought about Morgan's face as she walked out. It wasn't anger on her face; it was regret. And fear. And determination. That's what had bothered her so much. Morgan had looked as though she was doing something she had to do, rather than something she wanted to do. It wasn't a choice, but a necessity.

"I don't think you have bad judgment at all, Erin. Trust yourself. Trust her."

"I can't."

"Why not?"

"Because all this, however plausible it might sound and however forgivable it might be, you're guessing. We have no way of knowing if she was scared of something. We have no way of knowing if she was acting in our best interests. And we have no one to ask for corroboration because she can't remember even if we did!"

"Well, I suppose when you put it like that, you've got a point."

Erin let her head fall back against her chair and stared at the ceiling.

"You wish you didn't though, don't you?" Chris put his empty glass on the table.

"What?"

"You wish you didn't have a point. You still love her, don't you?"

"Why are you sticking up for her? And don't say you aren't, because you are."

"I want you to be happy. Apart from this last month or so, Morgan has always made you happy. Even when you got pregnant and stupidly left her, or you were arguing, or either of you were being moody. She still made you laugh."

"She doesn't remember any of that."

"And that hurts even more than her leaving you, doesn't it?"

"The Morgan I loved doesn't exist anymore. Seeing her yesterday made that so clear. My wife doesn't exist anymore, and the feelings I have about her walking out are never going to be resolved, because she doesn't exist to help sort them out. It's like she died. Like we had a fight and then she died." She closed her eyes and buried her face in her hands. "Seeing her yesterday, she was so different. She seemed so young, and she was so worried that the kids wouldn't like her. It was written all over her face and she seemed so vulnerable."

"Was that bad?"

"What? No. Just different. Not what I'm used to."

"She is different." He leaned his elbows on the table and waited until she looked at him. "Think about it. By the time we get to our age, we're shaped and molded by all the different things that have happened to us through our lives. I'm wary of getting involved with another woman because my last girlfriend cheated on me. I'm jaded, thinking every woman's going to do the same thing to me. You don't trust people because Dad was a knobhead, and Morgan left. These are big things that have had a deep impact on us, but really, they're fairly small everyday things that happen to just about anyone. Millions of dads leave their kids, billions of girlfriends cheat. Morgan's dad killed her mum, she testified against him, and he was sent to prison. For life, right?"

"Yes."

"That's not exactly commonplace, and it is hugely traumatic. This Morgan, the one you saw yesterday, that never happened to her. It hasn't had an impact in forming her thoughts, or her reactions, or anything."

"But she knows about it."

"And I know about the Second World War, and it makes me sad, and angry, and parts of it disgust me. But it doesn't affect me as a person. It doesn't change the way I'm going to live my life."

"But it's her mum."

"And she'll be grieving. But those images, those incredibly intense emotions that she must have felt, they aren't a part of her anymore."

Was that the difference? The thing that was missing? The insidious worm that had been eating Morgan's soul, stripping her of her passion, her confidence, and her spirit was a ghost, haunting her from the inside. Was this woman, this new Morgan, free of the shackles that had snared her before her life had really even begun? Was it this memory that had created the brooding, tortured soul that Erin had fallen in love with, wanted to heal, and needed to love her with an intensity that had taken her breath away?

"You still love her, don't you?"

Erin snorted. "It doesn't matter if I do or not. We've both said it in different ways but the result is the same. My Morgan's gone." She tossed the coaster onto the table. "I have to accept that and figure out some way of moving on."

CHAPTER EIGHTEEN

Morgan pressed the length of charcoal down the paper, loving the scratching sound it made as it left its mark. She used her thumb to smudge in the contours and create depth. Tiny touches added the impression of color to the eyes, bounce to the curls, and life to the page. She didn't remember being an artist, but the more she did it, the more natural it felt. It brought a sense of calm nothing else had, yet.

The sound of the doorbell pulled her from her reverie. She glanced at the page, frowning as she put it on the coffee table and went to the door. She smiled when she opened it.

"Hello, Maddie. What are you doing here?"

"Come to see you. Is that okay?"

"Course it is." She stepped back to let her enter. "Did your mum drop you off?"

"Erm, no." Maddie was in the front room and pulling off her coat. "Where's Auntie Amy and Auntie Nikki?"

"Out shopping. How did you get here?"

"I walked. It's only a few streets. That's Mum." She pointed at the drawing Morgan had left on the table. "Did you draw this?"

"Yes. Does your mother know you're here?"

"Have you done more in here?" Maddie lifted the sketchbook and turned the pages back.

"Does your mum know you're here, Maddie?"

"That one's me."

"Yes, it is. Now please tell me. Does your mum know you're here?"

Maddie shook her head.

"Where is she?"

"At home."

"So why didn't you ask her about coming here?"

Maddie shrugged.

"I would have come to get you, but you shouldn't sneak out."

"I didn't sneak." She put the book down. "I just opened the door. That's not sneaking."

"Maddie, you know what I mean, don't you? You should have told your mum where you were going, and you should have called me to come and get you."

"But I thought…"

Morgan waited, squatting next to her when she didn't carry on. "You thought what, sweetheart?"

"That I couldn't see you until Tristan said he wanted to. And he hasn't said yet, but I wanted to see you, and it's not fair if I can't because he's being a stupid-head, and I'm big enough to walk here, and I know the way, and I didn't get lost or anything."

"Hey, hey." Morgan pulled her into a hug and the tears started to fall. "It's all right."

"I'm sorry I didn't tell mum I was going out, but I didn't know if it was okay, and I really had something important to talk to you about."

"It's okay. You're allowed to see me anytime you want to. And we'll talk about the important things, but I think we should call your mum first. Let her know where you are, and that you're okay. Don't you?"

Maddie nodded against her shoulder. "She'll be mad at me."

"Well, maybe, but only because she'll be worried about you."

"Will you tell her?"

Morgan laughed. "Oh, you want me to do your dirty work for you, hey?"

Maddie looked up at her and nodded solemnly.

Morgan couldn't say no. "This time. But you pull this stunt again, and you're facing the music on your own, tough stuff." She tweaked her nose and grabbed the phone. Maddie told her the number and sat next to her flicking through the sketchbook as the phone rang.

"Hello." Tristan's voice welcomed her.

"Hi, Tristan. It's your mu—it's Morgan. Is your mum there?"

"She's going ape at the minute. Maddie's gone walkabout."

"She's here. It's lovely to hear your voice, Tristan, and I do want to talk to you, but can you please put your mum on the phone?"

"Yeah. Is she really there? With you?"

"Yes." She could hear him moving about.

"Just a minute." His words were muffled, but Morgan could clearly make out his voice as he shouted for Erin. "She's coming now. Did you come for Maddie?"

"What? No. Maddie just got here. She came by herself."

"So you're not kidnapping her or something?"

"What? No—"

"Morgan? Is she there?" Erin's voice was high-pitched and her breathing ragged.

"Yeah. She walked here by herself a few minutes ago."

"Oh, thank God. I'll come and get her."

"Erin, it's okay. I'll bring her back." There was a pause on the other end of the line.

"Are you sure?"

"Of course."

"Call me if she's bothering you, and I'll come get her."

"Erin, she isn't bothering me. I want to spend time with her. I'm glad she's here. I've already told her that she was wrong to sneak out without telling you, and that she's not to do it again, but I want to see her. Both of them. Anytime. We're going to have some pop, and then I'll bring her back. Is that okay with you?"

"Yes. Just a sec."

Morgan heard a muffling sound that she assumed was Erin's hand over the mouthpiece.

"We're having dinner at six, why don't you join us and bring Maddie back then?"

Morgan couldn't stop the grin that formed on her lips. "Is that okay with Tristan?"

"Yes. Do you want to?"

"More than anything. Do you need me to bring anything?"

Erin laughed. "Just our wayward daughter. See you later."

"Yeah." The soft click signaled the end of the call, and Erin's warm voice was gone. Maddie looked at her, a frown marring her forehead.

"Am I in a lot of trouble?"

"I think a firing squad was mentioned." Maddie's eyes widened, and her eyebrows shot up. Morgan laughed and tickled her ribs, loving the joyful sound of her giggles filling the quiet room. The squirming girl eventually managed to escape and sat on the far end of the sofa.

"I think you'll survive it, but it's going to be close. Your mum was really worried."

Maddie stared down at her shoes.

"You understand why, don't you?"

She nodded.

"Tell me then."

"Because there's weirdos out there, and I got to be careful and not put myself in dangerous situations and I have to make sure someone knows where I am so that nothing bad happens to me."

"Phew, take a breath, kiddo."

"I'm sorry mum."

"It's not me you need to apologize to. Tell your mum that when we go back, okay?"

Maddie made a cross over her chest. "I promise."

"So what's so important you risked the firing squad to get here?"

She grabbed her Scooby-Doo backpack and rummaged around before she pulled out a notepad with a pencil through the spiral wire at the top. The pencil had a big pink love heart on it. Morgan smiled.

"Do you make lots of lists?"

"Yup. So I don't forget stuff."

"My mum used to make lists all the time too." Morgan smiled to herself, remembering the notepad her mother carried in her pocket, and the second one that was attached to the fridge with a huge magnet shaped like a horseshoe. She remembered her rubbing it—for luck, she had said—and recalled the fleeting thought that the habit had never worked for her mother. She swallowed the bitter taste of loss and focused instead on what was important and right in front of her.

"She did?"

"Yeah. All the time." Morgan wrapped her arm around Maddie's shoulders when she got closer.

"You never told me that before."

"I didn't?"

"No. You didn't talk about your mummy very much. You got upset."

"I might still get upset, because she died."

"I know. But that was a long time ago. Before I was born."

"It was. I only found out a couple of weeks ago. So it's still really new for me."

"Are you sad now?"

"No, I'm really happy because you're here."

Maddie grinned and leaned into her, wrapping skinny little arms around her tummy. Morgan kissed her hair.

"So what's on the list?"

"This is my calendar." She opened the notebook to the first page. It was marked into a chart for the week, and each evening was marked with various activities. "These are the things I do. I go to Brownies on Mondays, gymnastics on Tuesday, swimming on Wednesday straight after school. Uncle Chris takes me to dancing classes on Thursday, and on Friday, I don't do anything after school. So can I see you then?"

"That sounds like a good plan. And maybe your mum could use some help with all the other stuff you do, so I could maybe pick you up or drop you off at some of this stuff."

"That's what you used to do."

"Then I'll definitely have to do that again."

"You used to do Mondays and Wednesdays because you worked on Tuesday and Thursdays."

"So Brownies and swimming. I can do that."

❖

"Do you have a key?" Morgan kept a tight hold on Maddie's hand and carried her backpack in the other.

"No. You said not until I got to secondary school, because there would always be someone home with me till then."

"Oh, right." Morgan nodded as though this made complete sense to her. "You can knock then." She pushed Maddie forward slightly and wiped her sweaty palms on her jeans. She frowned at the dark smudges and realized that she hadn't washed her hands after putting away her sketchbook, and the charcoal dust still clung to her skin.

Maddie pushed open the letterbox in the middle of the door and shouted through, "Tristan, can you let us in?" The door opened, and Erin smiled down at Maddie.

"No such luck, madam."

"I'm sorry, Mum. I was really bad, but I didn't think I was allowed to go and see Mum till Tristan said, but it was really important."

"And what was so important?"

"Mum's going to do Mondays and Wednesdays just like before." Maddie grinned, then stopped and adopted her serious face again. "But I'm sorry I scared you."

"Mmm." Erin crossed her arms over her chest.

"Can I come in yet?"

"I haven't decided." Erin winked at Morgan over Maddie's head before quickly looking away, a frown marring her beautiful face. The swift change caught Morgan by surprise and made her wonder what had caused Erin's angry reaction to her own playful behavior. Erin cleared her throat and turned a small smile on Maddie. "You might have to sleep in the backyard."

"Really? In the tent?" Maddie couldn't contain her enthusiasm for the proposed punishment.

Erin laughed and ruffled her hair. "Get in, rascal. Don't ever do that to me again. I won't stop you seeing your mum, but there's a right way to go about it and a wrong way."

"This was the wrong way. I know. I'm sorry. What's for dinner?"

"You'll have to wait and see." She turned back to Morgan. "Are you coming in, or shall I serve you out here?"

Morgan grinned. "I'd love to." She brushed by Erin as she walked into the hall.

"Why don't you hang your jacket over there?" Erin pointed to the coat rack. "And I'll get you a drink. Would you like a glass of wine?"

Morgan shrugged out of her leather jacket. "No, thanks. I don't drink wine." Morgan hung her coat up, pleased that she was starting to catch the vocabulary that was nothing but a reminder of her past. If she wanted Erin and her children to take her seriously as their mother, then she needed to try at least to sound the way mothers do. The way they remembered her. She turned to see Erin staring at her. "What?"

"You used to drink wine."

"Oh. I don't like the taste."

"When we met, you taught me about wine, how to taste it properly, and what made up a great bouquet." She laughed gently. "You told me that an ex-girlfriend taught you to appreciate wine, that she was a sommelier."

Morgan cocked her head. "A what?"

"A sommelier. A wine expert."

"Huh. Wonder how I ended up with one of them." Morgan felt her cheeks warming as she spoke.

"Come on." Erin smiled. "I hope you still like lasagna."

Morgan followed her down the hall, unable to tear her eyes away from Erin's denim clad backside, her hips swaying with each step.

Maddie was getting plates out of the cupboard to set the table when Morgan entered the room.

"Can I help?" Morgan held her hands out for the plates.

Maddie shook her head. "I've got it, thanks."

"Sweetie, go and get your brother when you've done that." Erin bent over to check the oven, and Morgan felt her mouth go dry.

"Okay." The clatter of plates snapped Morgan out of her staring and she rushed to help Maddie, despite her earlier refusal. Maddie smiled and disappeared up the stairs.

"Have a look in the fridge. See if there's anything in there you do like to drink." Erin smiled over her shoulder as she pulled the bubbling lasagna out and put the dish on a wooden board.

"Right, thanks." Morgan stuck her head inside the cold space and wished she could climb in. *Erin is not for drooling over. She's a gorgeous, brilliant woman who's made it clear that she's not interested. She didn't even want me to hug her at the football match, so get over it and behave like a damn grown up!* She grabbed a can of pop as Tristan and Maddie sat down. "Anyone else want one?" She held the can up.

Maddie nodded with a grin.

"Milk, young lady."

Maddie pouted as Erin handed a glass to Morgan. "Sorry" she mouthed to Maddie as she set the glass in front of her.

"Tristan?"

"I got it." He stood, clearly working hard to avoid touching her, and got himself a glass of fruit juice.

Morgan took a deep breath and slid into a seat.

"Oh, Morgan, before you leave later, there's a bag of stuff I need to give you." Erin placed the lasagna on the table and served portions onto the children's plates. "Make sure you eat salad too, Tristan." She kissed the top of his head. "When you were in the hospital, they gave me the things you were wearing when you were brought in. I meant to give them to Amy or Nikki earlier, but I kept forgetting."

Morgan smiled and held her plate out. "That's fine, thank you." She was so busy staring at Erin's lips that her words barely registered.

Tristan was watching her as she started eating.

Morgan cleared her throat. "So are you ready to go back to school next week?"

He shrugged and sawed a large section off his pasta.

"What year are you going into?"

"Nine."

Morgan frowned. "I don't know what that means."

"Third year at secondary school. They changed the system in 1992, but you probably wouldn't remember any of it." Erin smiled at Tristan as she filled in the blanks. "Later this year, Tristan gets to decide what he wants to study for his exams."

So much to relearn. "Oh, okay. So what subjects will you pick? Do you know yet?"

He shrugged again.

Erin frowned. "Tristan, answer your mum."

"It's okay. He doesn't have to." Morgan smiled sadly, first at Erin, then Tristan. "I'm sorry this is so hard for you, but thank you for trying." She looked down at her plate, wondering how she was going to eat enough so she wouldn't insult Erin, while her stomach was telling her it wasn't going to cooperate.

"PE, geography, French, and art. Those are the ones I get to choose, because we have to do math, English, and science."

Morgan turned her head. He was using his fork to worry a slice of tomato across the plate, but his eyes kept flicking up to her. "Art?"

He shrugged.

"Would you show me sometime?"

This time his eyes met hers and held as he nodded.

Progress. Baby steps, Morgan, baby steps. "Thank you."

"I'll show you mine, too, Mum." Maddie spoke around a mouthful of pasta.

"That would be wonderful."

Maddie carried most of the conversation through the rest of the meal, and Morgan felt she understood the finer workings of the British education system by the time they were done. Tristan's input was minimal, but he was visibly more relaxed and his plate was clean when he left the room.

"Can I help clean up?" Morgan pushed her chair back and started to gather dishes.

"No, Maddie's loading the dishwasher tonight. In fact, she's doing it for the next week." Erin grinned at Maddie, and the barest hint of a dimple creased her cheek. It was the first time Morgan had seen it, and she was fascinated. She wanted to smooth her finger over her skin and feel the softness she was sure she'd find.

"Aw, Mum!"

"It's dishwasher duty or no TV for a week, you pick."

"Dishwasher duty."

"I thought it would be. Go on, scoot." She tapped Maddie's bottom playfully as she got out of her chair, and winked at Morgan.

Her face felt hot, and she knew her cheeks were burning red. "I should get going then." Morgan opened her arms and lifted Maddie as she hugged her, the child's giggles warming her neck. "Phone me next time, and I'll come for you. Okay?"

"Okay."

"Go finish your chores." Maddie skipped back toward the sink and slowly rinsed the plates. "Thank you for having me."

"You're welcome." Erin's smile was warm and friendly.

She put her jacket on. "You said there was some stuff for me to get?"

"Oh, God, yes, just a minute." She climbed the stairs and Morgan heard a door open. She took a few minutes to study the photographs up the wall. Pictures of them all in staged poses, playing football, blowing out candles, and living their lives covered so much of the space she didn't have time to look at them all before she heard footsteps down the stairs.

She turned and was surprised to see Tristan. "Oh, I thought you'd be your mum."

"I've got her eyes, but that's about it." He smiled, a crooked little smile that made his face look younger.

"No, you've got her good looks too." She started to reach out, wanting to ruffle his hair, but she stopped, uncertain if her touch would be welcome or not.

"I've got something for you." He held out a slim square box.

She took it and slowly turned it so she could read the title. *Tristan and Maddie's baby films.* She didn't think as she pulled him into her body and held him tight. His arms were slow to come around her, but they did. His tears mingled with her own.

"Thank you. I can't tell you how much this means to me."

"It's just a DVD, Mum."

Morgan's heart soared. "No, it's not. But I didn't mean that. I meant this." She squeezed him tighter. "It's everything." She kissed his hair, stroked his precious face, and slowly let him go. "Thank you."

He looked down at his feet then sauntered off to the kitchen.

She wiped her eyes and stared at the box.

"Looks like he's forgiven you." Erin's eyes were bright with her own unshed tears.

"I wouldn't go that far, but I'll take it."

Erin handed her a bag. "I didn't open it, but I think it's just your clothes from the night you were attacked. I thought about washing the clothes for you, but..." She shrugged slightly. "It just didn't feel like—it didn't feel right."

"I understand. Thank you. For this." She held up the bag. "For tonight. For everything, I guess."

"I'll call you tomorrow about the kids' schedule. I'm glad you're up to helping out more often."

Morgan dropped her chin to her chest and left the house. The blow of the separation stung her to the core.

CHAPTER NINETEEN

Laughter greeted her as Morgan opened the door and stepped inside. The plastic bag containing her clothes banged against her leg as she dropped her keys onto the table and hung up her coat.

"It's just me."

Amy poked her head round the door. "Good. Glad you're back. We thought of something else that might stir some memories."

"Yeah, what's that?"

"A night out on the town, baby!" Nikki's voice reached her from the sitting room.

Amy's body jerked as if she were slapping at Nikki, then she started giggling. "Stop it!"

Morgan walked into the front room, laughing. Nikki was tickling Amy's stomach as she was slapping at her and trying to pull away.

"Nikki…stop. I mean it!"

"I thought you guys were old now?" Morgan grinned as both their heads snapped round.

"Who are you calling old?" Nikki looked outraged.

Amy managed to wriggle out of Nikki's grasp, and retaliated with a swift slap on her arm. "Yeah, you're older than both of us!"

"By six weeks!"

"Ow." Nikki rubbed her arm. "Six weeks, those make a huge difference, my friend."

Amy stretched her feet onto Nikki's lap. "So do you feel up to it?"

Morgan shrugged. "Yeah, why not. It's not as if I have to get up for work tomorrow."

"Good point." Nikki pointed at the bag in her hand. "What's that?"

"A bag."

"Oh, a comedienne." She turned to Amy. "Look, baby, our little girl's all grown up and trying to be funny."

Amy arched her eyebrow, a sardonic smile pulling at the corners of her mouth.

"Yeah, so anyway." Nikki turned back to Morgan. "What's in the bag, M?"

Morgan laughed. "Pressies."

"For me? You shouldn't have."

"Good, because I didn't." She pulled the DVD case out and waved it. "Tristan made me a video."

"We call them DVDs now that we're out of the dark ages."

"Amy, slap her again please."

Amy giggled as she complied and Nikki rubbed her arm as she pouted.

"Thank you. Tristan made me a DVD of them when they were little."

"Wow. Breakthrough." Amy smiled.

"I know." She bowed her head staring at the slim case, prying open the cover, only to snap it closed, over and over again.

"Want to watch it now?"

Morgan looked at the plastic disc. Such an innocuous looking thing, with its shiny reflective finish and matt underside, but she knew that this would be both crushing and overwhelmingly uplifting.

"Not right now, thanks. I think that's something I want to do when I can savor it."

She expected to see Tristan's first steps, with his chubby little baby legs running to keep him balanced. She wanted to hear the first words from Maddie's cherubic lips, her dimples etched in her cheeks, grinning at her own accomplishment. She knew all these moments, she'd seen them, heard them, known them before, but to discover them anew was something she needed to do alone. She already knew that she'd need time to mourn the loss of the memories even as she discovered the wonder of recapturing them.

"I understand. What else do you have there?"

"Clothes. The nurses gave Erin my stuff while I was in hospital. I'm going to put this all in the wash. Do you have anything to go in the machine?"

"Yeah, I'll go grab the basket." Amy left the room.

"You okay?" Nikki asked.

"Yeah, I'm fine." She pulled herself out of the chair and headed for the utility room. There wasn't a great deal in the bag. A pair of black ankle boots, a black denim jacket, and a pair of jeans. *Where's my top?* She unfolded the clothes to see if things had been tucked inside. *And my bra?* She checked inside the boots and squeezed the pockets in the jeans. She let her arms fall heavily back to her sides, causing a twinge in her healing shoulder. *They probably had to cut it all off and threw away the ruined stuff.*

She shook her head and stuffed the jeans into the washing machine. Morgan grabbed the jacket and checked the pockets. Something crinkled as she squeezed the fabric. She frowned as she fished the paper out and glanced at it as she stuffed the jacket into the drum, ignoring the blood that had dried around the collar and down the front.

It was an envelope. It was obvious the adhesive flap on the back had been opened repeatedly, since parts of it were torn and the edges refused to lay flat. There were dirty, smudged fingerprints in the corners and along the top edge. She frowned as she turned it over.

The red postal stamp, top center, caught her eye. June thirteenth. Manchester. Her name and address were hand written in neat block capitals. The second-class stamp, with its blue background and white Queen's head, looked slightly worn. Everything neat and proper and in its place, including the black box stamp in the top left hand corner. Four letters stood out, white on black.

H.M.P.S.

Her Majesty's Prison Service.

She felt as though the air in the room was too heavy, pressing down on her chest, making it harder and harder to breathe.

Instinctively she knew the letter was a doorway, a passage to her father. He was the only person she knew in prison. *I think.*

Her hands shook. The writing blurred as she stared at it, her eyes glazed and unseeing. It had to be important. Why else would she be carrying it on her at the end of July, when it's dated June?

"Morgan, what's wrong?" Amy put the basket down.

She turned and held the envelope out. "Do you know what this is?"

Amy looked down but didn't reach for it. "Other than a letter, I have no idea. What is it?"

Morgan pointed to the stamp in the corner. "Did I see him?"

"No."

"Did I want to?"

Amy shook her head and led Morgan out of the small room. "No. You didn't have any contact with him at all, and to the best of my knowledge, he didn't try to contact you either."

"So why do I have this?" She waved the envelope before dropping her arm back to her side and sitting on the sofa. "Do you know?" She turned to Nikki.

Nikki took the envelope and looked it over. "Not a bloody clue." She started to peel the flap.

"Stop!" Morgan's heart pounded wildly in her chest.

Nikki's hands froze and she looked up, startled. "We won't know what it is unless we open it."

Morgan stared at the white square of paper, but couldn't find the words to explain.

"Maybe that's the point, Nikki." Amy took the envelope from her and gave it back to Morgan. "Maybe she doesn't want to know right now."

Amy was right. She didn't want to know. Morgan Masters, the failed wife and mother, knew what was in that letter, and she kept it with her, guarded it more closely than she had her own children. The date on the envelope told her that. June thirteenth. *It had to mean something to me to be carrying it on me six weeks later.*

Secrets. Whatever was in the envelope was something she had kept from everyone who loved her. The secrets of a man, whom she hadn't even spoken to in twenty years, had been more important to that Morgan than anything else in her life. Morgan didn't know how she knew, but she was certain of it. Would she feel the same way knowing what was in the letter? Would she choose it over them again? It was a risk she wasn't willing to take.

"I don't want to be her."

Nikki frowned. "What do you mean?"

"Before the amnesia, I knew what was in that letter. I knew and I didn't tell anyone about it, but I left my family. Coincidence?" She shrugged. "Maybe. But I don't think so. What happens if I open that letter now, read it, and I feel like I did before? I don't want to be her."

"The old Morgan?" Amy sat next to her. "Why not?"

"I've already told you, she was a fucking idiot. You told me she was miserable. I don't understand why. She had a wonderful family, a good job, good friends. Everything that would be on my wish list, she already had, and she blew it. Why would I want to be her again?"

"But what if this is important?" Nikki frowned.

"How important can it be? You told me I hadn't had anything to do with him for twenty years. Now he wants to be pen pals? Well, I'm not buying it."

Nikki shifted forward in her seat. "M, hear me out. Your dad's not exactly going to be a spring chicken anymore; what if this is because he's ill, or maybe even the prison telling you he's died?"

"Nikki, don't say something like that!" Amy gripped her hand.

"I still don't want to know." Morgan didn't falter.

"How can you not want to know? He's your father."

"He is not more important to me than my children. I will not—cannot—do anything to screw up with them again. I honestly don't want to know anything about him. I know that probably makes me sound like a bitch, but he made the choices he did and he has to live with the consequences. I'm choosing not to be drawn into that old history. My old history."

Nikki was incredulous. "But aren't you even curious?"

Morgan laughed. "Curiosity is not what I'm feeling right now."

"Then what?"

"I'm terrified."

"Of a letter?" She waved the envelope.

"No. Of the possibilities. That letter is the proverbial can of worms. The second I open it, I know that I'm going to need to know things that I don't remember. Things I don't want to remember. Things that might make me her again."

"You don't know that."

"No. But I have a choice now. I can choose to learn the things she knew, and risk becoming her again. Or I can leave it all behind and be the woman she could never have been."

"Is that why you haven't read the transcript yet?"

"Yes." She grabbed the letter back from Nikki. "I don't want to be her. And now I don't have to be. I'm sorry if that's annoying for you. I'm sorry if you're dying of curiosity. And I know you want answers to why I left the way I did. Maybe those are in there."

"Maybe?"

"Okay, probably. But I still don't want to be her. I want to be better."

"Maybe that's good enough for you, M. But I don't think it's ever going to be good enough for Erin. She wants to know. She needs to know."

Morgan looked at the envelope in her hands, turning it over again and again. She knew Nikki was right. She knew that Erin wanted—needed—the answers.

"Maybe I should just let her read it and see if that explains everything to her."

"You want to just give it to her without even reading it?"

"It doesn't really feel like it's mine anyway."

"Of course it's yours. It's got your name on it."

Morgan shook her head. "No, it's hers." Morgan folded the letter in two and slid it into her pocket.

"You know, I can't get my head around this. One minute you sound like we did twenty years ago, and the next minute you sound more mature than you did a month ago. My head's starting to ache with it all." Nikki scrubbed her hand over her face.

Morgan laughed. "If that's true, then it's about time I grew up."

"Come on. Let's get ready and go have some fun. I need a break before my head explodes." Nikki stood and pulled Amy to her feet.

CHAPTER TWENTY

The doorbell rang and Erin looked at the clock. Eight p.m. "It's open." She dried her hands on a dishtowel and left the kitchen.

"Mum, I got a new badge at Brownies!" Maddie came bustling in with a panda mask on her face.

Erin smiled down at her. "You did? Which one?"

"World cultures. I made this panda mask on a balloon." She pointed to her covered face. "Pandas come from China and I like Chinese food. But I won't eat panda's 'cos they're endangered."

"I know." She lifted the mask and kissed Maddie's cheek, then hugged her tight. "I'm very proud of you." She looked up and caught Morgan watching them, a sad smile on her face. She patted Maddie's bottom. "Now go find a place to keep your mask safe and get your PJ's on. We've got your homework reading to do."

She waited while Maddie hugged Morgan and scampered up the stairs.

"You okay?"

Morgan shrugged. "I don't know. Can we talk?"

"I was just going to make some tea. The kettle's already boiled. Do you want a cup?" Erin made her way into the kitchen without waiting for an answer, her heart thumping. *What does she want to talk about? Has Tristan said something?* She made the tea and led them into the sitting room. It still felt strange seeing Morgan. Seeing a stranger in the eyes of a face she knew better than her own.

"Where's Tristan?"

"Basketball practice." Erin sipped her drink and crossed her legs, pulling at her skirt as it rode up. Morgan's eyes seemed glued to her thighs, and the familiar tingles of desire stirred in Erin's belly. *No. I will not go there.* She shifted in her seat.

"Oh right." Morgan started to fidget, her leg bouncing.

"You wanted to talk to me."

"Oh, erm, yeah." Morgan licked her lips. "I wanted…see I've been wondering…I…"

It was painful to watch. Morgan's vulnerability hung about her like a cloak. "Morgan, if you don't say what's on your mind, I can't help."

"What happened between us? When I left—what happened?"

She gasped and put her cup down, tucking her hair behind her ear before she sat back. Erin felt like she'd been punched in the gut.

"Why does it matter?" She twisted her ring around her finger while she waited.

"It's important."

"That doesn't answer my question."

"Because I don't understand."

"Like I told you, neither do I. So how do you expect me to explain it?"

Morgan got up from her chair and sat next to Erin. "Please, just tell me what happened."

Erin rubbed her hand over her face and sighed. "We had an argument. You'd been in a funny mood for a few weeks. You wouldn't talk to me, you were sulking about something, but— anyway, I told you to smile and at least pretend you were happy to be spending time with us. To pretend that we weren't making you miserable." She shook her head, willing away the tears. "I've played that conversation over in my head so many times."

She remembered the anguish and the sorrow. The loss, the sharp sting of disappointment, and guilt had hollowed out her heart leaving nothing inside but the empty chasm that Morgan had once filled.

"I—"

She waved her hand for Morgan to be quiet. "When I said that, it was like a red rag to a bull or something. You just flew off the handle. Said you couldn't stand to make us all miserable, that we deserved better than that. Better than you. No matter what I said—it doesn't matter now. What's done is done."

Morgan took hold of her hand. "When was this?"

The supple skin against her own made her flesh tingle. She wanted to squeeze her fingers to make sure she was real. "Does it matter?"

"Yes. I think it might."

Erin closed her eyes and leaned her head back against the sofa, wishing the conversation were over, but she didn't have the heart to pull her hand away. "Tenth of July."

"And you said I was in a strange mood for a few weeks before that?"

"Yes."

Morgan reached into her pocket and pulled out a slightly crumpled envelope. "This was in that bag of stuff you gave me from the hospital."

Erin glanced at it. "What is it?"

"A letter."

She raised her eyebrow. "I can see that. What does it say?"

"I don't know."

Erin frowned. "Then why are you showing it to me?"

"Look at the date."

Erin took the envelope from Morgan's shaking fingers. The prison stamp caught her eye first and she glanced at Morgan's face. She noted for the first time how pale and drawn she looked; the dark circles under her eyes were deeper than she'd ever seen them.

"Your father?"

Morgan grimaced. "I presume so."

Erin looked back at the envelope, trying to ignore the deep-set worry lines marring Morgan's forehead. The red ink stood out at the center, thirteenth of June.

Three weeks before she left.

"You think it was all about this?"

"I—yes, I think so."

"So why don't you open it and see what it was all about?" Anger welled in her chest. *She's come here looking for the answers she held in her own hands? Dragging up all the pain and the guilt that I've carried since then.*

"All I know about my father is that he killed my mum, and now he's in prison. I don't want to know any more than that."

Erin frowned. "Hiding from it all doesn't change it."

"I know that. But it might change me."

She uncrossed her legs and leaned forward, eyes narrowed. "Explain."

Morgan's leg bounced again. "The old Morgan knew everything that happened, she lived it, and survived it as best she could, but it scarred her. Right?"

Erin nodded.

"I don't have those scars. I don't remember any of that stuff."

"You don't remember the children, but you said you still feel that you love them. You can't have it both ways, Morgan."

"I don't remember them. And maybe it's about choosing to let myself love them, rather than remembering the specific emotion. I don't know. I just know that I love the bones of those kids and I will do anything to protect them, to love them, and to be there for them. Any way they want me. The more I get to know them, the more I love them. But I'm choosing not to know anything about him. I feel angry toward him, I feel hurt, I'm grieving for my mum. But I'm not affected by it the same way that she was. The old Morgan."

"You talk about yourself like you're two different people."

"That's how I feel." Morgan looked down at the floor. "She lived a life I never did."

Erin felt her heart clutch. "Is that a good thing or a bad thing?"

Morgan laughed sadly. "Both." She leaned forward and rested her elbows on her knees. "Maybe the price for losing the bad memories has been far too high."

Erin felt like she was falling when Morgan's gaze met hers. She wanted to run her fingers down her face and feel her skin. She longed to wrap her arms around Morgan and feel the warmth of her, the musky scent of leather that was like coming home. All the things she could no longer have.

"If you're choosing not to know about him, then why do you still have this?" She lifted the envelope in her hands.

"Because I think it's important. I was still carrying it more than a month after I got it. I didn't just keep it. I had it in my pocket. That means something, surely. It was important to her. My behavior change—it was a change, wasn't it? I wasn't always such a moody bitch?"

Erin smiled. "No, you weren't always that bad."

"But I was bad?"

"We all had our moments, Morgan. It's called life."

Morgan frowned but carried on. "I think that letter has something to do with why I left. Why else did I have it on me when I was attacked?"

"Do you think that this is why you were attacked?"

Morgan blushed and her gaze dropped to her hands. "I don't know."

"Do you know anything about the attack?"

Morgan visibly squirmed. "The police have some pictures from CCTV footage. They're trying to find the people who were there."

"They showed me the pictures. Asked if I recognized either of them."

Morgan flinched. "They showed you the picture?"

"Yes."

Morgan's face paled. "She was—I mean, we were—it looked like, maybe we knew—she might have been—oh God, I don't really know, but—"

Erin felt the knot of dread forming in the pit of her stomach. "What are you trying to say?"

"In the picture...the way we were together looked like..." Morgan frowned. "Didn't you think it was...I don't know, a little bit...erm...inappropriate for a car park?"

Erin felt the knot unravel. "The picture they showed me was of a woman's face and a man's face. I didn't see you at all."

Sweat beaded on Morgan's forehead. and Erin could practically hear the "oh shit" mantra going on in her head. "What were you doing with her?" Erin felt as though ice were flowing through her veins. "Talking to her?"

Morgan shook her head, just once.

"Kissing her?"

The blush deepened on Morgan's cheeks. "It, erm, looked like—"

"You were fucking her?" Waves of jealousy coursed through her and the cold numbness that had been invading her body fled before the burning tide of possession and fury.

"What? No."

"Then what?"

"My head was against her chest."

"Against her chest like you were hugging her? Or against her chest like you were fucking her?"

"I don't know."

"How do you not know? It's really fucking simple, Morgan. Did you have your arms wrapped around her, or were they between her legs?"

"It looked like they were on the car."

The picture formed in Erin's head of Morgan nuzzling the blonde's breasts and felt her worst fears coming true. She flung the letter at her. "You were fucking someone else in the car park three weeks after you walk out of here, and you want me to buy into that"—she pointed at the letter—"being the reason? Think again."

"I wasn't…it wasn't like that."

"Really? Then what was it like?"

"I don't know. I can't remember."

"No, you don't remember so that makes it all okay does it? That makes it understandable. Forgivable. Having no memory doesn't absolve you of anything, Morgan. It just means you get to forget the hurt you've caused."

"No. It doesn't mean that. It means I have no way of knowing what was going on. I can't imagine any version of me that would cheat on you, Erin. Never. But you're right. I don't know what happened. For all I know, I could have just met her in a bar or something. The doctor said I had that drug in my system, didn't she? Maybe it wasn't my fault."

"And that makes it all better, does it? Ifs, buts, and maybes, and it's all water under the bridge. I don't think so, Morgan. I want facts. I want tangible, concrete facts. And you want to know what they are?" She licked her lips and pointed at Morgan. "Three weeks. Three fucking weeks without a word. Your children didn't even know if they were going to see you again. We didn't even know if you were alive, and you think maybe is good enough." She grabbed the letter and tore it open. She pulled the page out and glanced over it quickly. Morgan stared at her the whole time. She stood up, grabbed Morgan's arm, and pulled her to her feet. "Get out!"

"It doesn't explain anything?"

"Nothing." Erin screwed it into a ball and tossed it at Morgan. She didn't try to catch it, instead letting it fall to the ground.

"But I thought it would."

Erin pushed her out of the room.

"Please, don't do this—"

"Me? I didn't do this, Morgan, you did!"

"I'm not her."

"You know something, my mum used to say if it looks like a monkey, and sounds like a monkey, there's a damn good chance it is a monkey!" She pointed to the front door.

"Erin, I'm different now. Please believe me. Whatever I did wrong before, let me put it right. I can't explain what I did then. If that letter doesn't make it clear then I have no idea."

"I do. It's blonde and lets you fuck her in car parks."

"I wouldn't do that to you. I don't know how I know, but I do. I wouldn't cheat on you. Not now, and I can't believe I would then either. Please. You have to believe me."

"Why? Why should I? Why is it so goddamned important that I believe you?"

"Because I love you."

Erin stopped and stared at her. It was ridiculous. This woman, who infuriated her in one breath, and enraged her in the next, stood in front of her, offering her the words she thought she'd never hear again. Morgan's face was open; there was no pretence, no hidden agenda, just her heart. And Erin wanted to believe her. She wanted to forget she'd ever seen that picture. She wanted to forget she'd ever heard the additional details. She wanted Chris's story to be true. She didn't want to believe it was true. She wanted there to be any other explanation, no matter how ludicrous. Her heart pounded and her breath was ragged in her chest.

Then Morgan's lips were on her own, soft and gentle, a tender sampling of her mouth. She heard the whimper before she realized it had come from her own throat. Her fingers itched to touch, to slide across silken skin, to twist and tug at Morgan's hair. She needed to feel, and the ache was just too much.

She pulled Morgan to her, moaning as her weight pressed them both against the wall. Passion drove her and she opened her mouth to Morgan's searching tongue as it flicked across her lips. Hungry, eager, demanding hands roamed freely, exploring arms, shoulders, faces. Erin couldn't think, desire flowed hot and heavy in her blood, and she wrapped her leg around Morgan's hip, groaning as her hand slipped down Morgan's back. Fingers squeezed her backside and pulled her closer to Morgan's body. The smell of leather and mint surrounded her, so familiar. Hot lips kissed her cheek, her neck, the small hollow at the base of her throat, and she was transported back in time.

She buried her fingers in Morgan's hair, pulling her until their lips met again. This was hers. Morgan was hers. She had never felt so possessive, so jealous, and so desirous. The need to feel every inch of Morgan against her blazed inside her as she started to peel the leather jacket from her shoulders.

"Mum." Maddie called from her room.

She froze. Slowly, she became aware of Morgan's body. That she was holding Morgan, their breathing harsh and in tandem. Her heart continued to pound, but the desire she had felt was gone, replaced by a sickening feeling of dread. A tender smile covered Morgan's lips.

Oh God, no. How could I be so stupid?

"Mum, I'm ready." Maddie's voice was increasingly impatient.

Erin took a deep breath, trying to sound as normal as possible. "I'll be right there, Maddie."

Morgan slowly lowered her leg, squeezed her backside tenderly, and kissed her lips before backing away. "I know we have a lot to talk about—"

"Morgan, this was a mistake."

"What are you talking about? No, it wasn't."

"Yes, it was. I'm sorry. I should never have let that happen."

"But I love you."

"We're over. Finished. Done. Understand? We are not a couple anymore. We are not together. We aren't going to be."

"But—"

"No. No buts. The only thing left between us are the kids. That's it. End of story." Erin waved her hand toward the door. "Now please go."

Morgan's eyes looked empty as she stared at her silently. She looked lost, alone, frightened. Erin ached to take that look away, but she knew it was beyond her. She couldn't let herself be vulnerable again. Morgan had proven to be untrustworthy, and she wouldn't give her a second chance. Her heart wouldn't survive losing her again.

CHAPTER TWENTY-ONE

Erin closed Maddie's bedroom door behind her and walked slowly down the stairs. The front room felt cold, empty, and lifeless. The cups still sitting on the coffee table were a scornful reminder of her failure. Her inability to protect her marriage, her children, and her heart left her reeling. Her reaction to Morgan's declaration left her dizzy.

The passion between them had always burned hot, and Morgan had been everything she could have ever wanted in a lover. She'd been tender, loving, exciting, and generous, with just enough edge to take her breath and keep her desperate for more. The need had never abated. *If tonight's anything to go by, it never bloody will.*

She bent to pick up the crumpled envelope and placed it on the table as she sat down.

Morgan's admission that she was with someone else in the car park when she was attacked was confirmation of her fears, yet the letter fit the timing of Morgan's abrupt change in behavior. The mood swings, the apathy, the depression. That all fit with the date of this letter. But there was nothing in the letter that explained those changes.

The more she learned, the more she realized she didn't know, and the more frustrating it became. She smoothed out the creases in the paper and unfolded the pages and wondered briefly if actually reading it would help Morgan get her memory back.

It seems like maybe I'm the only one who wants her to remember. And that's only so I can get some answers. In the moments where she let go of her anger she could readily acknowledge that Morgan seemed to be a happier person now. She was more carefree, better with the children, more patient and forgiving. And she certainly was trying her best with the kids.

Erin couldn't help but smile remembering Tristan giving Morgan lessons on the Internet and using Facebook. Morgan looked truly bewildered, but she sat with him for hours as he went through setting up a profile with her. Friending her. Showing her how to write messages. It was their preferred method of communication now.

It didn't seem to matter to them at all if she got her memory back. They were young enough to make new memories, to share in the future together. The only one who didn't have a future with Morgan was her. For a second, she felt jealous of her own children. Of the moments they would have with Morgan, the lifetime they would fill with laughter, tears, joy, and sorrow, and Erin felt the weight of it crashing down on her. She let the tears fall, knowing they wouldn't be the last.

"Mum, you all right?" Tristan sat beside her, his hair sweaty from practice as she ran her hand over his head and pulled him in for a hug.

"I didn't hear you come in, sorry. I'll be fine."

"What's wrong?" He pulled away, looking at her with a mixture of fear and determination in his eyes.

"Just feeling a bit sad tonight, kiddo. Sorry you found me like this." She tucked the papers back into the envelope and stuffed it into her pocket.

"I'm not a little kid, Mum. You can tell me stuff."

Oh, my sweet little man, I will keep you a little kid just as long as I can. "I know, honey, but I'm really fine. How was practice?"

He rolled his eyes but accepted the change of subject. He slouched back on the sofa as Erin wiped her eyes. "It was cool. Colin totally landed on his arse after a—"

"Don't swear."

"I didn't! Arse isn't a swear word."

"It's still not nice."

"But it's not a swear."

"You made your point. Now mine, use better English. You're a clever boy. Don't hide it under crass language."

He rolled his eyes again. "So, Colin landed on his bum after trying a jump shot. Twisted his ankle pretty badly and looks like he's not going to play for a couple of weeks. His mum was going to take him for an x-ray to make sure he hadn't broken anything."

"Oh God, that sounds awful. Was anyone else hurt?"

"Nope, but it means I'm going to play point guard in the next game."

"Is he going to be okay?"

"I texted him before, but he's not answered yet. He might still be at the hospital or something. I'm going to get a shower and go to bed." He kissed her cheek, a sure sign he was concerned about her. She smiled and patted his back.

"Do you want me to bring you a drink up?"

"Nah, I'm cool. Night, Mum."

"Night, honey."

She watched him go before she locked up and climbed the stairs to her bedroom.

She sat on her bed, pulled the envelope for her pocket, and unfolded the pages again. Two pages. One orange, one white. She picked up the orange page, the official stamp of Strangeways Prison glaring at her. The form held blank spaces where names, address details, and various other personal information was required to fill in the blank boxes. A visiting order. He wanted to see her. Why now? After all these years, why now?

She unfolded the white page:

Morgan,

I know that I'm probably the last person you ever expected to hear from again. I didn't exactly expect to be writing this. I made my mistakes and those are mine to live with. I don't expect you to forgive me. I never did, girl. But there are some things I need to tell you and I think they're best said face-to-face.

I've arranged a visiting order for you. You have to phone the number to book an appointment and they talk you through the rest of it.

You're probably thinking why the bloody hell should I go and see the old bastard. I don't blame you. I'd be the same if I were in your shoes. But there are things you and me need to discuss. Things I should have told you back then, things I regret not telling you.

There's things I'm sorry for saying to you. Things I wish I could take back, but I'll never be able to do that, and I'm not a young man anymore. I don't want to die with so many regrets on my soul. Lord knows, I've enough blackening it already. It's important that I see you, and I think you'd rather it was here than after I get out.

Yeah, that's right. I'm getting out. They don't tend to keep old fellers in when they're "no longer a threat." Sounds like they're putting me out to pasture, hey, girl? Well, there's still life in the old dog. Now, you come and see me, and we can get everything squared away once and for all. If not, I'll come and see you, on the out, as we say in here.

I expect you don't want your old man turning up on your doorstep, what with that pretty family you got there. Probably not even told them about me, have you? Well, I wouldn't blame you. I didn't tell the boys in here I had a dyke for a daughter. Probably would have gotten me more attention than I wanted, if you know what I mean. Pretty girl you got there. Very pretty. And kids too. That took me by surprise, I've gotta say. Good-looking kids. A man likes to see his kids do well for themselves. And I think you've done very well, Morgan.

I'll see you soon.

Dad.

She dropped the page as though she'd been bitten, staring at it with unseeing eyes. *Twenty years and then that. I don't know if it's an apology or a threat. I should have paid more attention earlier. I should have really read it.*

So many pieces fell into place and the tears came again. Morgan had been right. She had no idea how another woman fit into the picture, but it was so easy to understand why this letter affected Morgan the way it did. Was he threatening her? The kids? Was he threatening them at all? Or saying he was proud of her in a roundabout kind of way? She didn't know. But Morgan had clearly been terrified of him. She'd seen him angry and out of control, then watched the life flow from her mother's body, each beat of her heart pushing more blood between Morgan's fingers.

The look on Morgan's face when she had refused to speak about her father was etched into her memory, the pain so acute it had been crippling to see. She understood that it was this fear that had driven Morgan from them. What Morgan had seen was a horror embedded so deep into her psyche that it was always going to haunt her, and the damage had been done before they ever met. She finally understood. And now it was too late.

The blonde's face haunted her, and the image of Morgan touching another woman, burned in her imagination. She twisted in the inferno of jealousy as she tossed and turned in her bed—their bed. Had she slept with someone else there, between these sheets? She knew her imagination was running away with her, but she couldn't stand it any longer. She clambered out of the bed, stripping the sheets and covers, throwing them into the laundry basket. She grasped clean linen, determined to put all thoughts from her mind and rest. She had work in the morning. She needed to sleep. She flicked the sheet across the bed.

The plum colored sheets that they had picked out together. Morgan had smiled at her the whole day, and later made love to her on these sheets. She couldn't cry anymore. There were no tears left. She curled herself into a ball beside the bed, unable to convince herself that she needed to get in it. She wrapped the sheet around her body, and waited for the morning to come.

CHAPTER TWENTY-TWO

"Come in." Morgan turned to the door as Amy poked her head inside.

"Erin's downstairs. She'd like to talk to you."

Morgan knew she was grinning as she pushed herself off the bed. She hadn't expected to hear from Erin after the way they had left everything the night before. Erin had been clear that she didn't want anything to do with Morgan. Yet here she was. And all Morgan could hope for was a chance to put things right.

Erin was sitting in the chair by the fire, one leg crossed over the other, and her hands clutched the crumpled envelope in her lap. Morgan's heart sank.

"Good morning. Were you still asleep?" Erin asked.

"No. I didn't sleep very well last night."

Erin cocked her head to the side in silent question.

"Too many things on my mind."

Erin uncrossed her legs and leaned forward. "Me too." She held the letter out to Morgan. "This being one of the main things." She waved it when Morgan still hadn't taken it from her outstretched hand. "You need to read it."

"Why? You said it didn't explain anything."

"I think I was wrong." She urged Morgan to take it. "I'm hoping I was wrong. Please."

Morgan took it between her fingers, handling it as though it was toxic. She turned it over and peeled the flap open.

It felt strange to see her father's handwriting. She couldn't recall ever having seen it before. But seeing her name written by his hand caused the hairs on the back of her neck to stand up. Her heart raced and her palms were sweaty as she read each word over and over. She couldn't pull enough air into her lungs and the bold black ink on the page swam before her eyes. Everything in the room receded and she was back in her childhood home, the stench of ale and fear permeating everything in there. She could see her father sitting in his chair. The chair no one else was allowed to go near. She could hear sniffing from behind her and knew it was her mother; cowering for a nonexistent sin, and already smarting from the first of the night's blows.

He was picking at his teeth as he drank, laughing along to the TV sitcom. Laughing. His coal black eyes were as dark as his soul, and the smile that twisted his lips a sneering parody of true happiness.

"Morgan."

Hands shook her shoulders as she was yanked from her memories. She looked up to see Erin standing over her, a frown marring her beautiful face.

"Are you okay?"

"I...yeah. I think so."

"You looked like you were having a panic attack or something." Erin sat on the sofa beside her and placed the back of her hand to Morgan's forehead. "You sure you're okay?"

Morgan smiled gently. "Yeah." She waved the letter. "Just brought up some bad memories."

"You're getting memories back?" Erin looked hopeful and Morgan shook her head sadly.

"No, I don't think so. This was from when I was about twelve or thirteen. My dad sitting watching TV and my mum already nursing a busted lip. He'd come home and his dinner wasn't quite ready so he hit her."

"Jesus."

"That was pretty common. Anything that wasn't right, that he didn't like, he'd take out on us. Mostly Mum, but not just her. But I'm sure you know all this. Sorry to go over old ground."

"You aren't."

Morgan frowned at her.

"You never talked about it. It hurt too much. I knew he was violent because of the way your mum died, and I knew he had hit you on occasion, but you never spoke about it. You never told me details like that."

Morgan smiled sadly. "Maybe that's why you thought nothing of this then." She indicated the letter still in her hand. "I'm sorry. This is him threatening you and the kids if I don't do as I'm told."

"It reads like an apology."

"At the start it does. But everyone tells me I've had no contact with him since he went to prison. Correct?"

"Yes."

"Then how does he know about you and the kids?"

"I have no idea."

"Exactly. This was posted to our address. Our home address."

"He knows where we live."

Morgan knew that it was the shock of realization that had Erin stating the obvious. "Yes. I can see why this would make me feel I had no option but to leave."

"It's called running away, Morgan."

"No. Not running. Protecting you all."

"How the hell do you figure that when you just pointed out he knows who we are and where we live?"

"Right now my instinct is to put as much distance between you all and me so that he doesn't think you matter enough to hurt me."

"You know that's backward, don't you?" The crease between Erin's brows deepened.

Morgan laughed. "Yes. But that's how I feel now. I know what he did and I grew up there. He scares the crap out of me. But before I lived it all. I lived that night, and the trial, and everything else. I can only imagine the kind of fear this instilled in me then."

"I wish I knew more of what was going on in your head then."

"I'm sorry. I don't know anything else to tell you."

"I know." Erin sighed.

"Wait. I might have something." She stood up.

"Where are you going?"

"Upstairs. I might have something that could help."

Morgan quickly retrieved the transcript and held the file out for Erin.

"What's this?"

"It's the transcript of my father's trial. The evidence I gave against him. It's all in there." Morgan sat down again and ran her hands over her face.

"Becky?"

"Yes. She ordered it for me. I haven't read it. In truth, I wasn't going to."

"Why not?"

"I wanted to leave it all behind me as much as I possibly could. To try and live my life not…tainted by all that."

"And now?"

"I still wish I didn't need to know what's in there. But I think I do." She looked at Erin. "I think we both do."

Erin opened the cover and looked down.

"Before we do, there's just one thing."

Erin looked back at her. "What?"

"I'm scared that in learning the things in that file I'll become her again. The old Morgan. And I don't want to be her again."

"She wasn't all bad." Erin smiled sadly. "For the most part I thought she was wonderful. I even loved her."

"I want to be better. I wanted a chance to put everything right." She sidled closer to Erin. "Before we read this and everything changes again, I have to tell you that I love you." She took hold of Erin's hand and raised it to her lips.

"You don't know me." Erin's voice was barely a whisper.

"Yes, I do." Morgan pressed their joined hands over her heart. "This is yours." Tears filled Erin's eyes and slowly inched their way down her cheeks. Morgan wiped them away and leaned closer. "I really want to kiss you right now. But I won't." She could see the shock in Erin's eyes. "I won't kiss you again unless you ask me to." She brought Erin's hand to her lips again. "But I want to with all my heart."

Erin slowly pulled her hand away and cleared her throat. "We should look at this." She pointed to the folio.

"Do you have time to do this now, or do you have to go?"

"I'm fine. I'm not working today, Tristan's at soccer camp for the day, and Maddie's at her Brownie day thing."

"Okay,"

"Want me to read stuff first then pass it over if it's not too bad?" Erin asked.

"Yes, but no. Thanks for asking, but I think if I'm going to do this, I've got to do it all the way." She took a deep breath and looked down at the first page, her eyes struggling to focus.

"You'll need your glasses." Erin laughed.

"Yeah, right. I keep forgetting."

They pored over page after page of legalese, evidence, testimony, and dry, hard facts painting a picture of an abusive man who had terrorized his wife and daughter for the duration of their marriage. His defense protested his innocence to the very end, pointing the finger at his daughter despite every piece of evidence indicating that he was the murderer, including the ten-inch scar on Morgan's back.

Morgan's hands shook as she read her own testimony. She had to read it over and over. The words didn't make sense. They swam about her head and formed their own sentences, their meaning lost as she struggled to comprehend everything she had been through, everything she had seen. But she couldn't. There was no way to see it through the eyes of the teenager she had been and she let the tears fall as Erin read the final page out to her. Her father's final tirade as he was sentenced to life in prison. She could hear the anger of his words despite the soft tones of Erin's voice. In her mind she could see him banging his hands against the glass partition around the dock.

"I will make you pay for what you've done, girl. You'll be sorry you crossed me, you filthy fucking pervert. You've taken everything from me. I should've killed you when I had the chance. But I'll be there, Moggie. When you least expect it, I'll be there to make you

pay. You and anyone you ever care about. You're mine, Moggie. Mine. Do you hear me? Mine."

Those were his last words before he was wrestled from the dock and incarcerated.

Erin wrapped her arms around Morgan's shoulders and held her as they both cried.

CHAPTER TWENTY-THREE

Morgan held Maddie's hand as they walked, smiling and keeping up with her non-stop chatter. She kept looking over her shoulder, watching Tristan lag behind, his girlfriend hanging on to his arm. He managed to look both smug and embarrassed at the same time. Maddie was right. She was pretty, with long blond hair, blue eyes, and the look of the desperately smitten written all over her face. She'd yet to say anything other than "hello" and "thank you" to anyone other than Tristan, but she was here with him, and that said everything Morgan needed to know. *I think.*

The car park was packed, and she knew the indoor ski slope the kids had insisted they visit was going to be heaving with people. She also couldn't remember how to ski. Apparently, it was something she and Erin had learned together on holiday one year, and then taught the children when they had been old enough. Both had promised to teach her in return, though she now suspected that Maddie would be her instructor for the afternoon. She didn't mind; she was just happy to be with them both.

Thirty minutes later, they all stepped onto the slope, skis in hand and the world's most uncomfortable boots on their feet. *I enjoyed this? Jesus, I was a masochist.* Her ankles and calves were complaining at the unnatural position as Maddie showed her how to clip into her skis and start to move around in them a little. Tristan and Isabelle waved as they hopped onto the draglift to the short nursery slope to warm up. Maddie led her up a small rise, showing her how to walk sideways so she didn't slip straight down the hill.

She proved to be a patient teacher, demonstrating the technical "pizza" and "chips" positions of the skis before she made Morgan take her first five-foot slide down the fake snow.

"Now go to pizza to stop." The smile in Maddie's voice told Morgan she was proud of her student's progress. "That's it, now come back up and try it again."

Morgan started to turn but got her skis tangled and ended up on her backside. She laughed as Maddie appeared at her side.

"Are you okay, Mum?"

"I'm fine, kiddo. How do I get up?"

Maddie grinned and unclipped her skis for her. "I'll show you later how you can do it yourself, but I'll help you this time." She dropped the skis back on the ground as she reached for Morgan's hand.

Tristan stopped next to them, showering them with snow in an impressive display. "Mum, are you hurt?" He clipped his boots out of his skis and knelt beside her.

Morgan smiled at him. "I'm fine. Just a little fall. I expect I'll end up down here most of the time today."

"You never used to fall." He shook his head and started to stand up again.

She caught his hand. "Thanks for coming to make sure I was okay."

He nodded and then headed back to Isabelle waiting for him at the foot of the button lift up the main slope.

"Is he okay to go up there?"

Maddie giggled. "He's been going up there since we first came here. He's showing off today."

I just bet he is. "Okay, kiddo, pull me up." She held her hands out to Maddie, and they giggled their way back to the top of the small rise. After half a dozen successful attempts in a row, Maddie declared her good enough for the baby slope. Morgan looked up at the gentle incline, but the thought of coming down it with smooth wooden planks on her feet was intimidating.

"Why don't you head up and enjoy yourself. I'll wait for you at the bottom, then you don't have to worry about me."

Maddie shook her head. "I can't." She pointed to a sign hanging by the door. It was too far away for them to read. "I'm under twelve so I have to have an adult supervisor to go on the lift and the slope."

"I can supervise from here."

Maddie put her hands on her hips. "No, you can't. Don't be scared. You can do it."

"I'm not scared," Morgan huffed. *I'm terrified!* Maddie's head cocked to one side, and her little eyebrow rose. *Oh God, she got that look from Erin. No, I won't go there today. I will not spoil my time with the kids.* "Come on then, lead me to my doom!"

From the bottom, the slope looked mild and easy. At the top, Morgan's heart was pounding and her palms sweated inside her gloves. Maddie pulled her goggles down to cover her eyes and got herself ready to push off.

"Remember, don't push the first time. Just let yourself roll. Just slide off, and remember pizza to slow down. And don't fall."

"Slide. Pizza. Don't fall. Got it."

"Okay, you follow behind me, Mum."

"Right." Morgan bent her knees and stared down the hill. *What the fuck was I thinking? I can't do this. I'm gonna end up on my arse, in front of everyone, embarrassing myself, and the kids. I'll embarrass Tristan in front of his girlfriend. Oh shit! I should have stayed at ho—*

"Mum, are you ready yet?"

You can only die once, right? "Yep."

Maddie set off slowly, carving her path and flicking her eyes over her shoulder. Morgan took a deep breath, mentally crossing herself, and said the Lord's Prayer. She leaned forward and let the skis find their path. *That's what Maddie said, let them find their path, then pizza to slow the buggers down.* She quickly gathered speed.

"Pizza, Mum!" Maddie shouted as Morgan flew by her.

Morgan tried to create the triangle shape Maddie had shown her. *Pizza? Damn feet, pizza!*

She tried to force the skis into position, but the tips crossed and she hurtled forward even as her legs and skis planted firmly in the snow. She let go of her ski poles and tried to brace with her arms. Rolling and sliding down the length of the slope, she landed on her back gasping up at the high, corrugated steel roof. Her skis were still fixed to her boots and her legs were twisted in odd directions. *Ow.*

Maddie and Tristan both appeared at her side in seconds, their voices filled with panic. A wave of dizziness washed over her and she felt nauseous.

"Mum, can you hear me?" Tristan was out of his skis and on his knees. She blinked up at him, and reached out to stroke his cheek. "Are you all right?"

"Mum, say something." Maddie grasped her hand.

"Ow." They both drew back. Morgan shook her head. "My knee's killing."

One of the staff members stood over her, nodding down at her knee. "I think you're going to need an x-ray on that. I'll call an ambulance." He looked at Tristan. "If your dad's about, kid, you might want to call him."

Tristan rolled his eyes and smiled at Morgan. "We're all right, thanks."

"Your mum's gonna kill me."

Tristan grinned. "Nah, we'll say you were stunt skiing. You did cartwheels down that hill on purpose."

"I'm sorry, Mum." Maddie was crying.

"What are you sorry for? I'm the one who's spoiled the afternoon for you guys."

"I made you do it."

Morgan pulled her in for an awkward hug. "Nah, you didn't. If I really hadn't wanted to do it, you wouldn't have been able to make me. Dry your eyes, baby girl, it's not so bad." She didn't want to think about the angle her lower leg was lying at and tried to breathe through the pain. She looked at Tristan. "Where's Isabelle?"

"She's here." He pointed behind him, and the girl stepped forward.

"Isabelle, you'll have to come to the hospital with us, and then we can contact your parents. They can either come and get you, or we'll see if their mum can take you home. Okay?" The girl nodded, her hand on Tristan's shoulder. They smiled at each other, a sweet, tender kind of smile. Morgan closed her eyes and tried not to vomit from the pain and embarrass her son even further.

CHAPTER TWENTY-FOUR

Erin's heels clicked on the tiled hospital floor, again. She rolled her eyes when the same receptionist greeted her with the same saccharine smile, nasal voice, and couldn't-care-less attitude.

"Hi, how can I help you?"

"Morgan Masters. I got a call."

"Mum, we're over here." Maddie waved as Erin turned around. She smiled and shrugged at the receptionist before heading for the cubicle with its drab curtain surround. Maddie sat at the foot of the bed, painting Morgan's toenails with pink glitter nail varnish, while Morgan dozed. Tristan sat in the chair playing a game on his phone, the pretty blond girlfriend perched on the arm, leaning close to him and twirling her hair around her fingers, her fingernails covered in the same pink glitter color that was now decorating Maddie's fingers and Morgan's toes.

"Hey, so what happened?" She ruffled Maddie's hair and smiled at the teens in the chair.

"Mum did cartwheels down the baby slope." Maddie giggled.

"It wasn't cartwheels. That speed, they're more like somersaults." Morgan opened her eyes and tried to pull herself up the bed. "Thanks for coming."

Erin shrugged. "I was hardly going to leave you all to your own devices. God knows what would happen!" She winked at Tristan. "What's the verdict?" She pointed at Morgan's leg. The sturdy knee brace started at mid-calf and went all the way up her thigh, holding her leg at a thirty-degree angle.

"Not dislocated, but I've torn the medial ligament down the side. Not completely, so they don't want to operate, but I'm not going to be skiing again for quite a while."

"Ouch." Erin winced.

"Mummy, it was my fault." Maddie crawled along the bed and wrapped her arms around Erin's neck. Morgan and Erin spoke at the same time.

"No, it wasn't." Morgan reached for Maddie's hand.

"Why?"

"I made her go on the baby slope and she wasn't ready." Maddie's lip trembled.

"I would have said no if I didn't want to, Maddie." Morgan clasped her fingers across her stomach.

Yeah, not bloody likely. "See, sweetie, it wasn't your fault." She patted her back. "How long are you going to be in the brace?"

Morgan shrugged.

"The doctor said six weeks." Tristan looked up from the game he was playing on his phone. "Then physio."

"Six weeks? I thought you said it wasn't too bad?" Erin frowned.

"It isn't. The doctors are just being cautious." Morgan glowered at Tristan, who shrugged and went back to his game.

"Mummy, can she come and stay at home while she's sick, please?"

Morgan and Erin again spoke at the same time.

"I'm not sick!" Morgan pushed herself up in the bed.

"I don't think that's a good idea." Erin's heart raced. *I can't do it. I can't.*

"But I still think it was my fault and I should look after her. Please, Mummy." Maddie twirled her fingers through Erin's long hair where it lay against her neck. She lightly grasped her hand.

"Don't knot up my hair, sweetie. I don't think it would be a very good idea." Erin knew that having Morgan back in the house would be too difficult for her. It had been almost a week since their disastrous kiss, and she hadn't had a full night's sleep since.

"Why not?" Maddie picked at the tangle she'd made in Erin's hair, her tongue poking out as she concentrated.

"Well, our stairs are very steep, and your mum wouldn't be able to get up them very easily with the brace."

"The stairs are steeper at Auntie Amy's house, so she can't go there either then."

"I'm sure Auntie Amy won't mind if your mum sleeps on the sofa till she can get—"

"We have a sofa bed, Mum. She could sleep on that?"

Such clever kids "Yes, but recovery is usually faster when people can stay quiet and get lots of rest." *There, let's see what you think of that one. When did this become a competition with my own child?*

"But I can look after her so she can get lots of rest. And we'll be quiet. Won't we, Tristan?"

Tristan grunted without looking up.

"See? Please, Mummy. Please."

She was out of reasons that didn't sound like excuses, and she was quickly losing her determination in the face of Maddie's heartfelt insistence. "Maybe your mum doesn't want to stay on a sofa bed." She looked at Morgan.

Morgan's eyes were downcast, her voice placid as she spoke. "I don't want you to feel uncomfortable, but there is nothing I'd like more than to be with the kids as much as possible. I don't care if that means sleeping on a sofa bed." She finally met Erin's eyes. Resolve resonated from within her, and it left Erin breathless. "I think it's family that helps aid recovery more than anything else. It's your house, Erin; I'll do whatever you want."

Erin knew there was a far deeper meaning to Morgan's words. The look of determination on her face made it clear. It was also obvious that Erin was backed into a corner. She didn't want to say no to Maddie, knowing that the child was feeling guilty and trying to make amends for the wrong she thought she had done. She knew also that all three of them wanted more time together and the children's return to a normal school routine would severely restrict them. This seemed like a logical way to help them all—to help her children.

I can do this. I am a strong woman, I can resist. I will not—I cannot—let her hurt me again.

"Fine."

Maddie hugged her tight as she bounced on her knees on the bed. Tristan grinned before returning his attention to his game. Morgan's eyes didn't leave hers.

Oh God, please let me be able to do this.

CHAPTER TWENTY-FIVE

Erin pulled on the sofa to lift the bed platform out. She could hear Maddie fussing in the kitchen and Tristan was in his room. *Probably chatting online to Isabelle.* Morgan hobbled into the room. The metallic click-clack of her crutches preceding her, as they gave and strained with each movement. She carried on making up the sofa bed.

"I'm sorry for putting you on the spot earlier."

Erin laughed. "No, you're not. If you were, you wouldn't have backed me into a corner like that." She straightened the bedding over the thin mattress and threw pillows into place.

"Okay, I'm sorry for upsetting you."

"Same response." She tucked in the corners of the sheet. "Look, you got what you wanted. You're here, spending time with the kids. Fine. That's good for them, and that's what matters."

"It's not just them."

Erin shook out the duvet and pulled it into place. *I don't want to hear this. I know where you're going, and I do not want to hear it.*

"Please, Erin, can we talk about last week? About what happened?"

"There's nothing to talk about."

"Yes, there is. We kissed." Morgan shuffled a step closer. "I told you I love you, and then we kissed. You didn't stop me until Maddie interrupted—"

"It was a mistake." She stuffed a pillow into its case, glad to have something to do with her hands. Morgan was too close, to her—to the truth, to making her feel something other than anger, hurt, and disappointment.

"No, it wasn't. I felt it." She gripped her crutches so hard her knuckles turned white. "I felt you, and I know you wanted me."

"I wanted a fuck, Morgan." She threw the last pillow onto the bed with as much force as she threw the words at her. She needed control of the situation, of herself, and her emotions. "That's it. Sex. That's all you felt." She rounded the bottom of the bed. Adrenaline zipped through her veins, as an image filled her mind. "Just like you were doing in those pictures, right? In the car park."

She watched Morgan's face pale as her words wounded, and she didn't know if she felt elated or defeated. Morgan opened her mouth to speak, but Erin cut her off.

"Don't even start all that, I was a different Morgan, it wasn't me, I'm not her, crap again. Don't you see? Every time I look at you I see the woman who abandoned me. Then screwed someone else three weeks later!" She stalked to the door and pulled it open.

"Erin, I understand. But—"

"Enough. You left. You had a reason. Fine. I don't agree with it, but fine. You still left, when we could have worked it out." She pushed her fingers through her hair. "You still walked away. You never gave me a chance. You never gave us a chance. After fifteen years, you couldn't—you wouldn't even—"

Morgan rubbed her hands over her face, then pushed her fingers through her hair. "I'm sorry." She reached for her crutches. "I thought—" She shook her head. "Doesn't matter. I'll go back to Amy and Nikki's."

"What?" She couldn't keep up. The second she thought she understood where Morgan was coming from, she flipped it around, and did the opposite to what Erin expected.

"I know you only said it was okay for me to be here for the kids. I shouldn't have backed you into a corner like that. I thought if we could spend some time together you'd see that I'm different now. That I really have changed. But you're right. For all we know I was seeing someone else and I'm just a stupid fucking bitch. I just wanted—no, I want—another chance. For our family. For us. I thought that maybe we could get to know each other again—for the first time. I don't know what I was thinking. I've already lost you."

"I'm not yours to lose." Her voice was equally quiet, barely above a breath and tinged with sadness.

"That's not what my heart says." Morgan placed her hand over her chest. "I'll always be yours."

Tears clung to her thick, dark lashes, like dew drops on a spider's web. Her eyes, black as night, and as endless as eternity, offered Erin everything. Morgan's heart, her future, her soul were hers for the taking. The only thing she couldn't offer her was the past, already so tainted Erin couldn't let go of it.

"Do you still love me?"

Erin trailed her finger down Morgan's cheek, from the corner of her eyebrow down to her jaw. It would be so easy to say yes. To forget all the complications, and the duality of the Morgan she knew. But she couldn't. Her head just wouldn't let go, and her heart couldn't trust. "I don't know you, Morgan." She closed her eyes and kept the tears from falling by sheer force of will. "I loved the Morgan I knew. I *still* love the Morgan I knew." She touched her finger to Morgan's lips. Stopping the words she knew Morgan wanted to say. "But you're the one who keeps telling me you aren't her."

"Me and my big mouth."

Erin smiled, knowing that it reflected the sadness she felt. Her Morgan was gone and might never return. Did she want a replacement? A look-alike to replace her? She didn't know. There was just too much going round her head.

Morgan stood and tucked her crutches under her arm. Her slow steps toward the door played counterpoint to Erin's heartbeat.

She's leaving, just like I wanted. She's doing exactly what I wanted. Except I don't want her to.

Erin didn't want someone else to take care of her. She didn't want anyone else to...

"Do you know who she is?" She crossed the room quickly, putting her hand on Morgan's shoulder before she yanked it back.

"What?" Morgan turned to look at her.

"The woman. Do you know who she is?"

"No. The police were looking for her because they think she knew the man who attacked me. If they've found her, they haven't told me."

"Why hasn't she come forward? If you were seeing her, then surely she would have come forward, or tried to find out if you were okay. Did Amy or Nikki know anything about her?"

"No. They were as shocked as I was when the police showed us the pictures. I don't know anything more than what I've told you."

"Did they know about the letter?"

"No."

"I know I'm going round in circles, but I just can't get past it. I can't."

"I get it, Erin." She leaned forward and softly kissed her cheek. "I'm so sorry I hurt you."

Erin closed her eyes and breathed in the scent of her so close. "Stay. I can't get past what happened between us, but we can be friends. For the kids."

"Friends?"

Erin blinked. "Yes, friends." She hoped that Morgan couldn't see her pulse jumping in her neck, or her shallow breath as she tried to fill her lungs. "Nothing more."

"Is that what you want, Erin?"

She nodded, even as her body ached to reach out for Morgan. She tried to convince herself that it was habit that turned her insides liquid. Just familiarity that made her yearn for Morgan's touch. She knew she couldn't fool herself with her flimsy excuses, but she hoped she was able to convince Morgan.

"Friends it is then. I'll take whatever I can get."

CHAPTER TWENTY-SIX

Morgan pushed a pillow under her knee and tried to get comfortable on the thin mattress. Every time she moved, a different spring creaked, its complaint loud and clear. She pulled the cover up to her chin and longed to turn on her side and curl into a ball, and tried not to think about Erin. She knew it would only make sleep harder to find if she pictured her curled in her bed—the bed they had once shared.

I was a fucking idiot. I knew it before, but it's even clearer now. A prize fucking idiot.

She tried to turn onto her side and groaned at the ache emanating from her knee. Her head throbbed, and she didn't know if it was from the head injury or too much emotion. She did know it was a bloody uncomfortable headache, and that was enough to get her reaching for painkillers.

Her heart ached when she remembered Erin's words. *I loved my Morgan, but you're the one who keeps telling me you aren't her.* She'd made it clear she didn't want Morgan anymore.

No, that's not true. She does want me, but she doesn't want to want me. That's different, right?

Morgan stared at the ceiling. *And she doesn't trust her—the old Morgan. She won't give me a chance because she doesn't really believe that I've changed.*

Erin's words played over and over in her head. She knew she needed to prove to her that she was different, that she could be trusted. The question was how.

She pushed the covers off and swung her legs out of the bed, wincing as she hopped to the bookshelves and searched for a notepad. A pen was sitting on the coffee table and she grabbed it as she staggered back to the bed, flicking on the small lamp before she sat down. She drew two columns on the page and wrote in the headings. Old Morgan. New Morgan.

Under the heading Old Morgan, she wrote *was an idiot* before drawing a line under it and slowly adding all the details she had learned of her old self. The trauma that had led to her disillusionment sat at the top of the column. Each item added to the list built up a picture of a woman who had given up. She was someone who had suffered and never truly recovered from it, allowing herself to remain the victim of her own past, rather than flourish in the life she had built herself.

Glass half empty kind of girl. Always waiting for the bad news around the corner and not appreciating the precious gifts she had right under her nose.

At the top of the second column, she wrote *I will not give up.*

The youthful pride and optimism of her nineteen-year-old self fed her passions and urged her to seek the dreams and goals her old self had long since given up on. Dreams that had turned to dust and scattered on the winds of weakness, were rekindled, given life, and set free. Her art would have its voice again, and she would set it loose upon the world.

Her children were loved, and they would know it. They would never question her sincerity or her loyalty, and they would learn that they could trust and depend on her as never before. She wouldn't quit when they needed her, and she would be there if ever they wanted her.

Morgan wrote the words as she whispered them to herself. A vow, a promise, a binding contract that she set forth.

Then another name appeared on the page, one she didn't remember writing.

Erin.

She drew a big circle around it, before she finished her pledge.

Maybe she'll never love me back, but she will never again have cause to doubt that I love her. To the end of my days, I am hers.

CHAPTER TWENTY-SEVEN

Maddie shifted next to Morgan and dropped her hand to her knee. "Mum, can you help me with my homework?"

"First week back at school and you have homework already?"

"Yup, can ya help?"

"Sure, what've you got?"

She pulled a book from her backpack. "Math."

Morgan groaned. "I was never any good at math. Isn't your mum better at this?"

"Yep. But you should practice too. You don't want me to be smarter than you are, do you?" Maddie giggled when Morgan started to tickle her.

"Cheeky little madam. I'll give you practice."

The tickling continued until a cough at the door distracted them. Morgan looked up with Maddie sprawled across her lap, her feet kicking cushions onto the floor.

"We have company." Erin led two police officers into the room.

"I'm sorry, I didn't hear the door." Morgan helped Maddie back onto the sofa, careful not to jar her knee.

The taller officer took off his cap, tucked it under his arm, and held his hand out. "Ms. Masters. I'm PC Lock and—"

"PC Ward. I remember." She shook their hands before they sat down. "Maddie, why don't you go to your room and start on your homework? I'll come and help you when I've spoken to the police." Her uninjured leg began to twitch against the floor. Her playful mood evaporated, replaced by a sense of caution. The images the men had shown her at their last meeting still tormented her.

Maddie's cheeks were still red from her excitement, but her eyes were serious. She stuffed her book into her backpack, kissed Morgan's cheek, and then scampered out of the room.

Erin followed her toward the door. "I'll leave you to it."

"Please, stay." Morgan reached out and snagged Erin's hand. "I'd really like you to." Despite her trepidation, or maybe because of it, she wanted her close. Erin already knew they had pictures of Morgan with someone else; what could possibly be worse than that?

Erin paused, her cheeks coloring before she pulled her hand away, seemingly embarrassed by Morgan's pleading, and sat in a chair across the room.

Lock cleared his throat. "We have the man who attacked you in custody. We have to ask you to come and identify him."

"I don't remember him. I don't remember anything." Morgan pressed herself further back on the sofa.

"We understand that. But this is a formality." Ward leaned forward, his elbows on his knees. He had dark hair and eyes, thin lips, and a crooked nose, possibly the result of a well-timed fist.

"It's a waste of time." She picked at her nails, frustration coloring her voice.

Ward shrugged his hands. "Maybe, but in some cases, seeing their attacker helps people to recover their memories."

"That's in cases where drugs are involved, isn't it?" Erin asked.

"I will be able to answer more of your questions after the identity parade. But not before." Lock turned to face Morgan. "I'm sorry. I've been a police officer for fifteen years now, and I haven't come across a case like this before. None of us know what will work and what won't." He looked at Morgan. "It might do nothing, but it might help."

"How do you know it's him?" Morgan tried to stop her leg from jumping. The nervous twitch annoying her more and more.

"I can't go into details. Not until after the ID parade. Then I'll be able to fill you in on some of what we know." Lock's cleanly shaven scalp glistened slightly in the light from the bay window. Gray eyes watched her, calm, sincere, and open.

She glanced at Erin, at the tight frown knitting her brows together. She knew Erin needed answers more than she did. Would it help her forgive? Morgan had no idea, but she knew that she had to try to give Erin everything she needed. If that meant facing the man who had attacked her, then so be it. "When?"

"We can have the lineup ready in an hour or so."

"Now?" Morgan knew she was staring as he nodded at her. "I'm not…" She looked at Erin. "Will you come with me?"

Erin shook her head. "The kids are home—"

"Chris could come and watch them. Or maybe Amy?" Her voice sounded desperate, even to her own ears, but she didn't want to face this alone. The possibility that this might trigger her memory was as terrifying as the prospect of meeting the man who had beaten her. The thought of doing it without Erin made her heart race and her breathing accelerate. Her fear must have shown because Erin's face softened, sympathy—or was it pity?—etched in the subtle lines of her face.

"Is that okay?" Erin looked from one police officer to the other.

"Of course," Ward said. "If it helps, we could probably get a family liaison officer over to help out.

"No, I'm sure that won't be necessary. I'll just call my brother and see if he can make it." She pulled her mobile from her pocket, dialed, and waited for Chris to answer.

"Do I need to do anything? Bring anything?" Morgan couldn't take her eyes off Erin as she spoke quietly into the phone.

"No. When we get to the station, we'll go into a room. The glass wall will let you see the people in the other room, but they can't see you. It's safe. He won't be able to see you."

"But he'll still know it's me." She tried to recall the features of his face. The grainy picture hadn't been enough to fix in her mind. All she could see were shades of gray dots, white light, and black shadows. No face would come to her. *Was it my father? Is that what the letter was about?* She dragged her father's face from the depths of her memory and examined it as she remembered him. The shaggy, unkempt dark hair, the deep-set black eyes, and the chiseled features were so much like the ones she saw in the mirror every day.

She tried to picture him twenty years older. Twenty prison years older. Would that fit with the gray and black pixels on the page? "Did I know him?"

"I can't tell you anything until afterward, Ms. Masters. Then I'll be able to answer some of your questions."

"But not all of them?"

Lock smiled, an ironic little smile of agreement. "Probably not, no."

Erin ended her call. "He'll be over in twenty minutes or so." She looked at Morgan. "Do you need anything before I go and tell the kids we're going out?"

"No, just tell Maddie I'll help her when we come back if she still needs me."

Erin frowned and looked like she was about to say something, but she pressed her lips together and stayed silent.

"What?"

"Doesn't matter." Erin's voice was quiet as she left the room.

Ward stood. "I'll go and organize the lineup."

"Do you need any help?" Lock pointed to Morgan's crutches.

"No, I'm fine, thanks. Do we just meet you there?"

"That'll be fine. We'll see you soon, Ms. Masters. Maybe we can help you get some closure on some of this." Lock dipped his head as he left, the click of the front door signaling their departure from the house.

I won't hold my breath. "Right, thanks."

CHAPTER TWENTY-EIGHT

Morgan blinked against the harsh fluorescent lights that hummed overhead, plastic chairs creaked under their occupants' weight, and locked doors were everywhere she turned. Her gaze flitted around the room, and she stared briefly at posters stuck on notice boards, leaflets about the Crown Prosecution Service, legal aid, and bail bondsmen. The desk sergeant watched them, smiling sporadically as he leafed through his paperwork, his jowls wobbling as he moved his head.

A door to their left opened and PC Ward popped his head through. "This way."

He led them through a maze of corridors, each one white with strip lights, closed doors, and nothing to distinguish it from any other. They approached a small group of people standing and talking to PC Lock. He nodded as they got close.

"Ms. Masters, this is Mr. Harper. He's here from the Crown Prosecution Service, and this is Mr. James, for the defense." Lock indicated one after the other. "When we go in, you won't be able to see anything through the glass. Ms. Masters," he said to Erin, "I have to ask you to remain completely silent in there."

"That's fine," Erin said.

"When you're ready, we'll turn on the lights and get the men to enter the room. All you have to do then is tell us if you recognize anyone, specifically if you recognize him from the night you were attacked. Do you understand?"

"I do," Morgan said.

"Okay, take your time, Ms. Masters."

They filed in, one at a time. There were no chairs or tables in the room. Just a large, glass viewing window and an intercom on the wall beside it. *Looks like the snake enclosure at a zoo.* Morgan couldn't stop the shudder that scuttled along her spine. The small space was overwhelmed with the odor of cheap cologne, deodorant, and nervous sweat. The tension rolling through her body was an undulating ribbon of energy, palpable, unrelenting, yet elusive. Her hand shook as she grasped at Erin's fingers, searching for comfort, desperately seeking solace as she faced her fear. The shaking abated a little when Erin's strong fingers linked with hers, squeezing just enough to offer her reassurance.

"Are you ready, Ms. Masters?" Lock stood in front of her.

Morgan nodded and then jumped as the light went on behind the glass. The room was empty. More white walls and strip lights, the window barred. A buzzer sounded and the door opened. Six men entered the room in a long line, each holding a board in front of their chests. They were all between six foot and six foot three inches tall, they all had short hair in varying shades of brown. Some had tattoos, one had a pierced eyebrow, and several had earrings. All of them looked to be in their thirties.

One of these men attacked me. One of these men stole every blessed memory I had. Images from the DVD Tristan had given her flitted through her mind; she saw him slapping chubby baby hands into a birthday cake in the shape of the number one. She saw herself bending over a toddling Maddie, as she gripped onto her fingers and took unsteady steps around the lawn. There were pictures from their wedding. *One of them stole all that and so much more.*

She stared through the glass and the anger grew inside her, fear fleeing in its wake. She wasn't sure what she was expecting— hoping—to happen when she looked into the eyes of her attacker but she realized she had expected something. She wanted the movie moment where it all came flooding back in that moment of clarity. She wished she could turn to Erin and tell her she remembered it all;

every date, every kiss, every wonderful second that they had spent together. But there was nothing.

She searched face after face, hunting for a clue, a sign that this was the man who had taken her life and callously left her for dead. The features of each unrecognized visage jumbled before her eyes, twisting into a monstrous caricature of a man. A man who resembled everyone and no one.

Morgan ached to be able to say the words she knew everyone was longing to hear, that's him, number whatever. She hated the fact that it was ever more apparent that the day would never come when her memories would return.

She closed her eyes and let her head fall to her chest, despising her own inability to even accuse her assailant.

"Do you recognize anyone?" Lock stood close beside Morgan, his voice soft.

"No. I wish I did, but I don't recognize anyone." She turned her head to look at him.

Out of the corner of her eye, she saw Mr. James smile before he quickly covered it, his unprofessional display indicating that her answer was good news for his client. Mr. Harper made no indication that her response affected him either way, and she was glad he was the one fighting for justice on her behalf.

"Are you certain? Take another look and just make sure. Take your time. There's no hurry." Lock tipped his head toward the glass once more, directing Morgan's gaze back round. She followed his direction.

"Ms. Masters was perfectly clear." Mr. James stepped forward. "She doesn't recognize anyone. I think it's time to let my client go."

"I don't think so, Mr. James." Mr. Harper examined his fingernails, looking bored with the situation. "We have a witness statement that identifies your client, video evidence of him committing the offense, medical reports to corroborate Ms. Masters' amnesia, the blood and drug evidence found in your client's home." He inclined his head toward Morgan. "The CPS agreed to this identity parade, which you insisted upon, in the interest of justice, and in the hope that it may have had some benefit for Ms. Masters."

He opened the door and led them all out. "Mss. Masters, thank you both for your time today. I will be in touch with you in due course."

He ushered Mr. James out ahead of him. They were obviously deep in discussion as Ward and Lock led Erin and Morgan to another room. There was a table and chairs with a recording machine against the wall.

Ward indicated the chairs for them. "Can I get you a drink?"

Erin shook her head.

"Water, please." Morgan's voice sounded scratchy and hoarse.

Lock sat down as Ward left the room. He opened a file and placed the photograph of a man on the table—a mug shot. The man's hair was so short and dark it looked like a shadow on his head, and he had a tattoo crawling out of the neck of his T-shirt. It looked like a claw scoring the flesh of his throat. Morgan grimaced as she realized that this man had been standing in the room. His sneer was still etched in her mind's eye as he had stared through the one-way glass in her direction. She shuddered and wrapped her arms around her body, unconsciously trying to fight off the chill that was seeping into her bones.

"His name is Jimmy Davidson." Lock paused as Ward came back in the room and handed Morgan a plastic cup before sitting.

Morgan was pale and her knuckles had turned white around the grip of her crutches. "He's the man who attacked me?"

"Yes."

"Why?"

Lock flicked his eyes in Erin's direction then back at his file. He pulled out a mug shot and placed it on the table.

"This is his wife. Anna Davidson." He watched Morgan carefully, waiting.

"Do you recognize her, Ms. Masters?"

Morgan pulled the picture closer, studying it. She saw Erin press her hand to her mouth. She frowned as she looked at the image; blond hair, blue eyes, flawless skin, and high cheekbones stared back at her. She didn't know the woman, and she knew they could all see it on her face. She couldn't look at them. She didn't want to see pity on their faces.

"No, I don't think so." Morgan pushed the picture back toward him. "Should I?" She heard Erin gasp and turned to see her eyes wide and her jaw slack with shock.

"Anna Davidson was a model in a life drawing class you taught. She posed for the class for about six months." Lock tucked the picture back into the file. "The night you were attacked was the last class of term before the break for the summer. After the class finished, you and she went for a drink in a local pub."

"She was the woman!" Morgan's eyes widened and her cheeks burned bright red. She turned to Erin, but dropped her eyes quickly. "I'm sorry." She reached out to grab Erin's hand but stopped before she touched her. "I'm so sorry."

Erin stared at the table, arms folded across her chest, her mouth set in a thin line.

"I thought you said you checked with the security at the college and her picture didn't match." Erin's words were sharp, her voice sounding thinner and tighter than normal.

"The art models are contracted by the college, not employed as staff members. They don't have their pictures in any database; they don't have to go through the same security clearances." Lock shrugged. "So when we went and showed her picture around to the security people and to staff in the college, no one recognized her, and her face wasn't in the employees' or students' database. It seemed logical that she had no ties to the college so we turned our investigation in other directions. As there was alcohol in your system, we checked local pubs and found that you had been drinking in the Roundhouse. The bartender recognized both you and the woman as having been there that night, and he thought possibly the man, but he wasn't sure. He also said that he didn't know either of you and that he only remembered you because you'd asked him a number of questions about the wine they were serving." He smiled slightly.

"So I was out drinking with her?"

"Yes."

"How long…when did I start to…" Morgan motioned with her hands, obviously trying to expand her meaning.

Lock frowned. "How long what?"

"How long was I—"

"Oh, for God's sake. She wants to know how long she was screwing her. Right? Darling." Erin spat the words into the air, the endearment passing her lips with more venom than any four-letter word ever had.

Lock's eyes widened, but he showed no other reaction. "Mrs. Davidson stated that this was the first time they had been out together socially. All their other interactions had been work related."

"So I wasn't having an affair with her?"

"No. She admitted that you had no romantic relationship."

"I wasn't cheating on you." Morgan turned to Erin, she touched her cheek, lifting her face so there eyes met. "I wasn't cheating. I wasn't with her until after. She wasn't the reason I left."

"I'm not discussing this here." She folded her arms across her chest, and stared at the table.

"Ms. Masters, Mrs. Davidson has given us a full statement regarding her involvement and what happened that night. Whilst I can't tell you everything she said, I can tell you that they drugged you with a small amount of a Rohypnol derivative. Not enough to make you pass out straight away, but more than enough to make you amenable. She said she was acting on her husband's orders. And he had been instructed to gather evidence of an incriminating kind on you."

Morgan blinked rapidly. The date rape drug Dr. Bann had given her information about came flooding back to her. The reassurance that she hadn't been raped took a few seconds to settle in her brain. She took a deep breath and tried to calm her breathing. "So she drugged me to get me in a compromising position. Why?"

"She said her husband was acting under the orders of a third party. But all that was required was for them to get the photos. They drugged you because you were uninterested in Mrs. Davidson."

She turned to look at Erin, her face was flushed and her eyes wide, she felt vindicated, absolved of the sin she had never committed. The feelings of shame she had carried with her since seeing the picture of herself in another woman's arms lifted and she found herself wishing only for Erin to accept it, to look her in the eye and tell her that everything would be okay now. They could be together again, happy, in love. The shock still evident on Erin's face made it abundantly clear that wasn't going to happen. She choked down her disappointment and turned back to the two police officers.

"They had what they needed so why did he attack me?"

"Mrs. Davidson said that her husband is a very jealous man, prone to violence. We have had numerous call outs to their address from neighbors reporting disturbances." He left the rest unsaid. She understood the inference of domestic violence clearly and a tiny flicker of sympathy blossomed for the woman who had deceived her.

Ward cleared his throat. "Mr. Davidson was following his wife and attacked you when he saw you with her. You may recall Mr. Harper saying that we have Mrs. Davidson's statement, the CCTV footage of the attack, and we found clothes in his house with blood on it, and a small quantity of the drug too. We're waiting for the forensics team to confirm, but we believe the blood to be yours. With that, the CPS has more than enough evidence to try Mr. Davidson, with a very good chance of conviction."

"How did you finally catch them?"

The two officers glanced at each other before Lock spoke. "Mrs. Davidson came forward to make a statement implicating herself and her husband. She felt guilty. She said that Ms. Masters had been nice to her, treated her well while she worked for her, and she was very sorry that she had any part in this incident. She asked me to convey her deepest regret over everything that has happened to you, and she wishes you a complete recovery."

"Do you believe her?" Morgan swallowed the angry retort about it being too little too late and focused on more positive things. She knew from her own experiences and watching her mother that fear was a powerful motivator.

"Yes, I do." Lock met her gaze without compunction. "She is genuinely terrified of this guy. I think another reason she came forward is because prison will be a better place for her. She's already living in a prison with him." He shrugged. "One without him can only be a step in the right direction for her."

Morgan closed her eyes and allowed the wave of sympathy to wash over her. As drastic as it sounded, she knew he was right. In an official prison, she would be far safer than she had ever been as Jimmy Davidson's wife. She shook her head slowly. "I hope she gets the help she needs. What else do you need from me?"

"We don't need anything right now. We may need to speak to you in the future."

"Who were they working for?" Erin's voice was lightly hoarse and scratchy.

"Mrs. Davidson claims that she doesn't know, and Mr. Davidson has not yet revealed anything. Do you have any other questions?" Lock closed the file when they both shook their heads. "Thank you for coming in."

Morgan followed them through the building and into the car, as Erin drove in silence, her mind raced. So many questions had been answered for them all. So much doubt had been lifted from her mind. She hadn't been having an affair and she wasn't screwing someone else just weeks after leaving Erin. She had been targeted. Someone had set out to harm her, and her family. There was only one person she could think of who would do that.

CHAPTER TWENTY-NINE

Erin pulled up outside the house and held the door for Morgan as she struggled with her crutches before she opened the door to the house.

Chris was waiting. He kissed Erin's cheek and squeezed her shoulders. "You okay?"

She shrugged and walked past him into the house.

"Kettle's on. Maddie's in bed, and Tristan's chatting to his girlfriend. He was in a funny mood. Probably just back to school blues, but it might be an idea to have a chat with him later."

"I will. Thanks, Chris. I think I need something stronger than tea." She pulled the fridge open and grabbed a bottle of wine. She held it up to Chris in invitation.

"No, thanks. Hey, Morgan."

"Hi, Chris." Morgan hobbled into the kitchen and stood awkwardly by the table.

Erin poured a drink and stalked out to the conservatory. She sat on the window seat and stared out at the stars, blinking against the black curtain of the night sky. The wind had picked up and the tree branches shook and rattled against the glass roof, jarring her nerves further. Each mouthful of wine warmed her throat as she twirled the glass in her fingers.

"Penny for them?"

Erin startled as Chris pulled open the door, smiling slightly before he sat down.

"They're not worth that much."

"I beg to differ."

Erin rested her forehead against the cool glass and let the chill ease the pounding in her skull. "Did she tell you what happened?"

"Enough. She was drugged, she wasn't cheating on you, and they've got the people who attacked her. Do I need any more?"

Erin sighed. "I guess not."

"Do you?"

She turned to look at him and debated playing ignorant, but the look on his face told her she wouldn't get away with it. "I don't know. Every time I think I've got a handle on this whole situation it shifts and everything changes again."

"Like those kaleidoscopes you used to love when we were kids."

"This isn't a child's toy, Chris. This is my life, the kids' lives, we're talking about."

"I know that. What I don't know is what you want? And I don't think you do either."

"What are you talking about?"

"Correct me if I'm wrong here, but you wanted answers from her, correct?"

"Yes."

"You wanted to know why she left, if she was cheating, and whether or not she still loves you and the kids."

Erin laughed. "In a nutshell, huh?"

"Bullet points have always worked much better for you than long, protracted essays, baby sis." He grinned. "So, am I wrong?"

"No." She finished her drink and put the glass down.

"You have those answers now, don't you?"

Erin closed her eyes and let PC Lock's words play through her brain. Tricked, targeted, drugged, and left for dead. Morgan's only crime that night had been to trust someone she thought of as a colleague. There was no question in her mind that Morgan had been faithful to her, but the fact that she'd doubted her at all had guilt knotted in her stomach. The love in Morgan's eyes whenever she looked at Tristan and Maddie burned with an intensity that she had never seen before. She watched them constantly, and Erin could see her trying to commit every single thing to memory, and she accepted that her misgivings of letting Morgan back into their lives were unfounded.

Still, she distrusted Morgan. Her reason for leaving, while obviously valid to her, made Erin question the very foundation of the relationship they'd had. All Morgan needed to do was talk to her, to show her the letter, tell her what had happened with her father, and they could have dealt with it all. Instead, she had walked away and left Erin to question everything she had believed in. What was it that was so fundamentally wrong in their relationship that Morgan couldn't talk to her? Was she so unapproachable? Did Morgan really love her? Was it a convenient excuse? It seemed the more she learned, the less she knew.

"Want to try that one question at a time?" Chris smiled gently, his eyes filled with compassion.

"It won't make a difference."

"Do you believe she cheated on you?"

"No. She was clearly duped and then drugged. She was targeted by someone who the police have yet to identify."

"Progress. Do you believe she loves the kids?"

Erin smiled. "With all her heart."

"You know why she felt she had to leave?"

Erin felt the smile melt from her face and a frown tightened her brow. "I know her reason, but I don't understand why she couldn't talk to me."

Chris chuckled.

Erin glared at him. "It's not funny."

"No, it's not. It's actually pretty sad. How could you expect Morgan to talk to you about these things when you kept secrets from her too? You both came to an agreement, of sorts, in your relationship that incidents from the past stayed there. And now you don't understand why she couldn't talk to you about it?"

"But this was affecting our current lives, not just the past."

"So?"

"So our relationship was fucked up!"

"No, it wasn't. But you didn't have great communication with this kind of stuff. You wanted to leave your pain in the past, and Morgan obviously did too. I'm not saying it was right or wrong. It worked for you both for a very long time, and there was no real way for her to know that it was ever going to come back and bite you all. Plenty of people make threats like her father did and nothing ever comes of it. You know what they say about hindsight."

"Doesn't stop it hurting now, Chris." The tears were warm on her cheeks as she buried her face in her hands. She felt Chris's arms wrap around her as he rocked her gently and she let go, allowing the sobs to wrack her body. She knew Chris was right. They had each closed off parts of themselves to the other and contributed to the destruction of their relationship. They had both slowly allowed life to get in the way of their love, and she felt a fool for not seeing the cracks that had been steadily growing.

The little things that had slowly faded away when children got demanding and jobs took priority over them. The little text messages through the day, just to say I love you faded to nothing. The cuddle in front of the TV when the children went to bed, just to feel close, gave way to laundry, dishes, school lunches, and PE kits. And making love, while still good, had dwindled, sleep a more immediate concern.

"We let it fall apart."

Chris stroked her back. "It's not gone, Erin." He pulled back and wiped her cheeks and looked into her eyes. "Do you still love her?"

"Yes."

"Then please give me a chance." They both turned to see Morgan standing in the doorway, her grip on her crutches so tight her knuckles had turned white. She hobbled forward and slowly dropped to one knee in front of Erin, her braced leg stuck awkwardly out to the side. "I made terrible mistakes, Erin. I hurt you so much, and I will never be able to tell you how sorry I am for it all. But I do love you. Every second I spend with you makes me love you even more. I want to be everything for you. Everything I was before and more." She took hold of Erin's hand. "Please give me a chance to love you."

Erin tried to speak, but her mouth had gone dry. Chris left the room, closing the door with a soft click.

"Please, Erin. Please give me a chance."

Morgan's eyes implored her, and Erin wanted to give in. She wanted Morgan's arms around her never letting go. She saw nothing in those dark depths but sincerity, love, and hope, but she still couldn't let go.

"I don't know if I can trust you."

Tears welled in Morgan's eyes, but she didn't move. "Why not?"

"You hurt me."

"I know and I'm so sorry for that. So sorry. I'm asking for a chance to make it up to you. To put it all right again."

"Morgan, it's not as simple as that."

"It can be. Just give me a chance." She leaned forward and kissed her.

Erin closed her eyes, letting the tears fall as Morgan cradled her face in her hands and claimed her lips, her tongue flicking and sliding across Erin's lower lip. Erin moaned and let her in. She was helpless as Morgan pulled her closer, her fingers threading into her hair. All she wanted was to feel Morgan's hands driving away the nagging ache of her loneliness, to bring to life things she felt were dead inside. Her body responded to Morgan's touch, even as her brain demanded she pull away. Her body and mind fought a battle, and her heart was the trophy they both sought.

Morgan eased away from Erin's lips, kissed her gently on the forehead, and wiped at her tears with her thumbs.

"I love you." She kissed her lips again chastely. "Don't ever forget that. Don't ever doubt it. There will never be anyone else for me."

"Morgan, I don't—"

Morgan placed her fingers to Erin's lips. "Think about it. As long as you need. As slow as you want. Whenever you're ready. I'll be waiting." Morgan kissed her hand before struggling to her feet and leaving the room.

Erin picked up her glass. "Shit." She got up slowly and poured herself another drink. The stairs creaked as she climbed them, and she paused to look at some of the pictures. Their wedding picture caught her eye and she ran her finger over the glass. They were so happy then, the four of them. Could they have that again? Could it even be better?

She crawled under the covers and pulled an old T-shirt from under the pillow. Holding it to her face, she breathed in the scent of Morgan. Could it be better? *Maybe.*

CHAPTER THIRTY

The phone's shrill ring startled Morgan as she sketched. She reached for it, cursing as she smeared charcoal across her face.

"Hello."

"Hello, I'm calling from Marple Hall School. Can I speak to Ms. Masters?"

"I'm Tristan's mum, Morgan Masters. Is he all right?"

"Oh, well that's what we're calling about. I'm afraid he isn't in school. He attended on Monday, but hasn't been in for the past two days, and we haven't heard anything. I take it you didn't know he wasn't attending?"

Shit. "He left this morning in his school uniform, as normal."

"Ah. I think we need to discuss this unauthorized absence."

"It's unlikely that I'll find him right now, unless you can direct me specifically. I'm afraid I'm on crutches."

"Well, there are a number of places that the boys tend to go when they are truanting. But I suspect he'll arrive home as usual this afternoon. The head teacher would like to see you and Tristan. Would tomorrow be okay?"

Morgan quickly checked the calendar, grateful that Erin was due to work a late shift so she'd be able to come too. "First thing?"

"I'll make the appointment for you for eight thirty."

"Has Tristan had other unauthorized absences?"

"Tristan's attendance record has been very good prior to this."

"Thank you. I guess I'll see you in the morning."

She hung up and checked the clock. Erin was due home in the next half hour. She hoped Tristan was at least somewhere safe, since he wasn't at school. She sighed; figuring his change in behavior probably had to do with the chaos she had brought into their lives.

She tidied her sketchbook and charcoal away, then hobbled to the kitchen to wash up, setting the kettle to boil as she passed. She'd just finished making the tea when the door opened and Erin bustled in, dropped her bag on the table, and slung her coat over the back of the chair.

"Hi." She took the mug, sipped, and sighed appreciatively. "Bless you, I needed that." She took the other mug and placed it on the table. "How's the knee feeling today?"

"Aches, but it's fine." She sat down and propped the crutches against the back of the chair. "I had a call from Tristan's school a little while ago."

Erin set her tea down. "Is he sick? Do I need to go get him?"

"No. They rang to see if he was at home ill. He's ditching. Evidently, he ditched yesterday too."

"What? Why?"

"I don't know. Maybe it's stuff with me, but I thought we'd made progress on all that. I thought he was okay. The headmaster wants to see us in the morning."

"Yeah." Erin glanced at the calendar.

"I checked. You're on a late, so it's fine."

"Right, thanks." Erin frowned and chewed her lip.

Morgan grasped her hand and squeezed gently. "It'll be okay. It's been a tough time for him. I'm sure there's nothing to worry about."

"He could be anywhere. He could be hurt."

"If he was in the hospital or in trouble, someone would contact us. The police, hospital staff. Someone. I mean, how long did it take them to get in touch when they found me?"

"Not long."

"He'll be fine."

"I hope so. Then when he gets home, I can kill him."

Erin's stared into space, seemingly unaware that she was stroking the back of Morgan's knuckles with her thumb. Her natural physical action restored some of Morgan's hope that there was a future for them.

Erin finished her drink and stood, still holding Morgan's hand. She ran her fingers across Morgan's shoulder and kissed the top of her head. She froze and stepped away.

"Oh my God. I'm sorry. I wasn't thinking. Habit, or something…"

"Please don't apologize." Morgan stumbled to her feet and hopped to stand beside her. "I want you to touch me. I want to touch you. All the time."

"Morgan, we talked about this—"

"Have we? Really? Because all I remember is you being scared. I know I made mistakes, and I got it all so wrong. But I was trying to do the best for ever—"

"I know that. We really don't have to go over it all again. But that doesn't change the fact that you hurt me."

"And that's unforgivable? Whether I'm old Morgan or new Morgan makes no difference, does it? Have we never hurt each other before? Surely, we fought, argued, and screamed at each other in the past? Fifteen years, Erin, you can't tell me that we never hurt each other before?"

"What is it you want, Morgan?"

"You." Morgan pulled her close and kissed her. "Like I told you last night, I love you. I want you. I want our family, together, whole, and happy." She ran her fingers along Erin's jaw. "I need you." Erin's pupils dilated and her lips parted.

Morgan leaned in and claimed her mouth. She let loose the passion that had built inside her since she had opened her eyes and watched Erin sleep, curled in a hospital chair. She acted on instinct, holding Erin's face between her hands as she nibbled on her lips, before soothing each nip with the gentle caress of her tongue. She explored every millimeter of Erin's mouth, reveling in the taste of her, and relishing the tiny sighs and gasps that escaped her. She felt goose bumps erupt on Erin's neck as she drew her index finger down her cheek, along her jaw, and down the long column of her throat.

The silken flesh beneath her fingertip burned her skin even as Erin shivered against her body. And Morgan wanted more. She wanted all of her, and she wanted Erin to want that too.

She pulled back from the kiss, smiling when Erin whimpered, missing the intimate contact already. Her lips barely an inch from Erin's, she whispered, "We'll take this as slow as you need to, you have my word. But please, please give me a chance to love you." Morgan didn't care if she had to beg. Whatever Erin wanted, all she had to do was ask. "Erin, I love you."

"Don't hurt me." Erin's eyes sparkled with unshed tears.

"Never again."

Erin closed her eyes and threaded her fingers through Morgan's hair and tugged, closing the scant distance between them. The ferocious passion of Erin's kiss stole her breath; she felt her knees go weak and wrapped her arms around her shoulders to steady herself. Her lips burned with the fires of possession as Erin claimed her, branding her to the very core of her soul.

The telephone rang, pulling them both from the lingering kisses. They were both breathless, desire darkened Erin's eyes, her hair mussed from Morgan's fingers, her cheeks flushed, and Morgan knew she looked very much the same. The smile that spread across Erin's face stunned her. It was the first she'd seen that truly reached her eyes, making them sparkle and flash like sapphires held up to the light.

"I need to get that. It might be about that boy of ours."

Morgan nodded and watched her walk away, hips swaying, teasing, and promising with every step she took.

Oh fuck! Morgan froze. *I don't remember doing it before!*

Okay, breathe. Morgan dropped into the chair. *She's going to expect someone who knows what they're doing. She's going to expect the...lover...that you were.* She pulled the phone from her pocket and selected the message icon. She squinted at the small screen as she located Nikki's number and started typing.

Morgan: Need help!

Nikki's reply took thirty agonizing seconds, and Morgan drummed her fingers on the table, her eyes glued to the screen.

Nikki: What's the problem?

Morgan: I'm a virgin!

Nikki: RAOTFLMFAO

Morgan: What the fuck does that mean?

Nikki: Rolling around on the floor laughing my fucking ass off

Morgan: Thanks. Bitch

Nikki: So what do you want me to do about it? Amy'll kill us both if you even suggest I fix this problem for you.

Morgan: Ew. I just threw up a little. I need advice. Is there a manual I can read?

Nikki: What? Lesbian sex for Dummies? Lol!

Morgan: Lol? I don't know what that means either. Please speak English for dummies!

Nikki: Okay, spoil sport. Erin has quite a little library of lesbian romance novels. They're upstairs in her bedroom.

Morgan: How do YOU know this?

Nikki: Keep your hair on. She and Amy do swaps.

Morgan: Oh. Right.

Nikki: Your mission, should you choose to accept, is to study these guides. They will become your bible.

Morgan: I accept the mission.

Nikki: This message will self destruct in five...four...

Morgan: Right. Thanks.

Upstairs. In Erin's bedroom. She glanced at her crutches then at the ceiling. *Wonderful.*

CHAPTER THIRTY-ONE

Morgan slid her phone back into her pocket, and smiled as Erin came back into the kitchen. "Everything okay?"

"Yeah." Erin eased into her seat. "It was Chris. Apparently, Mum's not very well and needs to go to the doctor. He has appointments all afternoon, so he was phoning to see if I could take her."

"Is she all right?"

"Yeah, probably just a cold or something, you know what she's like—sorry." Erin grimaced.

"It's okay."

"I'm not trying to be insensitive or anything—"

"I know." She reached over to Erin's hand and ran her finger over her ring. "We'll get there again. But right now, I've never met your mother."

"Oh God. We have to go through all that again!"

Morgan laughed. "Was it bad?"

Erin groaned and dropped her head to the table. She felt Morgan's fingers brushing through her hair, sweeping it away from Erin's face. She shifted until her cheek rested on the back of Morgan's hand, and she smiled under Morgan's caress.

"Is this okay?" Morgan's voice was husky.

"Yes." Erin cleared her throat as Morgan's fingers worked through the long strands. Their gazes locked. "I'd never seen you so nervous. We'd been friends for quite a while before we got together. You knew that, right?" She raised her eyebrow.

"Yeah, Nikki and Amy told me a little bit."

"Hm, did they mention the stalking?" Erin laughed as Morgan blushed. "I'll take that as a yes. Well, you seemed to have some sort of phobia about meeting my mum. I suppose given what we now know about your parents, it's not much of a surprise, but it was bloody infuriating for me." She sighed and shifted a little closer to Morgan. "You came round one day when she was out."

"You were still living at home?"

"Yeah, I was only twenty-one then. I stayed at home while I went to uni. It was cheaper, and we were close to campus."

"True. What did you do at uni?"

"Mathematics and physics.

Morgan whistled. "No wonder you looked at me funny when I said I'd help Maddie with her math homework." Erin relaxed further under Morgan's ministrations.

"Yeah, sorry about that." She smiled sheepishly. "It's usually my job, and it was pretty strange to see you doing it."

"Why'd you go into air traffic control?" Morgan's curiosity was evident in the broad smile and her rapt attention.

"Long story. We'll get to that another time. I was telling you about my mum."

"Oh, yeah. So, me phobic, you living at home. Got it."

"Yes. You were picking me up. Said you had a whole day out planned, but I wasn't ready. You were sitting in the front room while I changed, and Mum came in. It was a Saturday, and she'd been shopping. She practically dragged you out to carry in bags of food. She loaded you up with all the tins and the heavy stuff, then made you sit in the kitchen. When I came down, you were as white as a sheet and looked as if you'd been tortured."

"Was she giving me the third degree?"

"I asked her later. She said she only asked what your name was, and she thought you were going to hyperventilate or something. So no, it wasn't that bad, but it was very difficult for you."

"Hopefully, I'll be better this time round."

Erin caught her hand, pulled it to her lips, and kissed her fingertips. "Hopefully, everything will be."

"What did I have planned for us?"

"That afternoon? You took me on a picnic."

"Really? Where?"

"To the duck pond where you saw the kids. You always loved it there. It's one of the reasons we moved here."

"It's a lovely house. When did we move here?"

"About ten years ago now. I had better go. Mum doesn't like to leave the house. I think it's some sort of agoraphobia that's developed over the past few years. It's hell to get her outside. I'll pick Maddie up from school after I drop Mum home. Tristan's supposed to be at basketball practice this evening, but he's not going after this mess at school. I should be back before he's due in, if not—"

"I'll tell him practice is a no go."

"You sure you're okay with that?"

"I'm his mum too. You don't have to be the bad guy all the time."

"Okay, gotta go." She stood, and Morgan kept hold of her hand. "I love you."

Erin put her fingers over Morgan's lips. "I know. And I still love you too, but I need to take this a little slowly. Okay? I need a little time to adjust."

"I understand. You let me know what you want—what you need from me, and I'll do it."

Erin smiled. "I know that too." She bent down and kissed her.

The kiss was sweet, and chaste, and over far too quickly.

❖

Time. I can do that. Time for research.

Morgan grabbed her crutches and struggled with the stairs, banging the crutches against each stair, and the walls, and even her foot. She gave up and crawled up on her hands, one knee, and shuffling up on her backside, dragging her crutches along with her. She was out of breath and sweating when she reached the top. The door to her left had a picture of Scooby-Doo, with pink glitter spots added to his neck and collar. *That has to be Maddie's room.* The bathroom door was open, and the one next to it was ajar. A black sock was part way across the threshold, like a wounded soldier trying to crawl for freedom. *Not that one either.* She slowly pushed open the door to Erin's room—their room.

Three walls had been painted a soft cream color and the fourth was a rich purple. The furniture was in chunky solid pine, with matching wardrobes, drawers, and dresser spread throughout the large room. A TV sat in the middle of a bookshelf, but the power cable lay coiled around the base of it. The rest of the shelves were filled with books. She hobbled over and started looking at titles. *Oh. My. God. There are so many. How am I supposed to find a manual in this lot?*

She pulled out her phone.

Morgan: There are hundreds here. Which one do I use?

Nikki: I don't know, read the blurbs on the back

Morgan: I'm not kidding, there are HUNDREDS. Ask Amy

Nikki: Amy says do you want a romantic story or a sexual how to guide?

Morgan: What does Erin like?

Nikki: Amy says it depends what mood she's in.

"Great, loads of help there, Nikki, thanks."

Morgan: Which one does she think is hot?

Nikki: Amy says that Erin has a few favorites, but they were all about the characters and not really about the smokin' hot sex scenes.

The phone buzzed in her hand making her jump before she could answer it.

"Hello."

"I swear you two are like kids." Amy tutted at her. "Are you in the bedroom looking at the shelf with the TV on it?"

"Yes."

"Would you like my help?"

"Yes."

"Then you need to answer three questions."

"What?" She could hear the laughter in Amy's voice and knew she was in trouble.

"No, I'm asking the questions. First, does this research trip mean that you and Erin are back together?"

"Maybe? I don't know. She wants to take it slow, but we kissed and she said she needed some time. So I think, maybe."

"I get the picture. So why do you need to raid her romance novels?"

"I—I don't remember—I hadn't been with—my memory starts before—"

"Oh, bless you. You've never had sex. Well, you have. Oh, that's so sweet. Nikki, stop laughing. So what do you remember?"

"Well, kissing."

"Yes, and?"

"And, that's it really."

"Just kissing?"

"Yeah."

"Oh, kiddo, you were so innocent. Nikki, get off the floor and behave yourself. Jesus, you're worse than a baby! So you need a guide to the birds and the bees of lesbian sex."

"No, I understand the—the principles. But Erin's going to remember what it was like before. She's going to expect me to know what to do. And I get the idea of what goes where and stuff, but, like, what do I do when I get there?"

"Well, I'd probably suggest asking Erin."

"I can't do that!" Morgan felt her face flush at the thought of asking Erin for intimate instructions.

"Why not?"

"Well, shouldn't I know this stuff? I'm going to look like an idiot."

"Morgan, Erin won't think you're an idiot for asking what will give her pleasure. I can guarantee that."

"Won't she think—I don't know. It's humiliating. I feel so… inept."

"Morgan, if I were in Erin's position, I'd think it was wonderful."

"Why?"

"Well, she'll be the only lover you know, and that makes it incredibly special."

"But what if I can't…you know?" Morgan waved her hands. *Idiot she can't see your hands.*

"What?"

"Make her…you know?" Morgan waved again, catching herself. *I'm losing it.*

"Orgasm?"

Morgan blushed. "Yeah."

"Morgan, you're almost forty years old."

Morgan could practically see Amy shaking her head. "I'm trying, Amy."

"I know. Look, Erin is a wonderful woman. You need to talk to her about your concerns. She'll help you, advise, teach, whatever. That really is the best way."

"So I shouldn't read any of these?"

"Oh, I wouldn't say that." Amy gave her a list of five titles to get her started and instructions to let her know if she needed any more help in the future.

Morgan found that going down the stairs on her crutches was much easier than climbing them and was almost at the bottom when Tristan breezed in, dumping his school bag and coat on a chair.

Show time.

"Hi." Her shoulders tensed as she hobbled into the kitchen behind him.

He ignored her and pulled open the fridge.

She took a deep breath. "I got a call from your school today."

He paused, shrugged, and pulled out a can of pop.

She'd spent enough time with him now to recognize that this wasn't his usual sullen silence. "They said you were absent and wanted to know if you were ill."

He continued to ignore her, sat at the table, and popped the can open.

Come on, Trist, at least grunt at me. "Where were you?"

He took a drink.

"Tristan, I asked you a question."

"And I don't want to talk to you." He slammed the can onto the table as he pushed his chair back. The table wobbled and the can tipped over, spewing its contents all over the wooden surface.

"Tough. Now sit down, and tell me where you've been."

He stared at her, defiance burned in his eyes, and his arms folded across his chest. They stood staring at each other, even as the door opened and soft voices whispered in the hallway. Heavy footsteps pounded up the stairs. Morgan felt Erin's hand at the small of her back, offering comfort, strength, a united front.

He glared at them both before dropping back onto his chair. Erin got a cloth and wiped up the mess. Morgan sat opposite him, her leg jumping with nervous energy.

"So where have you been all day?" Morgan tried again, watching him as he sulked.

"None of your business," Tristan mumbled, his chin barely moving from his chest.

"Tristan, enough!" Erin tossed the cloth into the sink and turned back to them. "Your mum asked you a question. Now answer her."

Tristan stared at Erin, eyes blazing with righteous anger. "I don't want to talk to her."

"Why not? I thought we'd gotten past this. I thought you were coming to grips with everything."

"It's got nothing—it's not about that."

"Then what?"

He looked away from Erin and glared at Morgan. His lips were pulled into a tight line, his jaw set, and the obstinate set of his shoulders so intractable that Morgan couldn't see any way forward. *What have I done?*

"Go to your room, Tristan. You can stay there until you're ready to talk to us." Erin pointed to the stairs. "No basketball, no TV, no phone, and no computer."

His eyes widened, and he looked as if he was ready to surrender, then he glanced at Morgan again, squared his shoulders, and stalked out of the room.

"I don't understand, what did I do?" Morgan wanted to cry. She felt as though all the progress she'd made with Tristan was crumbling.

"I haven't a clue. What did he say?"

"Just that he didn't want to talk to me. Then you came in."

"I'll go and talk to him. See if he'll tell me what's going on. Are you okay?" Erin touched her shoulder, rubbing small circles with her fingers.

"I don't know. Are you?"

Erin nodded. "Yes. He'll be okay, you know. He'll probably calm down and apologize before the night's out."

"Yeah."

Erin squeezed her shoulder before she left.

I hope you're right.

CHAPTER THIRTY-TWO

The ticking clock marked the passage of time, one second after the other, with its impudent click and thud echoing off the walls. Morgan's denim clad leg bounced. The three of them sat side by side outside the headmaster's office, Erin in the middle, Tristan still refusing to talk to her. She plucked at the sleeves of her leather jacket, then glanced to her left, her gaze fixed on Erin's crossed legs where her pale gray skirt rode up her thigh. The slender expanse of flesh hypnotized her, and the energy dissipated. She imagined running her fingers over the smooth skin and watching goose bumps erupt beneath her fingertips. She licked her lips, her eyes never wavering.

"Stop staring."

Erin's voice was close to her ear and low enough so only she could hear. She knew she was blushing as she looked up and met Erin's amused smile.

"Sorry." She grimaced, embarrassed to be caught, and let her head drop to her chest, unconsciously mirroring the posture Tristan had adopted the minute they sat down. He'd refused to talk to Erin at all the night before, so they'd left him alone.

"Hey." Erin scratched lightly at the side of her leg until she raised her head again. "I don't really mind, as long as you don't drool." Her lips parted in a slow, sexy smile that made Morgan's heart beat a little faster. The soft baby blue silk blouse made her eyes stand out as she winked.

"Mr. Parish will see you now." The secretary inclined her head toward the door, barely flicking her eyes away from the computer screen in front of her.

Mr. Parish was a short man, much younger than Morgan had expected, around his early forties, with sandy colored hair, green eyes, and a small paunch. He held his hand out to shake both of theirs before pointing to a seating area away from his desk.

"Mss. Masters, it's good to see you both again. I wish it were under different circumstances, but I'm sure we can get this sorted out."

"Mr. Parish," Erin said, "How long has Tristan been truanting?"

He frowned, casting a quick look at Tristan's sullen pose. "In his first two years at Marple Hall, his attendance has been exemplary. The new school year is less than a week old, but already Tristan has missed two full days." He flipped open a document file and pulled out an attendance record. "He was in Monday, but this is the first time we've seen him since then."

Erin turned her head to Tristan. "Why?"

Tristan shrugged and tried to burrow his chin further into his chest. His tie was askew and his blazer looked as if it had spent the night stuffed in his bag. Morgan wanted to wrap her arms around him and make whatever hurt him disappear. She wanted to recapture the look on his face when he had laughed at her cartwheeling down the ski slope, the gentle look of concern hiding his amusement.

"Sometimes…" Mr. Parish cleared his throat. "In cases like this, there is something worrying the young person. This is new behavior for Tristan. We would expect that there is a trigger of some sort. Can I ask how you hurt your leg, Ms. Masters?"

Morgan blinked. "I fell when we went to the indoor ski slope. It wasn't a particularly bad fall. I've just torn the ligament in my knee. I'll be fine—"

Tristan snorted.

They all stared at him.

"Tristan," Mr. Parish said, "Do you have something to say?"

He shrugged.

The tension and frustration in the room mounted. The air felt brittle, as if one wrong move would shatter it, piercing them with the shrapnel of exploded expectations.

"I think I can safely say that we all want what's best for you, Tristan." Mr. Parish continued, as Morgan and Erin both nodded. "We want to help you, but you have to tell us what the problem is before we can do that. Is it something at school?"

"No." Tristan's voice was little more than a mumble crawling from his chest.

"At home then?"

He shrugged.

It is me. Something I've done. Morgan swallowed her mortification., "I was attacked at the beginning of the summer. I suffered a head injury that has left me with amnesia. I'm afraid that I have no recollection of either of the children from before it happened." She watched Tristan as she spoke, looking for a reaction to confirm the amnesia was the problem. His sullen expression flickered and mutated, before it dissolved into rage.

"I don't care about that!"

"Tristan." Erin grabbed his arm and turned him toward her. "I thought we'd talked about all this. You said you understood that it wasn't your mum's fault, and you could work to get past all this with her. I know it's hard—"

"I told you, I don't care about that. It's got nothing to do with it. She's a liar!"

"A liar? About what?" Erin frowned, her confusion clear. Tristan closed his mouth, pulling his lips into a tight, thin line. He tugged his arm from Erin's hand and turned as far away from them as he could.

What the hell does he think I'm lying about? Morgan had been as honest as possible from the second she met them. As painful as those truths had been at times, she had known there was no other way forward if she wanted to be a part of their lives.

"Tristan, do you think she's lying about the amnesia? Is that what this is about?" Erin tried again, touching his shoulder gently.

Is it? Morgan's mind whirled, spinning, trying to grasp something solid.

He sat with his back to them, his shoulders pulled forward.

"If that's what you think, then you're going to have to trust me, Trist. The doctors have seen the brain scans. The damage is there. She isn't lying about it." Erin rubbed his shoulder again. "I believe her. So if you can't trust her yet, trust me, okay?"

He twisted his shoulders, shaking off her hands.

That's it, he doesn't trust me. Morgan could see it in every line of his body.

"Tristan, she isn't lying to you."

"Yes, she is." He turned back to look at her. "We can't trust her."

"Why not?"

Tristan shrugged and dropped her gaze.

"You can't just say something like that and not explain. You have to tell me what you think your mum's lying about."

He sat back in his chair again.

"Tristan, tell me." Erin's voice was getting louder, her mounting frustration more than evident.

Morgan looked at Mr. Parish. He had his hands clasped on the desk, staring at his hands as Erin continued to try to get Tristan to talk.

"Why won't you talk to me? I don't understand."

He looked out the window.

Erin blew out a frustrated breath and cast her eyes to the ceiling. Morgan reached for her hand, offering her support.

Mr. Parish said, "Tristan should work out of my office today. We have a zero tolerance policy here, and until he's caught up with his work, I'm putting him on academic suspension, especially since we don't know the reason behind his truancy. Once he's up to speed he can rejoin his classmates. Break and lunchtime will be held in detention for the next week. Do you understand, Tristan?"

Tristan didn't move.

Oh, Tristan, what have I done? Morgan finally looked away, her heart breaking as Mr. Parish lifted his hand toward the door and led them out of the room. Morgan hobbled behind him, Erin following.

Erin turned as soon as the door closed behind them. "Mr. Parish, I'm sorry. I don't know what's gotten into him."

"Please, Ms. Masters, there's no need. Clearly, this has been very difficult for you all, and Tristan is having a hard time adjusting. It's not unusual for boys his age to find it difficult to talk to his parents, especially when they have a lot to deal with too. I plan to keep him in my office for his academic suspension. I'm hoping if he stays with me today, he might open up a bit. Maybe once he starts talking we can get to the bottom of all this and help him."

"What can we do?" Morgan's voice sounded strange in her own ears, like she was listening to it underwater.

"Let him talk when he's ready. I don't think pushing him right now will do any good. He's a good boy. He's trying to deal with something that's difficult for us as adults to deal with. As a teenager, trying to understand that your mum doesn't remember you must be incredibly difficult."

"No, that's not it." It didn't feel right. Morgan knew it was difficult; she knew they had all struggled with her memory loss. But she knew they had been making progress. She knew Tristan was working toward rebuilding their relationship. This huge step backward didn't make sense without some other influence. "There's something else going on with Tristan."

"Like what?"

"I don't know. Something is making him not trust me. Even though the amnesia was difficult and painful, he still trusted me. Something's happened to change that." She could see that he was skeptical. The pinched look on his face convinced her of that.

"Perhaps, but until he talks to us, we won't know either way. Let's just hope he opens up quickly." Mr. Parish shook their hands and went back to his office.

Morgan nodded, shook his hand, and followed Erin out to the car. She glanced up at the headmaster's office window and saw Tristan staring at them. His gaze was fixed on Erin, a worried look on his face. When he looked at Morgan, the venom in his eyes took her breath away.

CHAPTER THIRTY-THREE

The silence in the car was oppressive. Like a boa constrictor, confusion tightened around Morgan, devouring her. She paid no attention to the streets they passed through, and their arrival home startled her. She followed Erin inside, stumbled into the front room and onto the sofa, propped her crutches next to her, and closed her eyes for a moment.

"Are you okay?" Erin finally broke the silence.

"Bit dizzy. It'll pass."

"Good, but I meant about Tristan."

She peeled open one eye and looked up at Erin. "I don't understand what happened. I thought we were getting there." She shook her head. "No, I know we were making progress. He was really trying. There has to be something that's changed."

Erin sat beside her. "Maybe…" Her voice drifted away as she twisted her ring around her finger.

"Maybe what?" Morgan reached for her hand, enjoying the warmth against her palm.

"Do you think he could have found out about her?"

"About who?"

Erin sighed heavily. "Her. Anna Davidson."

Morgan stared at her. It made sense. Would he assume that she had been having an affair, as Erin had? Would he assume that this was the reason for her leaving and his anger was about that, rather than the amnesia? In his place, she wouldn't know whether to trust her either. If it was true, one question remained. "But how could he have found out?"

Erin shrugged. "Maybe he overheard something with the police. I don't know. I can't remember what they said when they were here. Maybe he overheard us talking."

Erin squeezed her fingers before she turned her hand over and entwined their fingers. A wave of relief coursed through Morgan. She'd been so afraid that Erin would pull away from her at the mention of Anna's name.

"So what do we do? Try to explain to him what happened?"

Erin laughed softly, as she haphazardly stroked the back of Morgan's knuckles. "How? You don't know what happened to explain."

"Well, no, but we can tell him what the police told us."

Erin kicked off her shoes and tucked her feet underneath her, leaning against Morgan's shoulder. "I'm not sure that will help. We're only guessing after all. If we're wrong, and he doesn't know about her, do you really want to tell him, and make things even worse?"

"Oh, God, no. This is a minefield." Erin's hair tickled her cheek and the scent of apples and honey was a tantalizing distraction.

Erin turned her head until she could look into her eyes. "This is a family."

Morgan turned her head and whispered, "Our family?" Their lips were millimeters apart, so close they were breathing the same air.

"Yes, it is."

The first touch of their lips was as soft as a whisper, a fleeting promise with the heat of passion simmering beneath the surface. Erin twisted into a better position and slid her fingers into Morgan's hair.

"You need a haircut."

"Do I?"

"Mmm." She tugged Morgan's head closer, nipping at her bottom lip before flicking her tongue to soothe any hurt she may have caused. Morgan couldn't have stopped herself from moaning even if she'd wanted to.

Morgan rested her hand at Erin's waist, but the need to explore, to touch, was too great. She let her hands wander, seemingly of their own accord, and examine the long plane of Erin's back, the curve of her neck, and the tiny curls at the base of her skull. Their mouths came together again in a fiery kiss. Their tongues danced, teased, and retreated as Morgan panted and desire saturated her blood.

Erin's fingers scratched at her scalp, her breasts pressed against her side, her tight nipples straining through the thin silk blouse. She loved it. Morgan wanted to touch them, to reach out and run her thumb over the raised bump, hoping she'd hear Erin moan as she did so. Her own insecurity stopped her from trying.

She eased away from Erin's mouth, but missed the taste and feel of her so quickly, she had to go back for more. Tiny kisses, gentle touches, like the wings of a butterfly caressed her lips.

Erin smiled without opening her eyes. "I've missed you."

Morgan wanted to be able to say the same in return, but it wasn't true. What she felt was different.

Erin put her fingers over her lips. "I know. I just wanted you to know that." She leaned in and kissed her again, deep and possessive.

Morgan's insides had turned molten; her blood was a raging fire of desire flowing like lava through her veins. Erin's lips skimmed her jaw and down her throat, and Morgan slid her hand down to her backside.

Erin murmured against her neck. "There's some other stuff we need to think about."

"Now? You want to talk now?" She felt Erin nod against her throat. "Then I need to be able to think." She dragged her hand off Erin's arse and eased her body away. "Okay, what do you want to talk about?"

"Well, what you want to do."

"You mean for a job?" *Seriously?* "You want to talk about jobs now?" Morgan took a deep breath and willed her pulse to slow down. *How can she think about jobs? I feel like I'm ready to explode.*

Erin's cheeks were flushed and her eyes were dark, her desire evident. "Yes. Do you want to talk to the university about retraining to teach? They'll probably need to talk to you first, since it's unusual circumstances."

"I actually wanted to see if I could make a go at being an artist. I sort of made this promise to myself."

Erin untangled herself and moved to the far end of the sofa, shifting until her feet were resting in Morgan's lap. "What was this promise about then?"

Morgan frowned, feeling bereft of the comforting, maddening weight of Erin leaning against her. "Why have you gone over there?"

Erin's smile was slow and devastatingly sexy. Her blouse was rumpled, and pulled tight over her breasts. Her nipples were clearly visible beneath the thin material. "Because we really do need to talk about some things, and all I want to do is make love to you."

The words struck her with the force of a bullet to the chest. Instantly, she was exhilarated and petrified and her fear of not remembering how to please Erin perfectly balanced with her desire to try. "You do?" Her voice was a squeak that she barely recognized. *I sound like a teenage boy!*

Erin wiggled her toes against Morgan's thigh, and smiled when Morgan started to massage her feet. "Yes. But right now, tell me about this promise."

"I decided that I should never give up on my dreams. I have three."

"Three dreams?" Erin licked her lips and reached up to pull her ponytail out. She slowly combed her fingers through her long, soft curls, and they coiled in gentle waves about her shoulders.

Morgan nodded, unable to stop staring as Erin's blouse inched up her belly exposing her creamy skin and the shallow indentation of her navel. *I feel like I'm being seduced.*

"Tell me." Erin's voice was deeper than usual, and Morgan wondered how she would sound in the throes of passion. Would she call her name in deep, sensuous tones? Or would her voice hit a higher pitch, all breathless and cracking?

Morgan cleared her throat, determined to follow wherever Erin would lead them. "One, was to be the best mother I can be, for our children. And I will be. We'll figure this thing out with Tristan, and I'll do whatever he needs. We can go to counseling, or therapy, or something. Whatever it takes."

"Why is that a dream? It sounds more like a plan to me." Erin stretched her arm along the back of the sofa, and the top button of her blouse slipped open. A stunning expanse of cleavage peeked out from between the folds of fabric.

She's doing it on purpose. Morgan swallowed, throbbing inside her jeans. "Because it's my dream that they let me be their mum again. Better than before."

"And the next dream?"

She pressed her fingers into the pads of Erin's feet. *Two can play this game. I think.* She teased her fingernail down the length of Erin's sole, thrilled when she squirmed in her seat but didn't pull her foot away. "To make a living out of being an artist. Somehow. I might need to train in something, but I want to be creative with it. I want to draw, and paint, and see the pictures come alive under my hands. But I have to be realistic too; I have a family to support."

Erin laughed gently.

"What?"

"I was promoted to senior controller about six months ago. I make more than enough to support us if you want to work on building your reputation as an artist."

"Really? How much do you make?"

Erin shrugged, a playful smile tugging at the corners of her mouth. "A lot."

"Come on, tell me." She slipped her hands around Erin's ankle, working her fingers into the muscle of her calf, stroking from the tips of her toes, slowly all the way up to the back of her knee. Morgan smiled, enchanted by the happy, playful, seductive Erin.

"No." Erin pouted. "I don't want to think you only want me for my money."

Morgan stopped moving. "I don't."

Erin reached for her hand, entwining their fingers. "I know. I was joking."

"Do you want to know what my third dream was—is? It's the most important one."

"What?"

"To make you happy."

Erin tugged on Morgan's hand, pulled her close, and wrapped her arms around her shoulders. The kiss was pure passion, and Morgan was aching as Erin's tongue plunged between her lips. Someone groaned, and it took a second for her to realize that it came from her. She caressed Erin's shoulders before sliding her hands over her chest. She needed to feel Erin's breasts filling her palms. She wanted to feel her nipples, excited and wanting. Her chest heaved as she wrapped her fingers around the pliant flesh and heard Erin's breath catch.

Erin worked the buttons on Morgan's shirt, quickly pulling it free from her jeans and touching the bare skin of her belly.

Erin whimpered and jerked Morgan out of her lust induced haze and her anxiety tugged at her.

"Wait, wait." She leaned back, and let her hands fall from Erin's breasts to her stomach.

"What's wrong?" Erin was breathless, her chest heaving, her cheeks flushed, her lips swollen from their kisses. "I thought this was what you wanted."

"It is. I do. God, I do. I want you so much."

Erin cocked her head to the side. "Then what's wrong?"

"I want to please you." She reached out and tucked Erin's hair behind her ear, tracing the line of her neck before looking into Erin's eyes again.

"You were."

"I don't—I'm not sure—"

"Oh God, I should've remembered." Erin took her hand and kissed her fingertips. "You were a virgin till you were twenty." She caressed her cheek up to Morgan's temple. "In here you still are."

"I'm sorry." Morgan started to back away, but Erin held her in place.

"What for?"

"I feel so inept." She wanted to crawl away from Erin, almost as much as she needed to stay in her arms. She ran her fingers through Erin's hair. It was more than a desire to touch her, more than need; it was essential.

"Don't." Their eyes met and held, and Erin's lips quirked into a sexy smile. "It's kind of exciting, actually. I'm getting a new lover without having to trade in the old one."

"What if I do it wrong?" Morgan sounded pathetic to her own ears, but she couldn't help it. She wanted to be everything Erin wanted—needed. She wanted to fulfill every dream and desire, every fantasy.

Erin laughed softly and slid a finger from Morgan's lips to the waistband of her jeans. "Oh, baby, I'm not worried about that in the slightest."

The term of endearment startled her. It was the first time she remembered Erin calling her anything other than her name. "You called me baby."

"Hm, so I did. Problem?"

"No. I liked it. You can call me baby anytime you like." She smiled, still feeling shy and timid. "Why aren't you worried?"

"Morgan, we had a good sex life before. Why would I think we won't have that again?"

"Because I was experienced before."

"You still are. Your body remembers, even if your head doesn't. The way you were kissing me just now." She rubbed her fingers across Morgan's belly. "The way you were touching me. That isn't how it was when we first got together. It was much more similar to the way you touched me a couple of months ago. Before you left."

"It was?"

"Yes. Don't worry, or over think it all. Just relax and enjoy. You're very good at this."

"I am?"

Erin pulled her close and kissed her hard. "Yes. Now are you going to take me to bed or should I start taking your clothes off here?"

CHAPTER THIRTY-FOUR

Erin ached to run her fingers across Morgan's skin. The temptation of her downy covered abdomen was too strong to resist. She let go of her waistband and skimmed her fingertips across Morgan's belly, tracing the faint lines of muscle, the edges of her ribs, slowly getting closer to her breasts. Morgan's quick inhalation jolted her out of her sensual exploration. She looked deep into the coal black depths of Morgan's eyes and she was lost. Past, present, and future collided, fusing together to create a singular existence.

The weeks of uncertainty dissolved under the intense need radiating from Morgan's body. Her belly clenched as Morgan took her hand and kissed her palm, her wrist, and her fingertips.

They climbed the stairs in silence, Erin leading the way. She turned and looked over her shoulder, a part of her needing to see Morgan right behind her. She no longer doubted that she would be; she simply wanted to make sure it wasn't a dream.

She pulled the curtains closed, suffusing the light and blocking out the rest of the world, while Morgan waited just inside the door.

"You are so beautiful, Erin." She came further into the room. "You take my breath away."

Erin stepped forward and teased open each button of her blouse as she moved before she pushed it from her shoulders and let it fall to the floor. Morgan's desire for her was the greatest aphrodisiac Erin had ever known. To feel wanted, needed, and desired after the intense feelings of rejection made her feel powerful. It aroused her in a way she had never felt before, the taste of the fruit all the more sweet for having lost it once.

She pushed Morgan's shirt away from her body and dropped it carelessly, avoiding her skin. She knew once she touched her, she wouldn't be able to stop. She would have to satisfy the craving to touch her everywhere, but right now, she wanted to enjoy looking. Morgan wasn't wearing a bra, and her small breasts, tipped with stiff brown nipples that begged to be touched, made Erin want nothing more than to fill her mouth with them. To distract herself, she started to work on her jeans, flicking open the buttons and working them over her hips.

"Do you need to keep the brace on?" Her voice was deep and husky, dripping with lust and desire.

Morgan looked at it sheepishly. "Yeah, sorry."

Erin stepped closer, watching Morgan's nostrils flare as her satin covered breasts pressed into her. She moaned at the exquisite contact before dropping to her knees and working the denim from Morgan's legs. The scent of Morgan's arousal made her mouth water. Her heart was pounding in her chest, and her fingers shook as adrenaline and passion coursed through her. Morgan stood in nothing but her boxer briefs and her knee brace and Erin was glad she was already on her knees, since she was certain she wouldn't have been able to remain standing otherwise. She slid her hands up the back of Morgan's legs and palmed her backside, reveling in the way the muscles bunched and twitched in her hands.

"Please let me see you." Morgan's whispered words penetrated her brain.

She stood and quickly shed her clothes and moved back into Morgan's embrace, but found herself held at arm's length.

"You are truly stunning. Will you let me draw you?"

Erin shuddered. "Why?" Morgan had never asked her to pose for her before, and her own insecurities had prevented her from asking why. She didn't want to feel less than the models Morgan had sketched previously, and she was afraid that Morgan had never asked because she didn't think she was pretty enough.

"Because you are the most beautiful woman I have ever seen. The most beautiful I will ever see. I want to commit every inch of you to memory, and sketching you is the only way I can think of to do that."

"You don't have to put me on a wall to do that. I don't want to be displayed for other people to see."

"No." Morgan looked horrified. "I wouldn't display you like that. I don't want to draw you so other people can see you. I don't want to share you with anyone else." She wrapped her arm about Erin's back and pulled their bodies together. "You're mine."

Erin melted beneath her kiss. She wrapped her arms around Morgan's shoulders and relished the length of Morgan's body against hers. Breast to breast, thigh to thigh. Long moments passed as their hands discovered and rediscovered the supple contours and long planes of skin and muscle. Erin felt lightheaded from the lack of air and the overload of hormones saturating her blood.

"I need to lie down. I want to feel you on top of me," Erin whispered against Morgan's lips.

Morgan groaned and traced kisses down her throat as she pulled away and dragged the covers off the bed. She shed her panties and climbed in, smiling as Morgan groaned.

"God, you're killing me."

"Yeah, yeah. Lose the shorts and get over here." She stretched out on her side, one hand propping up her head as she watched Morgan push her underwear off, fighting with them as she tried to get them clear of the brace. Erin couldn't help but laugh as Morgan frowned and cursed her way to nakedness.

Morgan grimaced as she sat on the edge of the bed and shrugged. "Sorry."

"What for?"

"I kind of killed the mood."

"No, you didn't. Baby, we used to laugh when we made love all the time. It's supposed to be fun. A little laughter doesn't kill the mood. Sometimes it makes it better." She stroked Morgan's back and pulled on her shoulder. "I'm still very much in the mood. Now, come here and kiss me."

Morgan lay down and stretched out on her side as Erin had. "You'll tell me if I do something wrong?"

"Promise." Erin closed the distance and claimed her mouth, plunging her tongue inside. She tasted like mint, and coffee, and home.

Whispered moans filled the air as their bodies reconnected. Erin pressed her thigh between Morgan's legs, a slick abundance of arousal greeting her. Morgan's hands were everywhere. Grasping her buttocks and pulling her closer, caressing her breasts, pinching her nipples. But she wanted more. She needed Morgan to claim her, to own her body as she owned her heart. She needed everything.

She took Morgan's hand and eased it between their bodies, their gazes locked. She fought to keep her eyes open as their joined fingers pressed against her drenched sex. Morgan's eyes widened and she glanced down before she smiled and stared back into Erin's eyes.

"You're incredible," Morgan whispered before kissing her.

Morgan's gentle fingers explored every slick millimeter of her flesh. She hooked her leg over Morgan's hip and tried to get closer in the search for release. Then Morgan's hand pulled away.

"What? No—"

"It's okay. I just don't want to rush."

"Morgan, I need to come." She thrust her hips, frustrated to find nothing but air.

"Not yet." Morgan pressed her onto her back and rolled on top of her. "You see, I might be a bit unsure of what I'm doing, but I've been doing some research the last couple of days."

Erin spread her legs and sighed as her center connected with Morgan's skin. "Really? And what have you learned?"

Morgan grasped her hands and raised them above her head. "I was directed to some of your favorite romance stories." She nipped at Erin's throat as she clasped both wrists in one hand. "I noticed something in them."

"And what was that?"

"Well, Amy told me that the two of you would discuss which ones were particularly hot." She shifted and closed her lips around

Erin's nipple. She pulled the turgid point into her mouth and batted it with her tongue.

Erin closed her eyes under the sensual assault. Every swipe of Morgan's tongue left her feeling worshiped.

"In all those stories," she whispered and shifted to the other breast, kissing the outside, "the heroine." She sucked on Erin's nipple. "That would be you. She was always *claimed* by the hero." She blew cold air across the tip and Erin could feel her nipple tighten further. "That would be me." Morgan sucked hard on Erin's generous breast, pulling as much of it into her mouth as possible.

Erin moaned, wishing she could wrap her fingers in Morgan's hair and cradle her beautiful head to her chest. "What happened to shy and uncertain?"

Morgan released her breast, grinning. "No room for that when I'm making dreams come true."

"You read a few books and think this is my dream?" She flexed her wrists, still pinned beneath Morgan's hand.

"I meant my dreams. I want to make you happy, remember?"

Erin nodded. Morgan was so earnest, the yearning to make her happy so clear in her eyes, it was all Erin could do to stop the tears from falling as they welled in her eyes.

"Is this okay?" Morgan squeezed gently on Erin's wrist.

In that moment, Erin realized why she relished those stories. Why they were so erotic for her. It wasn't the heroine being overwhelmed by the strong hero, or the incredible eroticism. It was trust.

Trusting someone so completely that you never doubted—even for a second—that you were safe, adored, cherished, and loved. That was what turned her on. That was the element she craved the most, and she knew that it was still something she had never experienced with Morgan—with anyone—before.

There had always been something in Morgan that was hidden from her, a part of her that had remained untouchable. In response, Erin knew she had kept this final barrier between them. She had hidden her own secrets and let the gap between them widen. It was a heartbeat of time, but she understood that it was these barriers that had led to the destruction of their relationship. If they were to succeed now, there was no room for doubt. No place left for secrets or barricades. The trust had to be total, complete, and unshakeable.

She knew she wouldn't have been able to do it before, but trust shone in Morgan's eyes. She was offering Erin everything, and the walls shifted and crumbled.

Erin stretched her arms up and wrapped her fingers around the spindles of the headboard.

"This is more than okay."

Her skin burned beneath Morgan's hands, lips, and tongue. She writhed under a torrent of kisses covering her breasts, her belly, her legs. The first touches of Morgan's tongue lapping at her center made her shudder and call Morgan's name in a voice foreign to her own ears. Still she ached; she craved Morgan's possessive touch filling her.

"Oh, Morgan, please. I need—"

Morgan didn't make her beg. The swift penetration of Morgan's fingers pushed her over the edge. Wave after wave of delicious orgasm seared her, branding her soul with the insignia she would never lose. Morgan's.

CHAPTER THIRTY-FIVE

Morgan stretched, enjoying the slight ache of her muscles and the heavy limbed sensation that rode on the back of satisfaction. Erin's head rested on her shoulder, breathing the deep, even cadence of sleep.

It was nearly three thirty, and they needed to get up before the kids got home from school. She ran her hand down Erin's back, feeling the muscles flex as she arched beneath her touch. Erin's arms tightened around her, and she burrowed into Morgan's embrace.

Morgan kissed the top of her head. "The kids'll be home soon. We should get up."

Erin squeezed her a little tighter. "I don't want to."

Morgan laughed. "Me neither, but I'm pretty sure you don't want them walking in on us like this."

It was Erin's turn to laugh. "They've seen us in bed together more times than I can count, Morgan. It won't do them any harm."

"Oh, right. Course. Sorry."

Erin lifted her head and kissed her. "Stop saying sorry. I'm glad you're thinking about them, and what's best for them. But seeing us in bed together isn't anything to worry about. Now, figuring out Tristan's problem…" She shrugged.

"Yeah. I'll try and talk to him again later. Maybe he'll talk if we're alone."

"Okay." Erin threw off the covers and climbed out of bed. "I'm going to jump in the shower. I'd say join me, but that's probably not a good idea with your knee."

Morgan couldn't take her eyes off Erin. The rounded curves of her hip and breasts, her long, slender legs, and the soft, flawless skin begged for her touch.

Erin chuckled. "Stop looking at me like that, or we'll still be in bed when I have to go to work tonight, never mind when the kids get home." She stepped back to the bed, leaned down, and kissed her.

"Tristan can use a microwave, can't he?" She caught Erin's hair in her fist, deepening the kiss. Erin groaned before she pulled away.

"Come on, time to be grownups." Erin walked into the en suite leaving the door open.

"Being a grownup sucks!"

Erin laughed, climbing into the shower and running her hands over her body.

Morgan groaned and rolled to the edge of the bed. "And you're a tease." She grabbed her clothes and hunted for her underwear.

"In the chest of drawers under the window. Top drawer. There's clean underwear in there," Erin called, the cascading water almost drowning out her voice.

"Thanks." She dressed quickly and looked up in time to see Erin leave the bathroom, still naked, drying her hair with a towel. "God, you're beautiful."

Erin beamed. "A girl could get used to all these compliments."

Morgan hugged her, kissed her damp neck, her cheek, and then her mouth. "I'm going to put the kettle on before I can't stop touching you. Do you want coffee?"

"Please." Erin pulled her in for a final kiss, then pushed her away, laughing.

Morgan hummed a tune she couldn't remember the words to as she made the drinks and sat at the kitchen table. She started flipping through a magazine as she waited.

The front door opened and Tristan barged through, and then let it slam closed behind him. His angry stare fixed on her, his lips pursed in a thin line. He dropped his bag on a chair and stalked to the fridge.

"How was school?"

He pulled the fridge open and grabbed a drink without answering her.

Boy, does this feel familiar? "I asked you a question, Tristan."

He started for the door, but Morgan stood and blocked his path.

"Look, whatever the problem is, ignoring me and stomping around isn't going to solve it. Talk to me. Tell me what's wrong, and we'll figure out a way to fix it." She reached out to put her hand on his shoulder, but he backed away, flinching as he backed right up to the sink. *What the fuck?* She dropped her hand back to her side. "Tristan, please. Why are you acting like you're scared of me?"

"Get away from me! I won't talk to you. I wish you'd never come back!" He tossed the can in the sink, his eyes darting in every direction as he seemed to look for a way out.

"I thought we were past that. I don't have the answers—"

"I know the answers. I know."

Oh, fuck. It has to be. He knows about Anna. "Look, Tristan, just say it. Whatever you think it is, just tell me, and we can talk it out. If you know something about before, just tell me." Seeing fear in his eyes tore at her heart. *He's afraid of me. Why? Why would knowing about Anna make him scared of me? It doesn't make sense.*

Erin's footsteps sounded down the stairs and in the hallway. Morgan felt her hand at the small of her back, but she didn't take her eyes off Tristan. Erin slid her hand round and down her arm until their fingers entwined.

Tristan's gaze dropped when Erin appeared at her side, but Morgan had seen the look in his eye before he tried to hide it. Terror. He was terrified of something, but she had no idea what. *He's afraid of me, and terrified for Erin. What the hell is going on?*

He looked at Erin. "You're touching her."

Erin frowned. "So?"

"Like you used to touch her. Before she left."

"I say again. So?"

"Does that mean she's back?" He flicked his eyes in Morgan's direction, before stepping closer to Erin. "With you?"

"Yes. We love each other."

"No." Tristan's voice cracked as he shouted, panic clinging to every syllable. "She can't. You can't take her back. You don't have to." He grabbed hold of Erin's free hand and tried to pull her away from Morgan. "I don't want her to hurt you. I know now. We can make Maddie understand why she can't see us ever again."

"Tristan, stop. What are you talking about? She's your mum." Erin gripped his hand, but she wouldn't be pulled away from Morgan. "We're a family. She loves us."

"I don't care." He turned and faced Morgan. "I know the truth about you. I know what you did. I won't let you hurt her."

"Tristan, please tell me what you're talking about." Morgan felt everything crumbling around her.

He reached into his pocket and pulled out a photograph. He threw it at her. "I know what you did."

Morgan steeled herself. Erin hadn't seen the picture of her and Anna. She wished they didn't have to see this now, not after all they had shared earlier. She didn't want anything to ruin it. She glanced at Erin, but her eyes were locked on the picture in her hand. She could see Erin bracing herself and she took a deep breath and met Morgan's gaze. She nodded, clearly expecting to see Morgan in another woman's arms. Morgan wanted to scream, wishing she had any other option than hurting Erin, but she couldn't see any other option at this point.

She turned the picture over.

What the hell?

It wasn't a picture of her and Anna.

It was a picture of her as a teenager, her mother on one side of her, and her father on the other. She looked sullen and brooding. Her father had his hand on Morgan's shoulder. Her mother was slightly off to the side, her eyes sad, shoulders stooped, a fading bruise around her left eye almost covered with makeup.

"Tristan, what is this?"

"I know what you did."

CHAPTER THIRTY-SIX

Erin grabbed the picture from Morgan's hand, staring at it. "This is your dad?" She flipped the photo over and glanced at Morgan. Her face was white, sweat beaded on her upper lip, and her hands were shaking.

"Yeah."

"I've never seen a picture of him before."

Morgan turned her head quickly. "You haven't?"

Erin shook her head. "No."

"I wonder why." Sarcasm dripped from every word as Tristan grabbed for the picture, a sneer curling his lips. "That's mine. It was given to me."

"Who gave you this?" Erin pulled it out of his reach. "This has never been in this house. Where did you get it?"

"None of your business. Give it to me." He held out his hand.

"Oh, no. I'm still your mother and you will show me more respect than that, young man. Now sit down and start talking." Erin pointed at a chair, her chest heaving as she tried to retain control of her escalating anger.

"No. You let her back in here. You don't care about me. You don't care about us!"

Each word was an arrow slicing her heart and rending her soul. How could he think that? How could he doubt her love for him? For them both? When she opened her eyes, she could see her own wounded look reflected back at her. Tristan's sorrow marred his lovely face and festered in his eyes. She had to remind herself that the belligerent teen in front of her was actually her precious little boy. Confused, in pain, and scared, but the child she loved just the same.

"I'm going to pretend you didn't just say that, Tristan, because right now, you're angry, and people say things when they're angry that they later regret. When you calm down, you're going to regret saying that to me. When that happens, I want you to remember that I love you. I love Maddie. You both mean the world to me, and I would never knowingly do anything to hurt either of you."

She wanted to pull him into her arms, to wipe away the torment that made his shoulders inch toward his ears and body hum with tension. All that stopped her was the certain knowledge that her actions would push him further away from her.

"Will you please sit down so that we can sort this out?"

"I've got nothing to say to her." He glared at Morgan.

Erin flicked her eyes in Morgan's direction. "Okay, will you talk to me if Morgan goes into the other room?"

She could see Morgan nodding, but she didn't acknowledge her. The door clicked shut behind her and her hobbling steps could be heard down the hallway.

"Okay, it's just you and me. Now tell me."

Tristan wouldn't meet her eyes. His chin dropped so low it seemed stuck to his chest, and his arms folded across his body as he bit his lower lip.

Erin waited. This was a battle of wills she clearly couldn't afford to lose.

"Tristan, we can sit here all night. I don't care. But you will tell me what's going on. Where did you get this picture?" Erin placed the picture on the table.

Tristan stared at the picture, his leg jumping and twitching under the table.

He's just like Morgan with that nervous twitch. Still she waited, determined to get the answers she needed to help him. Time dragged. Every tick of the clock felt like an hour passing rather than the tiny second it was.

"Okay, we'll try a different question. What is it you think she's done?"

"I don't think, I know." His voice was strong and sure, certain in the knowledge he held. His body stopped shaking as his anxiety fled in the face of his truth. "He told me what she did."

"Who told you what?"

Silence. His leg twitched again.

"What are you so afraid of, Tristan? Morgan? Me? Or this mysterious him?"

Tristan still said nothing.

"If it's so awful that I need to keep her away from you, then you need to tell me. I can't protect you if I don't know what I'm supposed to protect you from."

"Who protects you, Mum? You can't let her hurt you." The words crawled out of his mouth on a pained whimper.

"Tristan, your mum won't hurt me. We've worked out the problems—"

"You don't have to take her back because you're scared of her. You're kinda pretty; you can find someone else."

"I don't want anyone else. And I'm not scared of her. I have never been scared of Morgan. Where's all this coming from?"

His features shifted from anger to failure, from fear to hate, in the blink of an eye. "I should have seen—I should have stopped—" He reached for the picture and ran a finger down the fading bruises of his grandmother's face. "Colin's dad hits his mum sometimes. He said she won't ever tell him the truth either. But he knows."

Erin was stunned. "Morgan has never hit me. Not once. She hasn't ever touched you in anger, and she never would. Why are you saying this, Tristan? Is this about Colin? Do you want me to talk to his mum?" Erin knew she was grasping, but none of it made sense. Why was he talking about this while stroking the picture of a dead woman? Why was he suddenly so scared of Morgan?

The realization struck her, and an explosion of images, words, thoughts detonated in her brain. She knew she should have thought of it before, but it just seemed impossible. *He's still in prison, right? He can't be the cause of all this, can he?* She jabbed at the picture.

"Where did you get this, Tristan? Tell me now."

The angry, belligerent Tristan was gone. The boy before her was resolute but sad. "No, I can't. I made a promise."

"And that promise is more important to you than we are? Your mother and me?"

The stubborn set of his mouth softened, obviously questioning the value he placed on his word. "You taught me to always keep my promises."

Shit. "Yes, I did. But I also taught you to think for yourself. To be kind and to know that your family love you. I thought I taught you to love us in return."

Tears dripped over his eyelashes, spilling a river down his cheeks.

"Do you still love me?" Erin knew she was pushing, but there had to be an end.

He nodded, the tears falling thick and fast.

"Do you think all this, all these secrets, are the best way to show me that?"

He dropped his head back to his chest, sobs wracking his body as he continued to fight the emotion. Erin wrapped her arms around his shoulders and held him to her.

"Tell me, Tristan. Who gave you this?"

"I can't." The words were muffled against her chest and thick with tears, but she heard them loud and clear.

"Why not? What are you afraid of?"

"I'm not scared!"

"Then tell me—"

"I'm the man of the house. I'm not scared of anything." He pushed away from her, quickly breaking her hold and jumping to his feet. The chair clattered to the ground behind him. "I'm not afraid."

Tristan ran from the room, leaving the picture on the table and avoiding Erin's hands as she reached for him. His heavy footsteps on the stairs weren't enough to drown out the pounding of her own heart or the resounding beat of dread bouncing around her brain.

CHAPTER THIRTY-SEVEN

Morgan pushed open the door to the kitchen. Erin had her head in her hands, her shoulders shaking as she cried. Morgan stood behind her, wrapped her arms around her shoulders, and kissed the top of her head. Erin gripped her hands and turned her head into her neck.

"Did you hear?" Erin's voice was muffled against her skin.

"Yeah. He thinks I beat you." *Please, God, don't let that be true.* "I know you told him I didn't, but I need to ask. Did I hurt you?"

"No." Erin pulled away and looked at her. Her eyes were unwavering, her jaw set in determination, her posture purposeful and steadfast. "You never raised a finger to any of us. When we decided to have children, you were definite that we wouldn't ever touch them in anger. I teased you once about spanking them if they were showing us up in the street or something. You were so upset you postponed the first IVF treatment." She tugged on Morgan's sleeve until she was sitting in the chair Tristan had vacated. "I would never let anyone be with our children, including us, if I didn't trust them completely."

"Thank you." Morgan leaned forward and captured Erin's lips in a slow, sweet kiss. "I couldn't hear everything. Who gave him the picture and told him all these lies?"

"He wouldn't say, but I think it's your dad."

Apprehension gripped her. "But he's in prison."

"Is he? He sent that letter in June, Morgan. It's September now. He said he was being paroled."

"Fuck!" How much more of this could they all take? It was just one thing after another. Every time she felt as though they were finding solid ground, it turned to quicksand beneath her feet. Morgan started to get up, but Erin caught her arm.

"Where are you going?"

"To ask Tristan."

Erin shook her head. "No, we need more than conjecture. He's as stubborn as we both are, and he's scared." Erin tugged her back into her seat. "Where's the letter?"

Morgan pulled it from her pocket, and handed it over as Erin cocked her eyebrow in question. "I didn't know where to put it that was safe, I didn't want the kids to read it. How much do they know about my dad?"

"Well, I think Tristan knows a whole lot more now than what we told him, but basically, we told them that Gran died before they were born, and we never actually mentioned Granddad. They know my dad left when I was a child, so I think they assumed it was along the same sort of lines. You never spoke of him. We never saw pictures, nothing. It was like he didn't exist for you, so he didn't for any of us."

"So, if my dad has spoken to him, or written to him—"

"Tristan will have no idea what to believe, other than we lied to him, and this person is giving him the information that is supposedly the truth."

Morgan pressed her fingers into the corner of her eyes. "I fucked it up so bad."

"Now isn't the time for blame, babe. We both thought that telling the kids would only cause them pain they didn't need to feel. We both made the mistakes. Now we don't have time to dwell on it all, because Tristan needs us to fix it." She pulled Morgan's hand to her lips and kissed her knuckles. "We need to call the prison and find out."

"Then what?" Her decision to flee in order to protect them all was becoming more and more understandable by the second. She knew she would never be able to make that same decision again, but she understood it now. She felt like an animal backed into a corner, with two choices, fight or flight. She'd run before. She refused to do it again.

She pulled her phone from her pocket and dialed the number on the visiting order. "Good afternoon, HMP Strangeways." The voice on the other end of the line was deep, gravelly, and slightly intimidating.

"Hello, I have a visiting order, and I'd like to make an appointment." Morgan's hands were shaking as she held the phone to her ear. She remembered her mother telling her that monsters weren't real when she was a child. That the boogie man didn't exist. She was wrong. *Some boogie men grow with us and just get more frightening.*

"What's the visiting order reference number?"

Morgan read off the number, then the prisoner reference number when prompted.

"Please hold."

Muzak blared down the line, some panpipe version of a popular song.

"Hello?" The gruff voice returned.

"Yes." Morgan's voice cracked as she spoke, then she held her breath, not sure what she was going to say if he offered her an appointment.

"I'm sorry, but that prisoner has been released on parole."

The world faded for a second and Morgan's blood pounded in her ears. "I see. I'm his daughter; can you tell me how I can get hold of him?" She didn't recognize her own voice as it cracked and faded to a whisper.

"I'm sorry. I can't give out any of that information. If you want to write him a letter, send it here and we can forward it to his parole officer."

"Right. Thank you." She said good-bye and hung up. She felt numb, her fingers nerveless as she dropped the handset and stared at the picture still sitting on the wooden table. "He's out."

"Shit." Erin wrapped her hands about Morgan's, entwining their fingers. "Okay, at least we know what we're dealing with now."

"Yeah. That doesn't fill me with confidence. He's done twenty years for murdering my mother."

"Look at me." Erin grasped her chin gently and tilted her head until she could see her eyes. "I won't let him hurt you." She pulled Morgan into her arms. "I won't let him hurt any of us." Erin held her until the shaking subsided, and kissed her gently. "I'll go get that boy of ours and see if he'll talk to us now."

Erin's footsteps lulled her turbulent mind into a moment of sweet oblivion as they echoed down the hallway. The things Tristan thought she had done burned at her. She wanted to know if it stopped at his suspicions of her beating Erin, or had her dad told him other lies?

"Tristan!" Erin's terror filled scream ripped her from her mental meanderings and catapulted her out of her chair. She hobbled to the stairs, looking up to see Erin's panic-stricken face, tears cascading down her cheeks.

"What?" Morgan dreaded the words she knew were coming. She didn't want to hear. The icy tendrils of fear swept along every nerve fiber in her body, paralyzing her in its wake.

"He's gone."

CHAPTER THIRTY-EIGHT

W hat do you mean, he's gone?"
"His room's empty." Erin's head spun until her brain shut down. Logic and sense vanished as she watched Morgan climb the stairs as fast as her crutches would allow. Erin couldn't move, but she could hear Morgan opening doors and slamming drawers. The dull, heavy thud of shoes hitting the wall tore her from the torpor that had caged her and she ran to Tristan's room.

"We have to call the police." Erin shivered, certain she wouldn't feel warm until she held Tristan in her arms.

"There's got to be something." Morgan didn't even turn around as she continued leafing through notebooks, piles of magazines. She pulled open cases to DVDs, video games, boxes—anything she could find.

"What are you doing?" Erin frowned, as Morgan grabbed his school bag and upended it. "Morgan, we need to call the police. You're wasting time."

"I'm trying to find an address, a phone number—something that will tell us where the old bastard's staying. Where Tristan is."

"You think there's something here?"

"I don't know, but if it was me," she said and reached into his blazer pockets. "I'd have the address written down somewhere." She held up the notepad next to his computer, angling it in the light. "There's something here." She grabbed a pencil and gently rubbed across the surface to bring the indentation into relief. "Four twenty-nine Offerton Lane. Mean anything to you?"

"No." Hope flared in Erin's heart and she had to fight the urge to run and find him. She wanted to lift every rock, open every door, and yell his name until she couldn't speak. Morgan's gaze locked on her, her determination palpable.

The slamming sound of a car door broke the tension.

"Mum, I got another star!"

Erin whirled around and ran to the door. "Upstairs, sweetie." Maddie ran up, grinning and holding out her piece of paper. Erin dropped to her knees and pulled Maddie into her arms as she entered the room.

Erin held Maddie's warm body cradled against her, her sweet scent filling the air. She carried her into the front room and sat down with her on her lap. She didn't care how heavy Maddie was now or how awkward carrying her was. She couldn't have let go if she'd wanted to. And she really didn't want to.

"Mummy, what's wrong?" Maddie stared at Morgan over Erin's shoulder. Her eyes were open wide, her lower lip trembling.

"Tristan's run off. We're going to get him." Morgan stroked the top of Maddie's head.

"Where's Tristan? Is he in trouble?"

"We don't know." Morgan gripped Erin's shoulder. "Do you want to wait here? I can call a taxi."

"I'm coming with you. It's faster if I drive." She loosened her grip on Maddie's slim frame and stood up. "We can drop Maddie with Chris on the way." She pointed at the page in Morgan's hand. "What if he isn't there?"

"Then we call the police and let them find him. But this isn't far away. Just a few minutes' drive."

They rushed to the car and were almost out of the driveway when Chris pulled up.

"What's wrong?" Chris frowned as Erin helped Maddie back out of the car.

"Tristan's run off. I was going to bring Maddie to you—"

"We'll be fine. Go. Call me."

Erin backed out of the drive and compressed the accelerator, urging the car over the speed limit, her eyes flicking to the side mirrors. *I will find my son, and if that bastard has harmed one hair on his head—*

"Erin, it's just up there." Morgan pointed to the left. "Just after the pub."

She scanned for somewhere to park and decided that the bar's car park would have to do.

The door to the house was a dingy brown, the paint chipped and peeling, the doorknocker rusted in place. There was a buzzer type intercom on the wall, "Jesper House" written in neat block letters in the small window. Morgan pushed the button and they waited.

Erin's palms were clammy, as she told herself over and over that everything would be fine.

"Hello." The static over the intercom disguised the voice on the other end. Erin had no idea if the speaker was a man or a woman. She didn't care, as long as Tristan was there.

"Hello, my name's Morgan Masters. I'm trying to find—"

"Masters. You looking for George Masters?"

Erin watched the color drain from Morgan's face as she gripped the doorframe. "No." Her voice cracked and she cleared her throat. "I'm looking for my son. Tristan Masters. I think he might have come here…"

The box vibrated and let out a strangled buzz until they heard the catch release. Morgan pushed on the door and it swung open on creaking hinges.

The hallway had black and white checkered floor tiles; magnolia colored paint haphazardly covered layers of woodchip wallpaper. The scuffed, off-white wooden banister was chipped, and one of the spindles was missing halfway up. The musky odor of rotting food emanated from further down the hallway, and unwashed clothing hung around the coats that clung to the pegs by the front door. The door closest to them opened and a man stuck his head out.

"In here." He inclined his shaved head toward the room behind him and held the door open for them. "I'm John Yorke. I'm the warden for Jesper House. This young man turned up about twenty minutes ago, looking for George."

Tristan sat in a chair in front of the window, his posture slouched, affecting the I'm-not-afraid-of-anything look that belied the nervousness in his eyes.

John was a short man with a matching girth. Thick muscles covered his chest, shoulders, and arms. "I was just about to call the police."

"Why?" Morgan frowned.

Erin crossed the room quickly, wrapping him in her arms, and kissing the top of his head before Morgan's question could be answered.

"We don't allow minors in the hostel. We have registered sex offenders in here. So no one under the age of twenty-one. He wouldn't give me his name, or your details, so I couldn't contact you. The only other choice I had was to call the police. It's for his protection, as well as theirs."

Erin pulled back far enough to look into Tristan's face. "Why?"

"Because you believe her." He flicked his eyes in Morgan's direction.

"I believe your mum because she told me the truth."

"So you lied to me too." It wasn't a question, and his words stung, but she knew they had to tell him everything now. They'd left it far too long.

"We didn't tell you some things because you were too young to know them. Too young to understand."

"He doesn't treat me like a little kid."

Erin shuddered. "No, I imagine he doesn't. I made my decisions based on what was best for you at the time. Remember that, Tristan. I was doing what was best for you. George doesn't have your best interests at heart, believe me."

"You don't know him" Tristan tried to pull away. "He said I was man enough to know the truth, and he told me everything."

Erin kept hold of him, knowing she had to get through to him.

"The truth. You want to know the truth?" She waited for him to meet her eyes. He was curious, receptive. *Good boy, Trist.* "The truth is your mum watched her dad kill her mum. She saw him hit her for years. He hit her, many times."

"He said she hit her mum. He said she'd hit you."

"It's not true." She looked away. "Morgan, show him your back."

"What?" Morgan frowned, her confusion clear.

"The scar on your back. Show him."

Morgan stepped forward. "I don't have any scars from him. He was always very careful about that."

"But you do. You told me that he cut you, but you refused to say any more about it." Comprehension dawned on them both as they stared at each other. "I'm so sorry, baby, but I have to show him. He has to know what your father did to you."

"It's okay. Where is it?"

"Down your right shoulder blade."

Morgan nodded and turned, pulling her sweater up her back. A thin pale line marred the smooth expanse of skin.

"He did this with a piece of broken glass." Erin turned back to Tristan. "Before she lost her memory, your mum never told me when he did this, but do you know how your gran died?"

He shook his head, staring at the scar on Morgan's back.

"Her throat was cut with broken glass." She took Tristan's hand and held him fast when he tried to pull away. "You can't cut yourself here, Tristan. You know that, right?"

Tristan's face turned ashen and his lips trembled, but his eyes never left Morgan's back. "He said he was covering for her. That she still had her whole life ahead of her."

Morgan dropped her shirt and whirled around, grasping his face in her hands. "I don't remember what happened, Tristan. I won't lie to you and tell you that I do, just to make this easier. What I can tell you is that he confessed."

Erin met her gaze before she focused on Tristan again.

"He said he confessed because the police suspected you."

"All the evidence says he did it. The glass had his prints on it. He'd beaten her so many times, I can't even tell you how many. He broke her bones, cut her, gave her concussions."

"He hit you too?" He wrapped his hands around her arms.

"Yeah, he did."

"I'm sorry, Mum. I didn't know. I didn't know what to believe. It was like he was the only one telling me the truth."

"He was lying to you, Tristan."

"Everything?"

"I don't know. What else did he say?"

"He said that you hit your mum. That he was sure you'd hit…" His gaze flicked to Erin. "He said you hit mum, because it was your nature. It's who you are. He said I should look after her, and Maddie, 'cos I'm the man of the house and that's what men do."

"Oh, Tristan." She pulled him into her arms. "I'm here to protect you. And I will. I swear I will not let that bastard near you."

The door creaked open behind them and they all looked up.

"You always did make promises you couldn't keep, girlie."

CHAPTER THIRTY-NINE

Cigarette smoke and gravel. His voice was deeper with age, more menacing with experience. It was the sound of the monster she had never escaped.

"Aren't you gonna say hello to ya dear old dad?"

Morgan tried to quell the shaking and focus on Tristan. She could feel sweat beading on her upper lip and trickle down her back.

"I have nothing to say to you."

"Really? I should think a thank you was in order."

She pulled Tristan against her, whispering in his ear, "Does he know about the amnesia?"

"Yes." Tristan's voice was just as quiet.

"Did he tell you that I killed my mum after he knew that, or before?"

"After." His response was instant, and as he pulled back, she saw the realization of what it meant register in his eyes. "I should have trusted you. I'm so sorry."

"It doesn't matter now. Right?"

Tristan nodded, tears rolling down his cheeks. He wiped them away with his sleeve.

Morgan let the truth warm her soul. She hadn't killed her mother, the gnawing fear receded, and relief washed through her like a tidal wave. She sucked in a deep breath, preparing herself to face her father.

"I have no reason to thank you." She stood up slowly, pressing Tristan into Erin's arms; she finally looked at her father.

Time and prison had been harsh mistresses for him. His once black hair was gray and thinning. The intense features she remembered from her childhood were more pronounced, and deep-set lines were etched into the skin around his eyes, nose, and mouth. The coal dark eyes she'd inherited from him had clouded with age, hatred the only emotion she could see within them. His brow looked permanently set in a deep frown, and the strong muscles that had terrorized their family were withered and wasted. He was little more than sinew and bone now, a shadow of the monster that haunted her dreams, an aged relic who deserved her pity more than her fear.

"What do you want?" Morgan shocked herself as her voice held steady.

He tilted his head back as he barked out a harsh sound, a poor approximation of a laugh. "I want my life back. Can you give me that, Moggie?"

She ignored the stupid question and waited. Her heart pounded, her body thrumming with nervous energy as her mind tried to find a reason that would explain what he wanted with them.

"Why did you want me to visit you in prison?"

"You owe me, girlie."

Morgan shook her head. "No, I don't. You killed her, you paid for your crime."

He laughed again. "You sure about that, Moggie? Because the boy there"—he pointed at Tristan—"told me you don't remember any of that."

"I'm sure." She knew it in her bones. "You pushed it too far, when you said I hit mum. It never happened. I remember all of that."

"Well, good for you. But your little…memory problem. It's enough to cast doubt on your testimony, see. Maybe get my conviction quashed."

Erin gasped. "You want money. That's what all this was about?"

Morgan frowned. "I don't understand."

"In the past twenty years, people who have had their convictions quashed or deemed unjust, but served time in prison, have received huge sums of money to compensate them for the time they've served. The longer they were inside, the greater the payout."

"But I didn't have amnesia when I got the letter. So that doesn't make sense."

"I was just going to ask you to help me out. Maybe lend me some cash. This is so much better." George sneered. "I'll have to thank Jimmy and that pretty little wife of his."

"Wait." Morgan whirled back to face him. "You know the man who attacked me?"

George stepped closer to her. "He was my cell mate for three years, Moggie. He owed me. What better way to pay his debt than by finding out all sorts of information about you? They were supposed to give you a little warning, leave you with a little message that it was in your own best interest to come and see me. To do me a simple favor."

"Give you money?"

George smiled. "Jimmy was supposed to take pictures when his pretty little wife seduced your perverted arse. A little insurance if you like. Jealous prick couldn't even get that right. Had to go all macho and beat you to a fucking pulp. Not that I don't understand the sentiment, girlie, but it wasn't what I told him to do. Deliver a message and get some insurance. That was it. Simple. Fucking arsehole." He closed the gap between them, his lips curled in a vicious sneer.

From start to finish, it was all a setup. I never stood a fucking chance. Anna, Jimmy, the beating. The only thing he didn't orchestrate was the amnesia, and the bastard's trying to use that to his advantage too.

"Why are you telling me all this now? With witnesses here."

"So that you know. So that you know it's me who beat you. Me who ruined your pathetic little life. Cost you everything you love, just like I promised I would."

Fury welled inside her, a ball of molten rage burning in the pit of her belly. Her hands shook as she curled her fingers into fists at her side as she looked beyond her fear for the first time and saw what she couldn't before. The thin, wrinkled skin that hung from his withered muscles made her wonder how she had ever feared this man. "You pathetic old bastard. You spent all those years plotting. And this is the best you could come up with?"

His lips curved into a cruel sneer. "I've done more than enough, Moggie. You'll be alone and pitiful. Your son wants nothing to do with you. Wife's kicked you out. I'm guessing that cute little girl of yours won't be too far behind her pretty mother." He looked beyond Morgan and looked Erin up and down, licked his lips, and blew her a kiss. "Want me to show you what you're missing, girlie?" He grabbed his crotch and thrust his hips in Erin's direction, laughing as she shuddered.

Morgan didn't realize she had moved until her fist connected with his jaw, and the sickening crunch of bone against bone couldn't be drowned out by Erin's scream.

Morgan stared at her trembling hands, the skin of her knuckles scraped and bleeding, one crutch fallen to the ground, and she couldn't believe what she had done. In a single instant, she had become everything she feared and despised. A single action and she had become the monster.

"See, boy. Apple doesn't fall far from the tree does it?" He wiped his mouth with the back of his hand then spat blood onto the floor. Morgan shuddered as the pink-flecked spittle hit her shoe. "Is that the best you got, Moggie?" He stepped forward, his face mere inches from hers. "Why don't you do a proper job, girlie? Use one of them sticks; show me how you really feel. Huh?"

He grabbed for her remaining crutch and tugged sharply, until their bodies collided, over balancing them both and toppling them to the floor. He landed on top of her and wrapped his hands about her throat.

"I should've put us both out of your misery a long time ago."

The room swam out of focus as he squeezed and she gasped for air, tears blurred her eyes. Time seemed to slow down as she tried to pull oxygen into her lungs. Panic rose inside her like a tidal wave, she could hear her heartbeat in her ears, and the rest of the room receded as she lifted her hands. She didn't think about anything but the need for air as she brought the metal crutch down against his head.

His grip gave way as he slumped against her.

Morgan struggled to pull her first breath into her lungs. Her throat burned, and her chest ached as his body was rolled off her.

The hazy blue of Erin's eyes replaced the view of cloudy magnolia woodchip. She wanted to reach up and wipe away the tears on Erin's cheeks, but her arms felt like lead. She wanted to smile, and tell her not to cry, but the muscles in her face refused to respond.

"You're okay, Morgan. It's okay." Erin cradled her head in her lap and stroked her hair off her face. "It's gonna be okay." She leaned down and kissed her forehead.

CHAPTER FORTY

"Tristan, call an ambulance, now," Erin said.

Tristan did as he was told.

"Morgan, keep your eyes open." She cradled Morgan's head.

"Tell them we need the police too." John's voice sounded strained as he shifted George to secure him better. George had come around and was struggling, crying out that she deserved it, that it was all her fault, and that she'd get what was coming to her one way or the other.

Erin stopped listening. She brushed Morgan's hair off her face, the red marks on her throat already darkening to purple. Morgan's breathing was steady, her pulse regular, but her skin was covered in a cold sweat. Her eyes were wide open but unfocused, her pupils dilated, and her hand gripped Erin's like a vice.

Tristan dropped to his knees next to them again. "They're coming. Will she be okay?"

"Yeah," Erin said without taking her eyes off Morgan. Tristan's hand rested on her shoulder and gripped Morgan's hand with the other.

"She's really cold." Tristan spoke quietly, like he wanted to avoid waking someone asleep.

"There's a blanket on the chair over there." John had pulled George's arms behind his back, clamped his wrists together, and held him in place with a knee in the small of his back.

"It's all my fault. I'm so sorry, Mum." Tristan took his hand from Morgan's shoulder and pushed his fingers into the corners of his eyes, obviously trying to stem his tears.

"No." Morgan's voice was little more than a whisper as she tried to shout.

Erin put her fingers to Morgan's lips, knowing her throat would be sore and need time to recover, and hoped that Morgan would take the hint. "Tristan, no. This isn't your fault. Why would you even think that?"

"None of you would have come here if it wasn't for me." The wracking sobs broke free of his tentative control. His body shook, and the tears flowed.

Erin stopped stroking Morgan's cheek and wrapped her arm around his shoulders to pull him into her. "This isn't your fault, Tristan. He manipulated you. This is his fault."

"But I shouldn't have listened to him."

"Not your fault." Morgan held his hand and tugged until he looked at her. "Tristan, I promise you, I don't blame you." Morgan's voice gave way to a series of wheezing coughs.

Erin helped her sit up a little until the spasm eased. "Morgan, please don't talk. You need to rest your throat." Morgan's eyes darted to Tristan as he continued to cry. Erin leaned down and kissed her head. "I know." She stroked Morgan's cheek. "Tristan, you didn't mean to hurt anyone, and you didn't cause this. Neither of us blame you, okay?" Erin struggled to find the right words. She needed to help him see that he wasn't to blame, and that she still loved him, the child in him cried out for it.

"It is my fault. You're all here because of me."

"No, this isn't your fault. He wanted to see your mum, and one way or another, he was going to do this. Look at him." She tilted her head in the direction of the snarling, prostrate man, grumbling under John's considerable weight. "This is all his doing."

"Why?" His body still shook, but he was listening to her now. His tears had subsided, and he was more in control of himself.

"Because he's a miserable excuse for a father and wanted nothing more than to make her pay for doing something he thinks was wrong."

"What did she do wrong?"

"She told the truth." Erin wiped his cheeks before she went back to touching Morgan.

"About her mum?" Tristan leaned back, looking down at Morgan, stroking her hand in his.

"Yes. She told the truth, and he paid the price. I don't think he's very happy about it."

Morgan squeezed Tristan's hand until she had his attention again. "I love you." Fresh tears rolled down his cheeks, and he dropped his head to her shoulder. She wrapped her arm about him and held him as close to her as she could.

"You make me fucking sick. And I thought you might have had a bit of mettle about you, boy. You're nothing but a fucking pansy arsed piece of shit. Just like your mother!"

"Shut up, George, or I'll knock you out." John shoved his knee further into the small of his back, eliciting a low groan.

Tristan lifted his head from Morgan's shoulder and looked her in the eye. "I'm proud to be like my mum." He spoke loud enough to be heard across the room. "She has more guts in her little finger than you'll ever have. She did everything she could to keep us safe from you—"

"Wasn't enough though was it, boy? I still got her. I still got you all." He laughed, then groaned as John thrust his knee again.

Morgan stroked Tristan's cheek. "But you didn't win." She smiled. "We're all still together, and stronger than before." She turned and looked at her snarling father. "You're just a pathetic old man who has nothing. I can't believe I was afraid of you." Morgan coughed again. "You know what? I actually feel sorry for you."

George roared and tried to buck John from his back.

"I feel sorry for you because I know things you will never know. I know what it is to be loved by my family. I know what it is to love them in return. All you ever knew was hatred and fear."

"I don't want your fucking pity."

"I know." Morgan smiled forlornly. "And that brings me even more sorrow." She turned to look at Tristan and Erin.

Erin saw the shift in her eyes. There was no more fear, no more sadness, and no regret. Instead, there was a certainty in them that Erin had never seen before.

Morgan turned her head and looked at her father. "I forgive you."

The air felt charged, crackling with the emotional energy between father and daughter. The rage in George was almost a physical force, pouring from him in hot waves of fury, and crashing against the peaceful calm that Morgan had become.

The door opened and the paramedics and police came in, breaking the spell that had Erin hypnotized.

Questions came from every direction. Morgan's pulse, heart rate, and pupil reaction were tested; she was strapped to a gurney, and Erin helped Tristan into the back of the ambulance.

"Ms. Masters, we need to go, but I need to have space to work in here."

"I'm not leaving her, and I'm not leaving my son."

The man held his hands up in surrender. "I wasn't going to suggest either. But would it be okay for the lad to sit in the front?"

Erin looked over at Tristan, pleased when he quickly climbed out of the vehicle. She heard the door slam behind him and the soft click as he fastened his seat belt.

The paramedic climbed back in and closed the doors behind him. "Good to go." The engine revved and the acceleration forced her back into her seat.

She looked at Morgan. The bruises on her neck were stark against her chalky white skin. Every piece of the jigsaw fell into place. Morgan's desire to protect them all, and what she wanted to protect them from, demonstrated so clearly for her. The manipulation of a bully—an abuser—trading on the fears instilled in Morgan since her early childhood. He had done exactly what Morgan must have feared he would do. He had attacked them from within and targeted their son. She had run away to keep it from happening, and it had happened anyway.

She brushed the tears from her cheeks.

"I'm gonna be okay." Morgan's voice was hoarse and scratchy, but her words brought a fresh stream of tears to Erin's eyes. "Don't worry. I'm fine."

The man slid a needle into Morgan's arm, removing it when the cannula was sitting in the vein.

"Do I really need that?" Morgan tipped her head toward the arm he was still holding.

"Given the recent history Erin gave us, I'm not taking any chances. Better safe than sorry in this line of work." The man winked at her and made some notes on his chart. "We'll be there in just a minute."

Erin stroked her hand gently. "I'm sorry."

"What for?"

"I should have trusted you more. I should never have doubted you—"

"Erin, I gave you no reason to trust me. I made so many mistakes. But that's all in the past now, right?"

"Yes." Erin's voice was thick with tears and emotion.

"Then it doesn't matter anymore. I love you."

Erin leaned forward and kissed her. "I love you too."

CHAPTER FORTY-ONE

Erin sat with her arm around Tristan's shoulders while they waited for news of Morgan, and for Chris to arrive with Maddie. She couldn't stop remembering her frantic visit the night Morgan had been attacked. The same leaflets were scattered about, the same magazines littered tables, and empty plastic cups marked their place with thick, dark rings, and the bitter aroma of stale coffee.

The doors burst open and Maddie flew down the corridor and into Erin's arms. Erin hoisted her into her lap, inhaling the scent of her hair as she tucked her head against Erin's neck.

"How is she?" Chris wrapped her in a tight hug.

"She's okay. The doctors are just checking out her throat. She's got some wicked bruises on her neck, her voice sounds like she's been gargling gravel, but she's fine."

Maddie's fingers twisted in Erin's hair, spinning the strands around her tiny fingers. "Can we see her?"

"As soon as the doctor finishes up we can." Erin kissed the tip of her nose.

Tristan buried his face in his hands, sobs wracking his body. Chris sat next to him and pulled him close.

"Hey, what's wrong?"

"It's all my fault." Tristan's words were muffled against Chris's chest.

"Tristan, I thought we talked about this. What's going on?" Erin stroked a hand down his back.

"She wouldn't have been there if it wasn't for me. It's my fault she's hurt. If she forgets us all again, it's my fault." He dropped his head to his knees, hiding his face in the crook of his elbow, his sobs uncontrollable.

She eased Maddie off her lap, nodding in Chris's direction. She sidled over to him as Erin pulled Tristan into her arms. She rocked him gently, the action born of years of comforting him, stroking his hair, and soothing the emotional turmoil raging inside him.

"Okay, now I want you to listen to me. You didn't cause this." He started to pull away but she held on tighter. "No, listen. Yes, you did things you shouldn't have done. You shouldn't have run away. You shouldn't have ditched school. You should have trusted us, and you shouldn't have talked to him. But all of these things are mistakes. And everyone makes mistakes."

"But she's hurt, and you were only there looking for me."

"Yes, we were, but George has been trying to get to see your mum for quite a long time. He sent her a letter when he was still in prison. That was why she left us. She was trying to protect us from him."

"And I let him get to her." His words were difficult to understand through his sobs.

Think, Erin. How can I make him see that he didn't start any of this? "Tristan, how did he find you?"

"He came to the house. He asked to see mum."

Fucking bastard! "When?"

"Just before school started back." Tristan's sobs eased a little as he answered her questions. "She wasn't in. You'd taken her for her appointment at the hospital, about her knee."

This is what we need, Tristan, good boy. "He came to see Morgan then?"

"Yes." Tristan's eyes widened as he realized the conclusion she was leading him to. "He could have come to see her any time. I didn't matter."

"I wouldn't say you didn't matter, kiddo. But in this instance, it was a question of when. You didn't give him an opportunity to get to her that he couldn't have arranged himself at some point.

Remember, he arranged for those people to beat her up. Do you understand? This was his doing, his fault, not yours."

Erin reached into her pocket for a tissue and handed it to him. "You should have told us when he came to the house. Why didn't you?"

He blew his nose and grimaced. "I'm sorry."

"I don't need sorry, Tristan. I need to know why."

He leaned back in his chair, slightly more relaxed as he started shredding the tissue in his hand. "The first time he came he just said not to worry about it and that he'd come back another day. He came back about an hour later and asked if he could wait."

"Oh, God." *I'll kill him.*

"It's okay, I said no. That I wasn't going to let a stranger in the house."

"Good boy." Erin breathed a small sigh of relief.

"He said he shouldn't have been a stranger. He said he was my granddad and that it was wrong that I didn't know him, or even recognize him, after everything he did for Mum."

Erin looked at Chris. His eyes were stormy. "Go on."

"I thought he was some crazy guy, so I told him to fuck off. I'm sorry for swearing but—"

"It's okay." *I don't give a flying fuck right now.* "What happened next?"

"He laughed and said I really was his grandson after all, that I had spunk. He got his wallet out and showed me the picture of him and Mum. It was definitely him and Mum when she was a kid. He wanted to know if she was all right and stuff. If she was happy. I told him she'd been in hospital. He's her dad. I didn't think I was doing anything wrong."

"Shh, doesn't matter. What happened next?"

"He said that he was dead sorry that she was poorly, so I told him she wasn't poorly, that she got hit in the head, and she had amnesia. He wanted to know what it meant. Like he didn't know what amnesia meant, so I explained it to him." He balled up the shredded tissue in his fist.

"He was still outside?" She hated the thought of him inside their home. It was their sanctuary, their private space, theirs alone. She didn't want the memory of him in it to taint what they had created.

"Yes, I never let him in the house. After that, he said it was probably best if he didn't see Mum. He said he should 'let sleeping dogs lie.' I wanted him to tell me what he meant by that, and he looked at me all funny. Like he was looking for something on me. He asked me if she hit me. I laughed at him and said no."

Erin closed her eyes. Even though she knew the information had come from Morgan's father, hearing how Tristan had learned it ripped her apart.

"He said it was probably because she knew how strong I was. That I was the man of the house, and she had to know that. He started to walk away and then he turned round and asked if she hit you."

"Jesus Christ. The bastard. Carry on, Tristan."

"He said she had a black temper when she lived with him, that she used to snap and lash out at her mum. I told him she'd never hit us. That she wasn't like that. He said it was all because the moods she had. He said her mum was the same. Got depressed and then angry, and lashed out, and then he asked if she still had her funny moods."

Erin held her anger in check as Tristan explained how he had been manipulated. She hated the way his childish innocence had been turned against him and knew that it had now been destroyed forever. Tristan would never again accept anything on faith as he had before.

"She does have funny moods sometimes, and I got scared. Everything was still…weird. She's Mum, but she isn't. And I didn't know why she left, and I thought maybe…I thought maybe she did hit you and you made her leave, but you didn't want to tell us that. He said that women are ashamed if their partners hit them, and they don't tell anyone. It kind of made sense. He said not to tell you that he'd been there because he didn't want any of us to get hurt, because of him. I was so stupid."

Erin pulled him into her arms. "No, honey, you trusted someone who abused that trust. You were vulnerable because of everything that was happening at home. That doesn't make you stupid, Tristan. It means I didn't do my job very well. I should have protected you better. I failed you, sweetie, not the other way around. I'm so sorry for that." She leaned back, cupping his face and looking into his eyes. "Can you forgive me?"

Tristan frowned. "You didn't do anything wrong."

"I left you at home, and that man came and got his claws into you." She let the guilt she felt fill her, hoping that he would see it in her face. He had to understand that even though they would all feel some measure of guilt for the part they played. That none of them bore any real responsibility for the result.

"You didn't know he was going to come around." Tristan put his hands over hers.

"It doesn't matter. I should have protected you. I should have taught you better, done something better—differently—so that you never doubted your mum."

"If she'd never left I wouldn't have." There was still the tiniest hint of anger coloring those words. Anger that Morgan had left them—him.

"She only left to protect us from him."

"I know that. That's why I said what I did to him." He wiped his eyes. "I get it, Mum. It all goes back to him. If she wasn't scared of him, the letter wouldn't have made her leave, and then everything else would have never happened. Him, not me."

She kissed his forehead. "Exactly. You get your brains from me."

He shook his head. "Nah, Maddie got your brains, I got your eyes."

Maddie climbed off Chris's knee and snuggled on the other side of Erin. "I got Mum's eyes."

Erin kissed the top of her head. "Yes, you did, sweetie."

Tristan smiled. "Does that mean I got Mum's brains…I forget."

"Very funny. I'll tell her you said that when she wakes up."

"Mummy, what if she has forgotten again?" Maddie kicked her feet under her chair, not quite able to reach the floor yet.

"Then we tell her who we are straight away. No waiting, like last time. If she doesn't remember, we'll remind her. She's ours, and we're not letting her go. Right?"

They both agreed. There would be time later to deal with her feelings of failure and the aftermath of the violence they had all witnessed. Tristan's feelings of guilt wouldn't just disappear, and she knew they'd have to be dealt with again. She rested her head against the wall and let out a huge sigh. Later. It could wait till much later.

CHAPTER FORTY-TWO

Morgan smiled as Erin pulled back the curtain and stepped toward her. "Hey. You okay?"

Erin smiled. "I should be asking you that question."

"Why? The doctors have already checked me over. Twice. Are the kids okay?"

Erin frowned. "Maddie's worried you'll have lost your memory again, and Tristan's having a tough time. He blames himself."

"Have you—"

"Told him it's not his fault? Only till I'm blue in the face."

"Sorry."

Erin waved the words away. "Doesn't matter. I think maybe seeing you on the mend will help."

"Bring him in."

"I will."

"Why does Maddie think I've lost my memory again?"

Erin shrugged. "Probably just because she hasn't seen you yet and you're back in the hospital. She's worried what to expect."

"Bring them in then."

"In a minute. We need to talk first."

"Those words scare the crap out of me. You know that, right?"

Erin smiled, cradling Morgan's hand in her lap as she sat on the edge of the bed. "Your dad's back in prison."

"Good."

"Jimmy Davidson's been charged with grievous bodily harm. He's been convicted twice before so the Crown Prosecution Service is throwing the book at him."

"Good."

"It's usually a five year sentence, but with the information that your dad set it all up and there was so much more to it, the CPS are trying to get more. Anna is being charged as an accomplice."

"Right." Morgan slid her hand over Erin's thigh.

"John Yorke recorded the whole thing on his phone. Your dad's confession and his assault on you."

"Really? Phones can do that?"

"Yes."

"Wow." Morgan tugged Erin closer to her and closed the distance between their lips. She felt possessive, needy, hungry. She caressed Erin's lips with her tongue, eliciting a beautiful whimper from Erin's throat. She drew her fingertips down her neck, relishing the tiny bumps that erupted in her wake.

"Morgan, we're still in the hospital."

She wrapped her fingers around the back of Erin's neck, holding her close. "Don't care." She placed tiny kisses down her throat. She could feel the muscles in Erin's neck working beneath her lips as she swallowed.

"I noticed." Erin groaned as she wrapped her fingers around Morgan's wrist.

"Good." Morgan traced her tongue from the small dip at the base of Erin's throat to her chin. She nipped with her teeth before soothing the tiny hurt with a kiss and then claiming her mouth again. It felt so good to feel Erin responding to her. Everything from the way she shifted on the bed, to the tiny moans, and soft whimpers, made it feel so natural, so easy to be with her. She knew she needed to stop—they needed to stop—she loved and respected Erin far too much to do anything else, but she knew she could have easily kissed her for the rest of her life.

"Oh, God, we have to stop."

Erin pressed her lips to Morgan's ear. "We'll finish this when we get home."

"Promise?"

"Definitely." She planted one final kiss on Morgan's lips and then backed away. "The kids are with Chris in the cafeteria. I'll go and get them."

"No, please stay with me." Morgan kept hold of her hand.

"Forever." She kissed the top of Morgan's head. "I won't lose you again."

Morgan looked up quickly at the sound of Erin's voice. "Are you angry?"

"Yes." Erin's eyes burned with rage.

"I'm sorry. I didn't realize you'd mind me kissing you here."

"I'm not angry about that." She kissed Morgan again, exploring her lips to emphasize her point. "I'm angry about what we lost. All these weeks, not knowing, thinking you were cheating on me, the kids, all of it—because he wanted some money from you!"

"It wasn't just about money. That was a bonus for him. He wanted revenge. He wanted to punish me. But, Erin, it's over now. We know everything that happened, we know why, and we can deal with it all." She held her hand out for her, wanting desperately to touch her. "Please don't be angry. Let this draw a line under it all so we can move on and be happy together, our whole family. Like cleaning the slate and starting over. My mum used to say that."

Erin took her hand and leaned down. "Okay. I just need to tell you that I'm really glad you punched the old bastard. If you hadn't, I was going to."

Morgan laughed as she brought Erin's hand to her lips and kissed her knuckles. "I'm glad you didn't. I have plans for these hands when I get out of here."

Erin's mouth popped open and her eyes widened. She leaned forward, but the door opening stopped them before they could kiss.

"Mum!" Maddie skipped into the room and hoisted herself onto the bed beside Morgan.

Erin leaned down and whispered, "Later."

"Do you remember us?" Maddie's forehead creased in a frown, her lips pouting slightly.

"Well, I remember Tristan, and Chris...I think you might be Father Christmas. So yeah, I'm good."

Tristan sniggered as he walked into the room. He met Morgan's eyes and tipped his head as Maddie launched herself at Morgan, knocking the wind out of her.

"Okay, you're a wrestler, not Father Christmas. My mistake."

"Mum! Stop it. I was worried." Maddie slapped her belly.

"I'm sorry, baby girl. I'm fine, and yes, I remember. Still got the big gap from the past, but no new ones." She held Maddie's hand, stroking across the back of it.

"When's my birthday?"

"Third of October." Morgan tickled her ribs, loving the way Maddie squirmed and giggled. *This is the only medicine I need.*

"What Brownie badge did I just get?"

"Something to do with pandas." She tickled more.

"World cultures." Maddie tried to push her hands away and catch her breath.

"But you had a panda mask. Do I pass the test yet?"

Maddie sat up, looking intently at Morgan. "Okay, you'll do."

"Well, thank you, Dr. Maddie."

Maddie laughed and snuggled beside her on the bed. "I might be a doctor when I grow up."

"If that's what you want to be, then you do it, kiddo." She looked over at Tristan where he leaned against the wall. She held her hand out. "Come here."

He walked forward slowly, taking her hand when he reached the bed. "I love you, both of you." She looked up at Erin. "All of you."

Tristan cocked his hip and perched on the edge of the bed. "I'm sorry, Mum. I didn't mean for you to get hurt."

She tugged him into her arms, hugging him awkwardly. "I know. It's not your fault, and I am absolutely fine. The doctors were being cautious because of last time. That's all." She kissed his head. "We're all fine, we're a family, and that is all that matters." She cupped the back of his head and looked into his eyes, determined that he see the truth of her statement. "I love you."

"I love you too, Mum." He wrapped his arms around her and laid his head against her shoulder.

Morgan took in her beautiful family and met Erin's tender gaze. *Home.*

Chapter Forty-three

Morgan shifted the pad on the blanket and breathed deeply as she drew her outline of two swans, swimming across the lake, side by side with their heads close together. She lay on her stomach, taking in every detail as Erin lay with her head resting on Morgan's back watching the children play across the field. The remains of a picnic were scattered around them, and the late September sun shone down on them all.

"Erin, I've been wanting to ask you something." She felt Erin's head move on her back.

"What?"

She pushed the pad aside and rolled onto her side to look at her. Erin looked at her curiously and propped her head on one hand. The sunlight made her eyes sparkle and her hair shone, and Morgan knew that forever with her wouldn't be enough. She took hold of her hand and brought it to her lips, turning Erin's wedding band around her finger. "Will you marry me?"

Erin smiled. "We're already married."

"I know." Morgan leaned close and pressed a gentle kiss to Erin's lips. "But I don't remember it." She kissed the band on Erin's finger. "And I really think I should remember one of the three most important days of my life."

"Oh, so you want a do-over." Erin laughed as Morgan turned her hand over and kissed her palm. "Well, I'm not going through labor again, no matter how much I love you."

Morgan grinned. "So will you marry me again?"

"Yes."

Morgan pulled her close and kissed her. Her tongue and lips soft and gentle until Erin parted her lips and let her in. The slow, tender kiss of lovers knowing they had the rest of their lives to touch, explore, to love each other.

"Oh, get a room!" Tristan's voice pulled them out of their miasma.

"Isn't it their bed time yet?" Morgan smiled against Erin's lips.

"You wish."

"Don't you?" Morgan missed her closeness as she moved away, smiling.

"Later."

"I'm going to hold you to that." She ran her fingers down Erin's cheek. "Hey, Tristan, want to be my best man? You're mum's agreed to marry me."

"What? Again?"

They burst out laughing. "Yes, again."

"Do I get to be bridesmaid again?" Maddie dropped down onto the blanket next to them and picked up a small bunch of grapes. Erin ruffled her hair.

"Of course."

"Cool." She munched away slowly. "Is this something you're gonna do over and over? I need to know so I can pick an extra special dress if this is the last time I'll get to be your bridesmaid."

"Oh no, this is the last time." Erin smiled over at Morgan and leaned in for another quick kiss.

Morgan smiled back. "This time is forever."

About the Author

A Stockport (near Manchester, UK) native, Andrea took her life in her hands a few years ago and crossed the great North/South divide and now lives in Norfolk with her partner, their two border collies, and two and a half cats (one isn't sure if she wants to be theirs anymore as the lady down the street feeds her Whiskas rather than whatever is on offer at the supermarket, like they do!). Andrea spends her time running their campsite and hostel to pay the bills, and scribbling down stories during the winter months.

Andrea is an avid reader and a keen musician, playing the saxophone and the guitar (just to annoy her other half—apparently!). She is also a recreational diver and takes an opportunity to head to warmer climes and discover the mysteries of life beneath the waves! Her first novel, Ladyfish , was the recipient of an Alice B. Lavender certificate for 2013.

Books Available from Bold Strokes Books

At Her Feet by Rebekah Weatherspoon. Digital marketing producer Suzanne Kim knows she has found the perfect love in her new mistress Pilar, but before they can make the ultimate commitment, Suzanne's professional life threatens to disrupt their perfectly balanced bliss. (978-1-60282-948-0)

Show of Force by AJ Quinn. A chance meeting between navy pilot Evan Kane and correspondent Tate McKenna takes them on a roller-coaster ride where the stakes are high, but the reward is higher: a chance at love. (978-1-60282-942-8)

Clean Slate by Andrea Bramhall. Can Erin and Morgan work through their individual demons to rediscover their love for each other, or are the unexplainable wounds too deep to heal? (978-1-60282-943-5)

Hold Me Forever by D. Jackson Leigh. An investigation into illegal cloning in the quarter horse racing industry threatens to destroy the growing attraction between Georgia debutante Mae St. John and Louisiana horse trainer Whit Casey. (978-1-60282-944-2)

Trusting Tomorrow by PJ Trebelhorn. Funeral director Logan Swift thinks she's perfectly happy with her solitary life devoted to helping others cope with loss until Brooke Collier moves in next door to care for her elderly grandparents. (978-1-60282-891-9)

Forsaking All Others by Kathleen Knowles. What if what you think you want is the opposite of what makes you happy? (978-1-60282-892-6)

Exit Wounds by VK Powell. When Officer Loane Landry falls in love with ATF informant Abigail Mancuso, she realizes that nothing is as it seems—not the case, not her lover, not even the dead. (978-1-60282-893-3)

Dirty Power by Ashley Bartlett. Cooper's been through hell and back, and she's still broke and on the run. But at least she found the twins. They'll keep her alive. Right? (978-1-60282-896-4)

The Rarest Rose by I. Beacham. After a decade of living in her beloved house, Ele disturbs its past and finds her life being haunted by the presence of a ghost who will show her that true love never dies. (978-1-60282-884-1)

Code of Honor by Radclyffe. The face of terror is hard to recognize—especially when it's homegrown. The next book in the Honor series. (978-1-60282-885-8)

Does She Love You? by Rachel Spangler. When Annabelle and Davis find out they are both in a relationship with the same woman, it leaves them facing life-altering questions about trust, redemption, and the possibility of finding love in the wake of betrayal. (978-1-60282-886-5)

The Road to Her by KE Payne. Sparks fly when actress Holly Croft, star of UK soap Portobello Road, meets her new on-screen love interest, the enigmatic and sexy Elise Manford. (978-1-60282-887-2)

Shadows of Something Real by Sophia Kell Hagin. Trying to escape flashbacks and nightmares, ex-POW Jamie Gwynmorgan stumbles into the heart of former Red Cross worker Adele Sabellius and uncovers a deadly conspiracy against everything and everyone she loves. (978-1-60282-889-6)

Date with Destiny by Mason Dixon. When sophisticated bank executive Rashida Ivey meets unemployed blue collar worker Destiny Jackson, will her life ever be the same? (978-1-60282-878-0)

The Devil's Orchard by Ali Vali. Cain and Emma plan a wedding before the birth of their third child while Juan Luis is still lurking, and as Cain plans for his death, an unexpected visitor arrives and challenges her belief in her father, Dalton Casey. (978-1-60282-879-7)

Secrets and Shadows by L.T. Marie. A bodyguard and the woman she protects run from a madman and into each other's arms. (978-1-60282-880-3)

Change Horizons: Three Novellas by Gun Brooke. Three stories of courageous women who dare to love as they fight to claim a future in a hostile universe. (978-1-60282-881-0)

Scarlet Thirst by Crin Claxton. When hot, feisty Rani meets cool, vampire Rob, one lifetime isn't enough, and the road from human to vampire is shorter than you think… (978-1-60282-856-8)

Battle Axe by Carsen Taite. How close is too close? Bounty hunter Luca Bennett will soon find out. (978-1-60282-871-1)

Improvisation by Karis Walsh. High school geometry teacher Jan Carroll thinks she's figured out the shape of her life and her future, until graphic artist and fiddle player Tina Nelson comes along and teaches her to improvise. (978-1-60282-872-8)

For Want of a Fiend by Barbara Ann Wright. Without her Fiendish power, can Princess Katya and her consort Starbride stop a magic-wielding madman from sparking an uprising in the kingdom of Farraday? (978-1-60282-873-5)

Broken in Soft Places by Fiona Zedde. The instant Sara Chambers meets the seductive and sinful Merille Thompson, she falls hard, but knowing the difference between love and a dangerous, all-consuming desire is just one of the lessons Sara must learn before it's too late. (978-1-60282-876-6)

Healing Hearts by Donna K. Ford. Running from tragedy, the women of Willow Springs find that with friendship, there is hope, and with love, there is everything. (978-1-60282-877-3)

Desolation Point by Cari Hunter. When a storm strands Sarah Kent in the North Cascades, Alex Pascal is determined to find her. Neither imagines the dangers they will face when a ruthless criminal begins to hunt them down. (978-1-60282-865-0)

I Remember by Julie Cannon. What happens when you can never forget the first kiss, the first touch, the first taste of lips on skin? What happens when you know you will remember every single detail of a mysterious woman? (978-1-60282-866-7)

The Gemini Deception by Kim Baldwin and Xenia Alexiou. The truth, the whole truth, and nothing but lies. Book six in the Elite Operatives series. (978-1-60282-867-4)

Scarlet Revenge by Sheri Lewis Wohl. When faith alone isn't enough, will the love of one woman be strong enough to save a vampire from damnation? (978-1-60282-868-1)

Ghost Trio by Lillian Q. Irwin. When Lee Howe hears the voice of her dead lover singing to her, is it a hallucination, a ghost, or something more sinister? (978-1-60282-869-8)

The Princess Affair by Nell Stark. Rhodes Scholar Kerry Donovan arrives at Oxford ready to focus on her studies, but her life and her priorities are thrown into chaos when she catches the eye of Her Royal Highness Princess Sasha. (978-1-60282-858-2)

The Chase by Jesse J. Thoma. When Isabelle Rochat's life is threatened, she receives the unwelcome protection and attention of bounty hunter Holt Lasher who vows to keep Isabelle safe at all costs. (978-1-60282-859-9)